THE COWBOY'S
PRAYER

LEE ANN SONTHEIMER MURPHY

This is a work of fiction. Names, characters, places, and incidents are products of the author's imagination or are used fictiously and are not to be construed as real. Any resemblance to actual events, locations, organizations, or persons, living or dead, is entirely coincidental.

World Castle Publishing, LLC

Pensacola, Florida
Copyright © 2024 Lee Ann Sontheimer Murphy
Paperback ISBN: 9798891262782
eBook ISBN: 9798891262799
First Edition World Castle Publishing, LLC, November 4, 2024
http://www.worldcastlepublishing.com

Licensing Notes

Cover: Cover Designs by Karen
Editor: Karen Fuller

Dedication: For my uncle, Darrell Neely, who lived and worked in Oklahoma for a while, who left me the legacy of a hand-tooled leather Western purse and stories about rodeos long gone but not forgotten.

CHAPTER ONE

First time he ever laid eyes on the kid, Lamont wasn't impressed. Scrawny as a scarecrow, the kid needed a haircut like last month. His eyes were too big for his thin face, and his clothes hung large on his skinny body. Teddy Anderson came to his place on Saturday to look at the old Ford Ranger pickup Lamont had listed for sale and brought the boy. Anderson, his loud-mouthed neighbor from down the road, reeked of beer and weed. He talked too much and twitched like he might need a fix. *Tweaker.* Had to be, and Lamont loathed illegal drugs of any type. As much as Teddy came on like a spring tornado, fast, furious, and out of control, the boy kept his distance. He said little, but Lamont would bet he watched everything and didn't miss anything.

The compact blue Ranger sat behind the main barn, weathered and worn. The paint job had taken a beating in a hail storm a decade earlier but despite having over 200,000 miles, it still ran well.

"I don't know," Teddy Anderson hedged as he walked around the old truck. "Looks awfully rough to me. How old is it?"

"It's an '85," Lamont replied with a sigh. "It's got a lot of miles, but it's still sound. Looks don't turn the wheels."

"I think you're asking too much."

Lamont squinted against the sun dropping low on the western horizon. He'd set the price below what the vehicle could bring despite an affection for the old truck. It had survived a tornado that took everything else on the place. "You don't have to buy it."

He doubted Anderson, a roofer who worked when the sun shone or, if he had the inclination, had the money in his pocket.

"I could use a truck, though. Would you consider payments?"

If Lamont did, he knew it was likely he would never get more than the first. Anderson was notorious for not paying what he owed. Lamont could remember when his neighbor competed in local or regional rodeos. On the circuit, Teddy borrowed often and seldom repaid, earning a poor reputation. Recent gossip that Lamont picked up from another neighbor indicated Anderson owed more than one drug dealer – but was unable to pay.

"Can't do it," Lamont replied. Right now, he wanted the man off his property and out of sight. The way Teddy jerked and trembled made Lamont's nerves jangle.

His neighbor's face twisted into a grimace. "Can't you give a fellow cowboy a break?"

Lamont Fortune rode saddle broncs for the last few years and bulls before that. Anderson used to ride bulls but hadn't in several years. Lamont recalled him from a long time ago but hadn't seen him compete for the last couple of seasons. Anderson sometimes showed up at rodeos to watch, envious as a hound eyeing a man devour a good steak. Lamont didn't remember ever seeing the boy, but maybe he hadn't paid close attention.

"No." Lamont's daddy had taught him no explanations or excuses were needed to refuse. "If you come up with the money, though, and it's still here, I'll sell to you."

Anderson mumbled and turned to go. When the kid hesitated, he whirled around. "Let's go. There's nothing for us here, so get moving."

"I don't wanna walk," the boy said. "My feet hurt."

Lamont glanced down and winced. The boy wore ragged tennis shoes, the kind bought at a dollar store that usually came apart in a month. Both toes were scuffed and one was worn through enough he could see a dirty sock. Holes dotted the sides of both shoes.

"You'll be all right," Anderson said. "Kid never stops whining."

"Your son?" Lamont asked, curious.

"Not mine, no. Stepson. I got stuck with him when his mom managed to get herself killed in a car wreck. C'mon, Shayne, let's make tracks."

That news wrenched Lamont's heart, strange when he could care less about most things. His former fiancée had ended their relationship before the planned wedding. Her parting shot had been that he had a cold, cold heart like in the old Hank Williams song. Maybe so because he'd shrugged and gone on with his life without Remy.

The boy gazed up at Lamont with brilliant blue eyes. He didn't resemble Anderson in the least. *I should have known they weren't related.* It also explained why he hadn't seen the boy until now, although he'd never known Anderson had a wife. "Mister, would you give us a ride back home? It's hot."

Teddy Anderson smacked the kid across the face. "Don't start begging. Ol' Lamont here ain't going to do anything to help, not when he won't let us have the truck."

Fury exploded through Lamont. He ached to punch his neighbor in the nose. "Don't hit the kid again, or I'll punch you. I'll drive you home. Just because I won't hand over the old truck for nothing doesn't mean I'm cruel."

Shayne rode in the middle when they climbed into Lamont's old Chevy truck.

"I'm Shayne Sawyer," the boy told him and extended his right hand. Lamont shook it.

"Lamont Fortune, and yep, that's my real name." People usually asked, so he got that out of the way first thing.

"Cool!" Shayne grinned for the first time. When he did, it lightened his face and made Lamont realize this was one good-looking kid. "Does that mean you're a lucky guy?"

"Maybe sometimes." Lamont didn't feel fortunate. He'd lost both his parents in a plane crash, the old family farmhouse had been destroyed by a tornado while he was on the rodeo circuit three years ago, and his fiancée bailed on him. That last, though, was a good thing because he doubted they would have made it as a married couple. He'd replaced the house with a brand-new home, nice, but so far it never had really felt like home.

The Anderson house was a mile down the road from his place. Until Lamon turned into the drive, he hadn't remembered how dilapidated it had become. The wood had weathered gray, and he saw at least one broken window patched with cardboard. He wouldn't want to set foot on the porch because the boards sagged, and the roof did, too. A strong wind or heavy snowfall might bring it down. A variety of junk littered the yard, everything from discarded aluminum cans and plastic jugs to a rusted washing machine and a motorcycle without wheels. A battered vehicle sat near the front door, and Lamont guessed it was the usual ride.

"Car's not running. Needs a battery." Teddy Anderson climbed out of the truck. "Thanks, Lamont."

"No problem. Let me know if you decide to buy the Ranger."

Teddy responded with a bitter laugh. "That's about as likely as pigs flying, but sure, I will. Get out of the truck, Shayne."

Shayne hadn't moved from the cab. With his head bent, Lamont wondered if he had been praying. The boy scooted across the seat to exit from the driver's side and when he did, he slipped a folded piece of notebook paper to him. "Thanks for the ride."

"You're welcome."

The folded square fit into his hand, and Lamont kept it

concealed. He didn't open it until he'd parked the trunk under a big oak tree at home.

"Mister, please call my aunt Matilda Mannheim. She lives in New York City."

Lamont read the childish printing twice, then sighed. The cryptic note disturbed him. If he had to live with Teddy Anderson, he would want to escape, too. He wondered about the boy's mother and tried to imagine what kind of woman would have married Anderson. He crumpled the note, then paused. Maybe the boy needed a rescue, and this aunt was someone who would deliver him from Anderson's clutches. But she might also be another tweaker. Lamont decided he'd ponder it before deciding. He had too much to do to worry about it.

He was already late heading out on the circuit. Although it was just April, he should have been gone by mid-March, but a late winter bout of flu had laid him low. Lamont planned to leave within two weeks. He always came home when he could, but he'd be on the road most of the season, driving from one rodeo to another.

The kid haunted him, though. Lamont couldn't forget the way Anderson had smacked the boy or spoken to him with distracted cruelty. By now, if he'd found any money, Anderson was probably high. He considered calling the authorities to report possible child abuse, but that wasn't his way. He preferred to handle things himself. After two days, Lamont plucked the note from his dresser. It appeared to have been written sometime back. The folded creases were deep. *The kid must have carried it around until he found someone to hand it to.* With a deep sigh, Lamont set out to locate Matilda Mannheim. It took less than a half hour with his computer to track her down. Mannheim wasn't a common surname.

Matilda Mannheim lived in midtown Manhattan. He'd figured she would have some highfalutin career, a model or a fashion photographer or a up and coming actress. Instead, her name was associated with a bakery where she made specialty cakes.

Allowing for the time difference, he made the call after evening chores. Lamont sat down in his favorite overstuffed armchair and propped his feet on the hassock. He took a long, deep breath and dialed the number he located, hoping he would make a connection and even more than the woman would care about her nephew.

"Hello."

Lamont had expected some fancy New York accent, not a sweet tone that sounded like pure Texas. "Is this Matilda Mannheim?"

After a pause, she said, "Yes, it is. Who's calling, please?"

"My name is Lamont Fortune, and your nephew asked me to give you a call."

She gasped. "Shayne? You know where Shayne is? Oh, thank God. Is he all right? Where is he?"

The series of questions caught him by surprise. "Whoa, now, lady. Give me a second. One question at a time. He lives down the road from me with his stepfather, I guess. He's pretty skinny but as far as I could tell, he's okay. I guess this confirms you are his aunt."

"I've been trying to find him since my sister died." Her voice broke as she spoke and Lamont realized she wept. "Where do you live? Is he still in Texas?"

Flustered, Lamont babbled. "Ma'am, I live in Oklahoma. The closest town of any size is Claremore. Teddy Anderson's been my neighbor for a few years but I didn't know he had a stepson until they came over to look at a truck I have for sale. I don't really have any answers for you beyond that. The kid handed me a note that asked if I could call his aunt. He gave me your name, but I had to figure out the number myself."

"I'm glad that you did. I'm coming out there as soon as I can book a flight. Can I fly to what was it, Claremore?"

Lamont hated flying. He didn't like it, and since his parents died in a plane crash, he didn't plan to ever take a flight again.

"No, you'll have to fly into Tulsa," he told her. "Tulsa International Airport."

First, he heard a pen scribbling on paper, then the click of computer keys.

"Got it. Tulsa. I'm booking a flight for tomorrow. I'll rent a car and come find Shayne."

Matilda might be from Texas but she didn't sound like a country girl. "Miss Mannheim, I don't live in Claremore. My place is out in the boondocks, and your nephew lives down the road. I don't think you'll be able to find it without getting lost."

"I can use GPS."

Lamont laughed. "Around here, GPS will take you on a wild goose chase about half the time. How about I come pick you up at the airport?"

When she huffed into the phone, Lamont rolled his eyes and wanted to throw up his hands. *She's gonna be difficult.*

"I'll rent a car so I can get around without relying on you or anyone else."

"Then pick up one in Claremore. You're not familiar."

"And you are?"

Lamont closed his eyes and counted to five so he could avoid smashing something or throwing the phone at the wall. "I've lived here all my life, so, yeah, I am. Text me what time your flight will arrive, and I'll be there."

Matilda said nothing for a few seconds, and when she did, her voice had an edge that could cut a good steak. "I've booked it online. My flight arrives in Tulsa at 9:38 p.m. tomorrow night."

"Then I'll be there."

He ended the call with a sigh. The last thing Lamont

wanted to do was face Tulsa traffic or navigate the airport, but he would do it. Since he hadn't eaten supper yet, Lamont made a thick bologna and cheese sandwich with a handful of chips. He parked at the table to eat, but he hadn't taken more than three bites when someone beat on his door.

"Mister, are you there?" a young voice shrilled. It was the boy, Shayne Sawyer.

Muttering, Lamont opened the front door. "You got good timing, kid. I just talked to your aunt, and she's coming out here."

Gasping as if he'd run from his home here, Shayne shook his head. "It's not that. It's, it's…."

Shayne choked on a sob. Lamont realized not only was the boy's face brick red, but he'd been crying. His guts tensed as he realized something must be wrong. "What's the matter?"

If Anderson had beat the child, Lamont would have it out with the man.

"It's Ted…Ted…Teddy," Shayne cried.

"Did he hurt you?"

The boy shook his head fast and furious. "I think he's dead, Mister Fortune."

It took a moment for it to sink it. "Dead? Teddy Anderson's dead?"

"I'm pretty sure," the kid stammered. Still wheezing, Lamont thought he appeared to be on the edge of collapse or a meltdown.

"Come inside, and you can tell me what happened." Why did this have to happen to him? Lamont liked minding his own business and keeping out of trouble. It appeared he wouldn't be able to do either.

In the living room, Shayne stopped and stared, then parked himself on the loveseat. Lamont sat upright in his armchair.

"Are you all right?" he asked, realizing he should ask.

"I guess. Yeah, maybe."

"Do you want a soda pop or a sandwich?" Lamont had lost his appetite, but maybe the boy needed something.

"I don't think so, thank you."

"Tell me what happened."

The story was short and terrible. Not surprisingly, Anderson had been high on meth.

"Sometimes he smoked it, sometimes he used a needle," Shayne said. "It seemed like it took more and more of it to get him high. He'd shot up several times, and I'm pretty sure he'd taken some fentanyl, too. He fell over on the floor."

When his stepfather collapsed, Shayne figured he had passed out, which wasn't uncommon. But this time, he made some gurgling sounds, then went quiet. "I thought he'd gone to sleep," Shayne told Lamont. He twisted his hands together as he spoke. "He usually left me alone when he got high and when he was sleeping it off, so I didn't bother him. But that was last night, and he ain't woke up yet. His lips are a funny color, and he's stiff. He kinda smells weird, too."

If he were still a praying man, Lamont would have been on his knees. Instead, he reached for the phone and called the county sheriff's department. He told them what Shayne had told him and promised to meet them at the Anderson place.

He didn't think the kid should go, but he had no place to leave him, and besides, the deputies would want to talk to him.

Lamont pulled his boots back on and wished he was a drinking man. Right now, he could use a beer to mellow his nerves, but he'd given all that up a long time ago. "C'mon, kid, we gotta go over there."

"Are you gonna make me stay there, even if he ain't dead?" The question came in a harsh whisper.

Lamont made a swift decision, one he would keep. "No, you're not going back once we get done with the Sheriff. Until your aunt comes, you can stay here."

He just hoped he could make it happen.

CHAPTER TWO

Shayne strutted in new blue jeans. His feet sported brand-new shoes with no holes or rips, and he wore an Oklahoma Sooners jersey. It had taken a lot of fancy talking to keep Shayne out of Child Services custody. Since Sheriff David Wills was Lamont's first cousin, he'd leaned on the authorities more than a little to persuade them that Lamont could take the kid home.

"His aunt's coming and she can file for emergency custody," Lamont had told Davy.

"Bring her to my office first thing the morning after she's arrived," David had replied. "We'll get it sorted out one way or another."

Shayne shadowed Lamont, sticking close to his side. That grated on Lamont's nerves and made him antsy. He lived alone, and even on the rodeo circuit, he kept to himself.

But he took the kid shopping for clothes at a local discount store because everything he owned had been fit for the rag bag. After a quick fast-food supper in Claremore, Lamont headed for Tulsa.

He navigated the airport, found parking, and located the concourse where Matilda Mannheim would arrive. Both took a seat on the hard plastic chairs and waited. It would be more than an hour until her flight was due. Being in an airport made him antsy although he could manage. Seeing and hearing planes land was one thing – flying would be another, and that wouldn't be happening in this lifetime.

"You'll recognize your aunt, won't you?" Lamont had

seen her photo online, but she'd been wearing a double-breasted white chef's garb, a chef's hat, and an apron. Her face had been in shadow and the focal point of the picture had been the cake, not the baker. He might not spot her in normal garb.

"I don't know," Shayne said. The more time he spent with Lamont, the more he talked. "I haven't seen her since I was a little kid. I don't really know her."

Lamont shot a look in Shayne's direction. "Then why did you want me to call her?"

Shayne shrugged. "I figured she might come get me. I don't have anybody else except you."

"How long had you been toting that note?"

"I've always had it. My mom told me that Aunt Matilda would come if I ever needed her. She had me write that note. Mama said to give it to somebody when it was time. Teddy was gettin' worse, and so I handed it to you. He beat me a lot."

If Lamont thought much about that, he'd get mad, and now wasn't the time to be angry, not waiting to pick up a city woman likely to look down on both him and Oklahoma.

"She's your mom's sister, right?" Lamont didn't count on anyone, and he'd rather Shayne not depend on him. He wasn't family.

"Yeah, Matilda and Melissa. My mom was Melissa, but everyone except Teddy called her Lissy. Is she taking me back to New York?"

"I don't know." Lamont hoped so. He didn't want the responsibility of a child or to deal with the woman who had seemed difficult on the phone.

"I want to stay here." Shayne spoke those four words in a quiet voice, each one dropping like a pebble into water. He gazed up at Lamont as he spoke, his eyes soft and filled with trust.

Lamont didn't know what to say. He cleared his throat and took off his cowboy hat, then put it back on his head, then pretended not to understand. "Here at the airport?"

"No, in Oklahoma, with you, Lamont."

They'd made the leap from Mister Fortunate to Lamont. That made him glad, but the rest of it didn't. It scared him. He parted his lips to tell Shayne that wasn't an option, but something about the boy tugged his heartstrings. "We'll have to see what your auntie thinks, buddy."

Buddy. That had been his nickname as a child. Both his parents and his granddaddy had used it more often than his name. His brother and sister still did on occasion.

"Okay," Shayne said and yawned. The flight was delayed, and the kid fell asleep. Every passing minute increased Lamont's anxiety. He didn't do well with most women, and his broken engagement proved it. Remy's accusation that he had a cold, cold heart hit the mark. He could have his pick of buckle bunnies when he was out on the rodeo circuit, but Lamont ignored them. Somewhere along the lonesome way, he'd given up on finding a woman to date or marry.

When he came down with a bad case of flu earlier this spring, Lamont had wished for a woman. Soft hands to soothe him would have been welcome. Someone putting a cold compress on his feverish head and bringing him a cup of tea with some over the counter meds would have given comfort. Somebody who asked how he felt and worried over him a little would have been nice. Instead, he had weathered being sick alone and was miserable for the better part of two weeks.

When the flight arrived, and the passengers streamed into the terminal, Lamont stood after nudging the boy awake. His eyes darted from side to side, seeking a woman that resembled the one he'd seen online and watched Shayne for any reaction. He dismissed one woman after another. Two were much too old, gray hair revealing their age. Another had to still be in her teens. Three walked beside small children. One of the last passengers to appear wasn't as tall as he would have guessed, a brunette with short hair somewhere between her ears and shoulders. Despite her petite size, she toted a carry-on bag and rolled a huge suitcase along.

"Mama!" Shayne shouted with more delight than he'd heard from the kid. "It's Mama."

Since Lamont knew his mother was deceased, it wasn't her. Shayne ran forward, and the woman halted. Her bags were abandoned as she rushed forward and knelt to hug the child.

"Shayne, oh, Shayne!"

The boy drew back and stared at her. "You're not Mama. I knew that, but for a second, I thought…"

"I'm your Aunt Matilda. It's been too long, but I'm glad I'm here. You're so tall for ten."

After glaring, her nephew said. "I'm twelve."

Shayne pulled away from her and stood at Lamont's side, edgy like a frightened animal, ready to bolt at the first hint of danger.

Uncomfortable and feeling awkward, he extended his hand. "I'm Lamont Fortune, Shayne's neighbor from down the road. We talked on the phone."

"Matilda Mannheim." Her brown eyes shone with unshed tears. "Thank you for coming to pick me up. I didn't know you planned to bring my nephew."

Honesty was best, even when blunt. "I didn't, but things changed. His stepfather died."

"Tim Anderson is dead?" Her mouth hung open with surprise. "What happened?"

"Drug overdose." Lamont picked up her bag and put it over his shoulder, then maneuvered the larger case. He headed toward the exit.

"When?"

"I heard about it right after I talked to you last night." He kept his tone level. "Buddy, there, he came to tell me."

Her lips twisted into a frown. "And so, you brought Shayne along with you? I hope his stepdad isn't lying cold and dead in some hovel."

Hovel was an apt description of the place her nephew had been calling home, but her assumption that Lamont might be an idiot who didn't report the death rankled. "No, he isn't because I called the sheriff's department. They took Anderson's body away and did an autopsy early this morning, which confirmed it was drug related. Shayne's been with me."

He raised his voice a fraction, then remembered they were still at the airport and lowered it. Lamont glared at her and she sent an evil look in his direction.

"Lamont bought me some new stuff, and I got a haircut," Shayne said, the first time he'd spoken directly to her since her arrival. "He said I don't have to go back to the house at all if I don't want to go there."

"Did he?" Her tone had softened a fraction.

The boy nodded. "I've been staying at his place. I want to keep staying there."

Matilda wrinkled her forehead and gawked. "I thought you'd want to be with me."

Tired, ready to go home, and irritated with the woman for no valid reason, Lamont asked, "Where did you book a room?"

He would deliver her to the hotel of her choice, leave Shayne with her, and then he'd be finished with his good deed.

She wore heeled fashion boots, which tapped out a rapid rhythm on the tiled floor, but the question brought her to a halt. "That's what I forgot," she said, in such a low voice, Lamont wasn't sure if it was meant for him or if she talked to herself. "I didn't make a reservation anywhere. I'm sorry."

"It's all right." It wasn't, but he could roll with the unexpected.

"Is there a hotel nearby?"

They reached his vintage truck, a 1970 light green Chevy that he had restored. Lamont put her luggage in the back. Matilda paused, then followed Shayne into the cab. "Several," he said. "But it'd be easier if you stayed in Claremore – it's about thirty minutes away from here, but it's closer to my place. You're welcome to stay with me. I have three extra bedrooms."

As soon as the words flew out of his mouth, he couldn't believe what he offered. Yeah, he had four bedrooms and two baths plus a den, along with the usual living room and kitchen, but Lamont didn't have many guests. Once a year, his older sister, Lanelle, came to visit for a week, usually around Thanksgiving. His brother, Logan, came more often, sometimes to fish and to hunt every deer season. Sometimes, one of Lanelle's kids accompanied her which didn't happen often. Logan's wife, Tatum, occasionally came with him. So did their daughter, Paisley, age six.

As he waited to hear her reply, Lamont pulled out of the parking area and headed for the main road. He glanced over Shayne's head. Matilda chewed her lip as she stared through the windshield. She didn't say anything as he turned onto Airport Drive, but after five long minutes, she said, "I'm not sure that's a good idea. I don't see any hotels, at least not on this road. And I don't know you."

To be fair, he didn't know her either. "Maybe you should have thought about that before you agreed I'd pick you up at the airport. Do you know anyone in Oklahoma?"

She raised her hand to her lips and nibbled at a hangnail. "Just Shayne."

Lamont laughed. "You don't really know him."

"Yes, I do, he's my nephew..."

"And he must have been a little guy last time you saw him. You thought he was ten years old, and he's twelve. You didn't even know where he was until I called."

He didn't intend to be rude, just honest, but Matilda squawked and clutched her purse tighter. It sat on her lap as if she thought he might snatch it and steal anything of value.

"Stop!" she shrieked. "Stop right here and let us out. I'll call for a taxi or an Uber or something. I'll hitchhike or walk."

Beside him, Shayne stiffened and leaned closer to Lamont. "I don't want to get out," the kid mumbled. "I'd rather stick with you."

Lamont jerked the truck onto the shoulder of the four-lane major thoroughfare. "Okay, Tilly, you listen, and you listen good. I understand you're here for this kid. You want to do right by him. So do I. But let's get something straight. You don't know me, but I'm not some criminal that you can't trust. If I take you to a hotel, you're gonna be stuck there until you can rent a car. You're not familiar with Tulsa or Oklahoma. I am. So why don't you just chill out a little and come home with me tonight? Tomorrow, the sheriff wants you at his office to talk about custody. After that, you can figure out what you want or need to do."

Matilda tried to open the passenger door, so he locked it. She kicked her feet against the truck floor and made a wild noise. "I can call 911."

Lamont wanted to beat his head against the steering wheel. "If that's what you want, call but the kid's under my temporary custody per order of the Sheriff. Calling 911 is more likely to hurt your chances, not help them. Besides that, you don't want out here – look around. Do you see anywhere to go? That's Mohawk Park across the road. You want me to tell you some of the crimes that happen there? I wouldn't go there at night unless I was armed, and I sure am not about to let you take Shayne over there."

She twisted around to stare at him. "How do I know that's true?"

"How do you know it's not?" he asked. "Why would I

lie?"

Shayne pouted, his lip jutted out, and his arms folded. Matilda looked at her nephew, then at Lamont. She sighed, long and hard. "I guess I don't, and I can't think of any reason you would. Maybe I'm overreacting."

Maybe? Definitely. Lamont removed his hat long enough to run both hands through his short, blond hair. "Look, it's late. I bet you're tired and maybe hungry. Can we start over?"

He suggested it for the kid's sake. He'd just as soon drop her off at a hotel or return her to the airport and never see her again. Beside him, Shayne offered a thumbs up.

"We can," Matilda said after a few moments of silence. "I haven't eaten at all today, and that's probably part of the reason I'm cranky. I think this is a different time zone. This situation is more than I expected. I'm pleased to meet you, Lamont Fortune and glad you are helping my nephew."

She stuck out her hand to shake and he took it.

To his way of thinking, there wasn't a situation, just a boy who needed someone, a kid who'd been mistreated by his now deceased stepfather. "No problem, Tilly."

"It's *Matilda*. Matilda Mannheim."

"I got that, Tilly. It's a nickname, woman, because the other is a mouthful."

She almost smiled. "I suppose it is."

"Why is your name Mannheim, not Sawyer like me?" Shayne questioned.

Matilda blushed and Lamont realized under her gruff exterior, she was quite pretty.

"It *was* Sawyer but I was married for a very short time to a German baker, Freddy Mannheim. I always planned to take Sawyer back but I never have gotten around to it."

So, Shayne's mom hadn't been married until Teddy Anderson. Interesting. And Miss Matilda had survived a brief marriage. Lamont wondered why it ended, but he wasn't about to ask and start any fresh contention.

"Let's go find some food," he suggested. "Then we'll go home. Do you like hamburgers?"

If she asked for a salad or organic food or yogurt or tofu, Lamont thought he might yell out loud and drop her at a hotel anyway.

"I do," she replied. "That sounds good. I'm sorry if I've been difficult. I didn't mean to be."

Her quieter tone softened his attitude. "*De nada.* It's all a lot to deal with."

Despite the late hour, the hamburger joint in Claremore had a full parking lot. Once inside, Lamont ordered them all burgers, family size fries, and chocolate malts. Seated at a table, Lamont dived in, but Matilda bowed her head and reached for their hands.

"Thank you, Lord, for this food, for the kind man who provided it, for being reunited with my nephew, and for whatever happens with Shayne. To God be the glory, in Jesus Name, Amen."

Surprised, Lamont removed his hat at the last moment before she asked a blessing. Shayne goggled at his aunt, apparently as unaccustomed to saying grace as Lamont.

"Can I eat now?" Shayne asked as he pulled his hand free.

"Of course," Matilda replied.

As they ate, the kid devouring his burger with speed, Lamont realized they must look like a family. At first, the idea made him a little uncomfortable, but then he liked it, at least a little. He could imagine family life, something he'd once wanted. Of course, it would have to be with a different woman, not some city slicker who pitched a fit before they were two miles from the airport. Lamont needed a country gal or a small-town woman, someone who knew how to nurture and make a man feel better, not worse. So far, this Tilly hadn't done a lot for his self-image.

Having a kid, though, he liked that idea a lot. Shayne seemed like a fine boy, one most men would be proud to call son. Lamont didn't like the way Anderson had treated the child or how he'd made sure to mention Shayne was his stepson. Steps were something you went up or down, in Lamont's opinion. They had nothing to do with a relationship. It was your kid, or it wasn't, he figured.

"This is delicious," Matilda said, blotting her lips with a paper napkin.

Lamont liked the compliment on the humble fare and liked her a bit better for it. Then she ruined it with her next comment.

"It's basic, but I never expected anything this tasty in the wilds of Oklahoma," she said between bites. "It's not wagyu beef, and although it's not topped with anything like shallots, Gouda cheese, Shitake 'shrooms, or a special mustard, it's actually yummy."

"Food doesn't have to be fancified to taste good."

To him, the double meat burger topped with grilled onions, lettuce, pickle, tomato, and American cheese on a toasted bun came near perfection. Maybe by New York City standards, the burger seemed basic, but to Lamont, it was prime eats.

"I like it just fine," Shayne said. "Fries are good, too."

"Darned straight," Lamont said.

Matilda glanced up with a frown. "I didn't say that food had to be gourmet. I *like* it."

"I'm glad it passes your Big Apple approval," Lamont said, allowing sarcasm to flavor his words. "I might just have me another one."

He didn't, though. This late, another burger on top of the fries and shake would be too much. They spent the rest of the meal in silence, broken only if Shayne said something and Lamont answered. As soon as the last morsel of food passed between Matilda's lips, he gathered their litter onto the plastic tray and headed for the nearest trash can.

"Let's get a move on," he said. "I'd like to get some sleep before morning. We gotta be at the sheriff's office by 9."

The woman slung her purse onto her arm and stood up. "I'm ready."

Once all three were in the truck, Lamont fired the engine. He drove through Claremore and headed for home on the two-lane. When he turned onto the gravel road that would take them to his place, Matilda sat up straight.

"I didn't realize you lived this far out."

"It ain't all that far," he said, dropping into cowboy talk on purpose. He figured it would irritate the city gal. "I like having some space. Never been much of one for town living."

"It seems remote, that's all."

Probably did, he realized. He'd been to New York and had ridden once in a rodeo at Madison Square Garden, back when he rode bulls as well as broncs. All those skyscrapers and apartment buildings hadn't impressed him. Lamont had hated the traffic clogged thoroughfares, the crowds, and the never-ending noise.

"That's what I like about it."

Lamont vowed he would say as little as possible until he got shed of this woman. With any luck, after they met with the Sheriff and probably a social worker, Matilda Mannheim would get custody of the kid. Then they both could ride off into the sunset, and he'd be done with them.

He rolled the truck to a stop. "We're home," he said. "Come on."

After retrieving her luggage from the truck bed, Lamont led them up the wide steps to the side entrance. They came through the den, his favorite room, then his office space, and through the kitchen. He put down her bags in the living room.

"My room's through there," he said, indicating the master

suite. "Shayne's been staying in the smallest bedroom on the other side. You can take your pick of the others, Tilly. One has a bathroom."

Matilda glanced around, eyes wide. "This is nicer than I imagined."

Because he wanted to go to bed, Lamont swallowed the hot words that sprang to his lips. *She's clueless and suffers from foot in the mouth syndrome.* "Glad you approve," he told her. "Good night."

With that, he headed into his bedroom, shut the door, and shucked his clothes. After a long, steaming shower, he crawled into bed, but he had trouble falling asleep. His mind spun in circles. To help a kid, he'd landed himself in the middle of one hot mess. The sooner they could work through it and get custody resolved, the better.

After Remy, a Dallas socialite, wealthy from her family's oil money, he'd had his fill of highfalutin women. He would be glad to see the last of Matilda Mannheim.

She might be pretty, but she was as prickly as barbed wire, difficult and edgy.

CHAPTER THREE

Lamont woke thick-headed with no desire to climb out of bed. He almost rolled over and went back to sleep until he remembered Shayne. He squinted at the clock and groaned. It was 7:12, and if they were going to eat breakfast, then make it to the sheriff's office by 9, they didn't have time to spare. He grabbed a fresh pair of faded blue jeans and reached into the closet for a shirt. Once dressed, he slid his feet into his boots.

The unmistakable aroma of bacon wafted through the air. Lamont sniffed again, thought he must be hallucinating, then headed for the kitchen. Shayne sat at the bar, drinking chocolate milk, watching his aunt bustle around the kitchen. Lamont halted and stared. Matilda wore a pair of black jeans that fit her trim figure and a long-sleeved crew neck blouse with the top two buttons undone. Her hair was pulled up into a messy knot and held in place with a plastic clip. He watched as she turned bacon over in the skillet and put slices onto a paper-towel lined plate. Then she pulled a pan of biscuits from the oven and set it on the stove.

He found his voice. "I hope there's coffee."

"Good morning," she said, more polite than he'd been. "Yes, I made a pot. How do you like your eggs?"

"Fried over easy," he said. "Morning. Thanks for making breakfast. I didn't expect you to do that."

She shrugged. "Shayne said he was hungry, and you were still asleep. I didn't think you'd mind, and it's one way to pay back some of your hospitality."

"I don't," he said. He poured a cup of black coffee and settled down at the table. "I appreciate it. I probably would have just grabbed a sack of sausage biscuits on the way to town or got out the cereal."

"I like to cook. In the city, I'm a baker."

He glanced up and almost smiled. "You make cakes, right? I saw some pictures online, fancy stuff."

Her lips lifted upward. "I do, now. I've been a chef, too. I can cook. Melissa, Shayne's mom, and I didn't grow up rich, not by any means, so we learned how."

"Do tell." Lamont wouldn't have guessed that from her manner, which screamed urban and well-off.

She put a plate down in front of him with two biscuits, four slices of bacon, and two eggs cooked the way he liked. Shayne brought over the butter and a jar of peach preserves. Matilda joined them, and Lamont noticed she had one biscuit and scrambled eggs. She bent her head and prayed before she ate. He'd already been chowing down and felt like a heel, but she hadn't asked him to join her.

"You don't like bacon?" he asked.

"I do, but I try to limit my fat intake."

He looked her up and down. She looked slender and shapely. Lamont decided not to comment. "Food's good," he said after he'd downed most of it. "Even though it's just hypocrite biscuits."

Matilda choked on a sip of coffee. "What?"

"Canned biscuits," Lamont said with a light laugh. "We always called them 'hypocrite biscuits.' Mama always made them from scratch. I don't even think she needed a recipe."

Thirty minutes later, they drove into Claremore and to the sheriff's office. His cousin, the current sheriff, offered them coffee, which Lamont accepted, but Matilda declined.

"Grab a seat," Sheriff Wills said. "The social worker will

be here any minute. Lamont, this is the kid's aunt?"

"Yeah, Tilly, meet David Wills. He happens to be my cousin as well as a lawman."

"Matilda Mannheim," she said and extended her hand, which David ignored.

"Good to meet you. Lamont, I explained the situation to Donna Wellington from social services, and we have some issues."

Lamont's chest tightened. "Like what?"

"I'll let her explain when she arrives."

Donna Wellington had to be close to retirement age, Lamont figured, with short-cropped gray hair and a lined face. She wore a sour expression as she got to the heart of the matter without preamble.

"I can't grant emergency custody to someone from out of state," she said in a nasal whine. "Ms. Mannheim is a resident of New York, I understand. I also understand that she is not very familiar with the child. The child needs to remain here until he's either placed in a foster home or some type of permanent custody arrangement or an adoption can be made."

Lamont knew little about foster care, but his overall opinion wasn't positive. He'd heard too many tales of neglect or poor treatment, foster parents who valued money over the child. There had to be good scenarios, too, but he hated to see Shayne shuttled away to strangers. He'd suffered enough with a horrible stepfather. A quick glance at the kid broke his heart. Shayne appeared near tears, his face set tight in sad lines.

"What are the options here? I think we both have the best interest of Shayne Sawyer in mind."

Ms. Wellington glared at him. "There aren't many, Mr. Fortune, if that's your actual name, which I doubt."

Irritated, Lamont came to his feet. "It's my real name. I'd be happy to show you my driver's license or birth certificate if you want. Or you can ask the sheriff, here. His mama and mine were sisters. He can vouch for the fact that I was born a Fortune right here in Oklahoma. Case you're not aware, the family dragged it over from Ireland more than a hundred years ago."

Without another word, he hauled out his billfold and retrieved his license, then handed it to her.

She flushed and nodded. "My apologies, but I had to ask. The best interests of any child in the system is always my first and foremost priority."

"Options?"

The social worker twisted her lips together and read from a paper in her hand. "If there are any close relatives who reside in Oklahoma who are citizens in good standing, we could place Shayne there. I understand you were granted emergency custody on the death of the child's stepfather. Are you related?"

He could lie, but the truth would be revealed. "I'm a neighbor."

"A neighbor. Hmm. The other option is to place this child in an approved foster home, a temporary one until we make a longer placement."

Matilda rose. "I'm his aunt, as far as I know, his only living relative. My sister was killed in a car wreck. She was his mother."

Ms. Wellington nodded. "I see that noted here. However, you're not an Oklahoma resident."

"But…"

"You're not a viable option," the social worker snapped.

"Then who is?"

"Mr. Fortune is the sole possibility," Ms. Wellington stated. "He would have to be approved if he wishes to become a long-term foster parent or consider adoption, but we could upgrade the emergency custody order that the sheriff approved to temporary custody. That is if the Sheriff would vouch for this individual."

"I do," David said. "Absolutely."

"Before we go any farther, can't I take Shayne home with me?" Matilda asked.

"To New York? No, not at this time because he's a ward of the state of Oklahoma." Ms. Wellington told her. "Do you own a home in New York?"

"I rent an apartment."

"It's a moot question, but do you have a bedroom for your nephew?"

Matilda's cheeks turned crimson. "No, I live in a one-bedroom studio apartment in midtown Manhattan."

"You wouldn't qualify even in New York City, I'm afraid. Mr. Fortune, are you willing to take on this responsibility?"

There didn't seem to be any other choice. If he said 'no,' Lamont figured they would haul the kid away here and now. "Yes," he said, voice as firm as he could make it. "Yes, I am."

If he thought it would be simple, it wasn't. First, there was endless paperwork to complete. He had to provide banking information and have his assets confirmed to make sure he could provide for the boy. Ms. Wellington set up an appointment to come see his home, and he agreed to have both a mental and physical assessment with qualified medical personnel. Matilda drummed her fingers against her knees and fumed during the lengthy process.

As Ms. Wellington reviewed the applications, her eyebrows rose. "You're a bronc rider?" she asked. "That's your primary source of income?"

"I have land and assets," Lamont said. His jaw hurt from clenching it tight. "But, yes, that's my occupation. I usually would be on the circuit by now, but I was delayed this year."

"May I ask why?"

He drew a harsh breath and held it for a moment, then exhaled. "I had a bad case of the flu."

The woman pursed her lips together in a tight line. "I don't know. I'm not sure that occupation will be considered stable enough…"

"Are you aware that this man is the national PRCA saddle bronc champion for the last two years?" Sheriff Wills said in a slow drawl. "I imagine he's got more in the bank than you do. Can you expedite the paperwork, or do I need to make a phone call to your supervisors? I'm talking at state level, by the way."

Ms. Wellington huffed and puffed, reminding Lamont of something about to explode. He squelched the desire to laugh.

"I'll get the emergency approval before 5 p.m. today," she said. "I will be at your home tomorrow morning at 9 a.m. for a home inspection. If that passes, then you have two doctor's appointments, both in Tulsa. I will give you the times later. Once the department has the results in hand, if all goes well, then you'll be approved as a foster parent with temporary custody."

"Sounds like a plan," Lamont replied. "Just to let you know, I plan to visit a lawyer with the goal of adoption. I'm fond of this kid, and I'd rather not see him spend the next six years in the system."

He didn't really realize the latter until he spoke, but Lamont realized it was true.

Shayne's face lit like a Fourth of July fireworks show. Matilda gasped and put one hand to her chest.

"Awesome," the boy cried and raised his fist to bump against Lamont's.

"I could…"

Lamont had an idea where she was going, and he shook his head. They could talk about it later, but in front of the prissy social worker didn't seem to be the time or place.

"Ms. Wellington, I'll see you tomorrow morning at my place. Do you need directions?"

"I have GPS."

"All right." It might work, likely wouldn't but he wasn't going to argue. He would save that for more important battles. Although Lamont would have preferred to go home, he headed for what he liked to call the "cut-rate supermarket" to stock up on groceries. If he was going to have Shayne, he'd need additional food. He would feed Matilda, too, for a couple more days if necessary.

"Are you really a national champion?" she asked as they traveled to the store.

"Saddle bronc champion? Yeah, for the last two years and once before that," Lamont replied. "Didn't you notice the belt buckle?"

He wore it often, with some pride. It was big and gaudy so hard to miss. If she paid any attention at all, Lamont couldn't figure how she didn't notice.

She ignored the question.

"Does that make you famous?" Shayne asked.

"In rodeo circles, yeah," Lamont told him.

"Awesome possum!"

"Where are we heading?" Matilda asked.

Lamont sighed. "Grocery store — you don't need to threaten to call 911 again."

"I wasn't planning to – I just asked."

"All right," he told her. He hadn't slept much, and he'd just committed to adopting a child he barely knew. For once, he wished he'd listened to advice his dad had handed down – before opening mouth, engage brain. Lamont had no clue how to parent and wondered what he'd do with Shayne when he headed out on the rodeo circuit. As much as he loved rodeo, he doubted it was the best environment for a 12-year-old kid.

At the store, he climbed out and slapped his oldest cowboy hat on his head. "Let's go. Shayne, you'll have to show me what you like to eat."

When Matilda didn't get out of the vehicle, he added, "And you can pick up what you want to cook, Tilly."

Lamont took charge of the buggy and let the other two shop free range. Shayne brought several packages of cookies over, but he approved only one. "You don't need to fill up on sweets, kid," he told him. "Maybe get some snack crackers if you like them. What about cheese?"

Matilda put wholewheat bread into the buggy and then visited the produce section. She brought back five pounds of potatoes along with apples, celery, onions, bananas, tomatoes, green peppers, a few lemons, two cloves of garlic, and some fresh mushrooms. She met his gaze as she put her selections into the cart, but he didn't complain. He'd told her to choose what she wanted.

By the time they headed to the checkout, the buggy was heaped high. Cheeses, boneless chicken breasts and thighs, lean turkey lunch meat, several steaks, some ground beef, and some fresh rainbow trout filled one corner. There was milk, brown rice, butter, eggs, and dry goods. From what he could see, she'd added staples like flour, sugar, baking powder, canola oil, and more. Shayne had added pudding cups, orange juice, hot dogs, hamburger patties, some sausage, frozen chicken nuggets, frozen fish fillets, and several boxes of macaroni and cheese. When he held up a box of ice cream bars, Lamont nodded. Kid needed a few treats, he thought, and he liked ice cream, too. After a moment's hesitation, Tilly added some vanilla ice cream, orange sherbet, and some turkey sausage. He drew the line at that and plucked it out of the buggy.

"Sausage comes from pigs in my house. Turkey is for Thanksgiving or maybe a sandwich. Everything else is fine."

Lamont had chosen some dark roast coffee, a bag of fried pork rinds, the ones he called "piggy pops," rippled potato chips, a carton of sour cream and onion dip, plus a few frozen pizzas.

"I can make pizza that will taste about ten times better than that," Matilda said. "I bought yeast for dough and everything."

"I'll get one," he said in compromise. "For emergencies."

The total came out triple what Lamont spent on an average store trip but there were three to feed, not one. He had the money, so he didn't complain. At his place, they carried in the groceries. Shayne helped his aunt put the things away, then Tilly made sandwiches for lunch.

Lamont opened the chips and dips to enjoy with the sandwiches. He was about to pop the first chip into his mouth when Matilda again folded her hands and bowed her head. With a groan, he put his head down, too, and waited.

"Amen," he said when she finished. "Let's eat and talk. There's a lot we need to discuss."

Matilda had been quiet since they left the sheriff's office, saying little, but it had been the calm before the storm. "Yes, we do. I don't begin to understand why I can't be his foster parent or guardian or something. He's my nephew."

Lamont resisted an urge to throw his sandwich across the room or smash a cup. "I know that. The authorities know that, but they have rules to follow, Tilly. Shayne's a great kid, and I don't want to see him go into the system, then be stuck there till he's 18. I stepped up to prevent that. I ain't planning to cut you out of his life. You can fly out here and see him whenever you want."

"But, Lamont, that's not the same thing."

Good Lord but the woman was obtuse and stubborn as a billy goat. It was the first time he noticed she used his name, though.

"Honey, we aren't going to keep beating a dead horse. As far as the state of Oklahoma is concerned, you can't be a foster parent. You might get an adoption lawyer to listen to you, but it would be a long and costly process. I have deep pockets – do you?"

Her face fell like a rock dropped in a pond. "Not really."

"Then listen up. I have Shayne's best interests in mind. I'm doing this for him. I'm worn out, didn't sleep worth a flip, and I have the home visit plus two trips to the doctor to deal with. Let's talk about something else, okay?"

"All right." She nibbled at her sandwich like a mouse, head down. Her voice sounded muted.

After a few moments of heavy silence, he asked, "What are you fixing for supper?"

"Lemon piccata chicken," Matilda told him. "With rice pilaf and a vegetable."

It had to be a fancy dish, he thought. It couldn't be good old fried or barbecued chicken. He preferred mashed potatoes with milk gravy instead of rice, and he didn't even want to guess what the vegetable might be. Still, he steeled himself not to complain. "Sounds tasty."

When she offered nothing more, he made another effort. "So, where in Texas are you from?"

"My sister and I were brought up in Marshall," Mathilda said. "Just a small town on Highway 80, another one of the exits off I-20."

"We lived at Jacksonville," Shayne said, reaching into the bag of chips and grabbing a handful. "I don't remember a whole lot, though. After my mama died, Teddy moved us here to Oklahoma, first up around Miami, then here. I was nine when she got killed in that wreck."

That had been about three years ago, Lamont figured. Nine was young to lose a parent. He'd been older – almost twenty – when his parents died, but it had still been a crushing blow. And three years seemed like a coincidence – that's how long it had been since the tornado took out the old home place.

"Did you know his stepfather?" Matilda asked.

"He was a sorry excuse for a man," Lamont replied. "I knew him by sight. I didn't pay much attention to him even though he lived just down the road. I knew him from the circuit before that. We became neighbors about three years ago, though, after the tornado."

Matilda put down her sandwich. "Tornado?"

The two sandwiches he'd wolfed down lay like rocks in his belly. Lamont didn't like to remember the tornado. "Yeah, one hit three springs ago, took out the old farmhouse where I was raised. Cut a swatch about five miles wide, but it didn't touch the old shack where Anderson lived. That's when I built this house. Got a storm shelter, too. I wouldn't expect a New York city gal to know much about tornadoes, though."

Matilda shot a look in his direction that should have seared him. "I'm from Texas so I'm familiar. Did you lose much?"

Lamont snorted through his nose. "Everything but the clothes and gear I had with me and what bits I could pick up out of the debris. And an old Ford Ranger that somehow wasn't smashed."

Shayne's eyes were huge. "Was it scary?"

"Probably. I wasn't here, though. I was out on the rodeo circuit. Came home when I heard the news to find everything destroyed. That wasn't one of my best years."

It hadn't been a champion year either, although he'd earned that back.

"I'm sorry," Matilda said. "That had to be a terrible experience."

A headache pounded inside his skull, and he'd had enough conversation for now.

"I'm going to go watch television in the den, probably take a nap," he announced. "Didn't sleep much last night. If I'm not up, wake me when supper's ready."

"I will, Lamont," she said and reached across the table to

touch his hand.

Invisible electricity crackled between them, but he ignored it. He hadn't decided if he liked the woman, and even if he did, she would leave soon. Lamont didn't need any more complications in his life, not an attraction to a stubborn urban woman who lived 1500 miles away.

He took two aspirins and dozed off before the program got past the opening credits.

The lemon piccata chicken turned out to be delicious, and the rice wasn't bad. He'd expected some strange vegetable, but she had fresh peas, which he liked.

Over the supper table, Shayne chattered, and Tilly sometimes spoke. It wasn't perfect, but he could tolerate it. That made for a fair start.

CHAPTER FOUR

Lamont woke up at five-thirty, got out of bed at six, and sat down for breakfast at seven. Matilda baked banana muffins, and although the fruit wasn't usually one of his favorites unless it was served in a banana split, he liked them. She offered him eggs or oatmeal on the side, and he chose the cackleberries. She and the kid ate oatmeal.

He drank coffee, and so did Matilda, but Shayne dug in the refrigerator, wanting soda pop.

"For breakfast?" Lamont questioned, with one eyebrow raised. "Not here. Milk or coffee."

With a sigh, the kid settled for a glass of milk and Lamont had to wonder what other dietary disasters Anderson had allowed. Soda pop for breakfast! Not even on the circuit had he ever indulged.

While she cleaned up the kitchen, Lamont ran the vacuum and had Shayne sweep the kitchen floor. He wanted everything spick and span for the social worker who rolled down the driveway at a quarter of ten. He stepped onto the porch to greet her.

"Good morning, Ms. Wellington. I expected you at 9."

Her already stern expression hardened. "I had to backtrack. I missed the correct turnoff the first time. I'm ready, however. I certainly hope you are."

He hid a rush of annoyance behind a fake smile. "Ready as I'll ever be. Come on in."

She stalked through the place, one room at a time,

including every bedroom and each bathroom. If she had donned white gloves to check for dust, he wouldn't have been surprised. Ms. Wellington peered into the fridge and opened the freezer. She pulled open cupboard doors and asked about the large gun safe in his bedroom, even trying the door, which was locked.

"Are there firearms inside?" she asked, her tone sharp enough to slice a Sunday roast.

If he hadn't figured sarcasm would infuriate her, Lamont would have told her, no, it's filled with gold bricks or something just as nonsensical. "Yes. I have several hunting rifles in there. Two are antiques, family heirlooms that I was able to retrieve after a tornado took out the original house on the property. Do you need to see them?"

"I'd rather not," she said with a sniff. "I'm not sure about safety if there are *weapons* in the home."

"It's a gun safe, and I keep it locked," Lamont said with growing impatience. "They're legal and registered to me."

She scribbled something on her notepad, but she continued with her inspection. After a very long hour, she returned to the living room. There were a few more questions, how many acres did he own, what was in the outbuildings, and the proximity of the closest neighbor. Lamont mentioned the storm shelter, figuring it might bring some brownie points.

"So, did I pass?" he asked.

Ms. Wellington's lip curled upward. "Yes, for temporary custody. That will be for three months. After that, you will be re-evaluated as a potential foster parent, or the child will be moved to a suitable location. The background check came back clean. You still must complete the physical exam and the psychological evaluation. I scheduled both for this afternoon in Tulsa. All the information is on this sheet."

She handed him a paper with the printed details. "Both doctors will send their findings to me and to the state," she said.

"Although it isn't mandatory, I wanted to ask if you live here alone."

Lamont ached to tell her, no, there were seven dwarves who shared the living space or maybe an alien or two. "Yes, but now it'll be Shayne and me."

"Is Ms. Mannheim a current occupant?"

Matilda's cheeks flamed crimson at the question. Lamont couldn't decide if she was embarrassed or angry.

Lamont shook his head. "Tilly is visiting her nephew, that's all. She doesn't live here."

He came close to adding, "and that's some more of your business," but didn't. He figured Tilly – *Matilda* – would hot-foot it back to the city as soon as temporary custody was settled. Maybe she'd come back to see Shayne, but maybe not. After all, she hadn't seen him for at least three years. It might be another five before she returned.

"Very well," Ms. Wellington snapped faster than she popped the gum in her mouth. "Then I'm finished, here, for now. I will email the temporary custody documents, and you can print them. They will also arrive in the mail. There will be a follow-up visit before you become more than a temporary foster parent *if* you do. I will be waiting to get those medical reports, and I'll be in touch as needed."

"All right," Lamont said. "You know where to find me."

He waited on the porch, arms crossed, until the social worker's vehicle passed out of sight, then came inside. Shayne and his aunt sat in the living room.

"Let's get around," he said. "We gotta head to Tulsa before long so I can make these two doctors' appointments. I'm gonna splash through the shower and change clothes, but I figure we can leave in thirty, forty minutes."

"Does that mean you want us to go with you?" Matilda asked, a frown crinkling her forehead.

"Yeah, it does," Lamont told her. "Afterwards, I wanted to stop somewhere and buy Shayne some more duds. He doesn't have that many clothes. I thought we'd catch lunch on the way and eat supper somewhere in Tulsa before we head back here. Unless you have something else planned?"

He knew she didn't unless she'd booked a flight back to New York. If so, he could drop her off at the airport.

"I don't," she replied. "I didn't want to assume anything or tag along if you'd rather we didn't."

"If I didn't, I'd say so straight out."

He took a swift, hot shower, then put on his best Wranglers and one of his favorite dress Western shirts. After consideration, he chose his finest boots, too. When he came out into the living room, he found Shayne wearing his new jeans and the one button-down shirt he'd bought for him. Matilda had changed into a navy sleeveless dress that didn't reach her knees.

"Looking fine, Tilly," he said without thinking, then winced in case it offended her.

Instead, she offered him a small smile. "Thanks. I wasn't sure what to wear."

Lamont grabbed his keys and billfold. As he started out the door, Matilda called his name.

"What?"

"While you were in the shower, someone named Lanelle Karnes called. She wanted you to call her back."

"She's my sister," he said. Lamont had no idea why he felt a need to explain, except Matilda probably figured he had women on the string. "I'll phone her on the way."

Once they merged onto the Will Rogers Turnpike, Lamont pulled out his mobile phone.

"This isn't the same way we came from the airport," Matilda said, glancing around as if he might be taking her hostage.

Lamont sighed. "It's not. That was the back way. Since this

Schusterman Center is downtown, taking the turnpike is quicker. Do you want to navigate?"

She shook her head. "I wouldn't have a clue where to tell you to go unless I looked it up on my phone."

"Give me some credit for having a brain," he returned as he punched in his sister's number.

"Hey," Lanelle said. "What's up, Lamont? I talked to Suzi-Q, and she said you've taken in a kid? Whose is he? Is it yours from some buckle bunny?"

"You know better than that." No one could get under his skin like his sister, but he loved her. "He lived down the road in a bad situation, but his stepfather just died... It's a long story, but yeah, I've got temporary foster custody, but I plan to adopt him. He's a good kid – name is Shayne."

"Wow. That surprises me. I never thought of you with a child. Who's the gal?"

Lamont pretended to be stupid. "What gal?"

"The one who answered the phone."

"That's Tilly," he said. "Shayne's aunt from New York City."

Lanelle groaned. "Don't tell me she's another uppity airhead like Remy."

"No, she's originally from Texas. Lanelle, I'll tell you all the details later. I'm on the way to Tulsa now, got some doctor's appointments."

Concern gentled her tone. "Are you sick, Lamont?"

"No, sis, I'm not. I'm fine. It's a routine physical and a mental evaluation for the custody thing."

"Thank God," Lanelle said. "I worry about you. You just got over that flu, and you've been injured so many times."

"I'm good, I swear. Talk to you later."

Lamont ended the call before his sister asked any more questions or referenced God again. They'd been raised in church with Christian parents. Lanelle and his brother Logan still believed. It wasn't that Lamont didn't – he had lost his trust in the Lord. He couldn't trust, not after his parents died and a tornado took out the old homeplace. Then Remy broke off their engagement. He'd wondered what kind of God would allow such things or for him to get mangled in the arena so many times. During the two weeks he'd been so sick with flu, he'd felt like Job.

"How long till we get there?" Shayne asked, bouncing on the seat in his excitement.

"About half an hour to Tulsa, another ten minutes to get downtown. We'll grab a bite to eat before I go see the doc."

"Hamburgers?" Shayne sounded hopeful.

"I thought chicken this time around. There's a regional chain serving chicken chunks instead of nuggets and a lot of other things, too. I figured we'd try it."

"We had chicken last night." Matilda's tone was quiet, but he wondered if she was offended.

"And it was delicious," Lamont said. To his surprise, it had been. "This is different but if you'd rather just grab a burger, we can. This place also has catfish, chicken fried steak, and dumplings."

"It's fine," Matilda said. "I like that kind of food."

His first appointment was at two, and it was twelve thirty when they pulled into the casual restaurant. Lamont ordered chicken chunks with potato wedges and fried okra. Shayne did the same but asked for corn, not okra. After a few long moments of deliberation, Matilda ordered catfish with potato wedges and pea salad. Although Lamont didn't comment and refused her offer to pay, she said, "Thank you. It smells great here. I haven't had catfish in years."

"It's good. You'll like it."

He was prepared this time for the blessing and bowed his

head at the right time. Her prayer surprised him, though, and touched his heart.

"Bless this food that we are about to eat, oh Lord, and bless us all. Watch over Shayne and Lamont. Let his doctors' appointments go well, and let him be healthy. Bless him and his home every day. Thank you for the safe journey here. In Jesus' name, I pray, amen."

"Amen," Lamont echoed. First time he'd said an amen in years. It seemed strange on his lips but, at the same time, somehow right.

Another issue cropped up during the conversation over the meal. Matilda asked Shayne where he attended school. When he told her he was in 7th grade at the junior high in Claremore, Lamont realized the kid hadn't been to school all week. He wondered if Shayne had attended on Monday. That evening, Teddy Anderson had collapsed on the floor dead from an overdose. So Shayne came to him for help.

Tuesday, he'd bought clothes for the kid, then picked up Matilda at the airport. Yesterday, they'd gone to the sheriff's office and met the social worker. Today, she'd come to inspect his home, and he had the appointments to keep.

"It's Thursday," Lamont said.

Matilda glanced up. "Yes, it is. Are you okay?"

He nodded. "I just lost track of my days with everything that's happened. I just realized Shayne's been out of school all week."

Shayne avoided meeting his eyes, and Tilly frowned. "He can't miss classes!"

"I know that." He clipped the words out fast and short. "I'll call the school and explain it. Maybe I'd better call David first."

"David?"

"The sheriff, my cousin," Lamont told her. "It was his wife

that told Lanelle about Shayne. That's why she called."

He'd lost his appetite. Here he hadn't even got started as a foster parent and had already screwed up. "Hey, David, it's me, Lamont. I haven't sent Shayne to school all week. Is that going to be a problem? I never even thought about it."

Sheriff Wills laughed. "No, it's not an issue. I had one of my deputies inform the school that Anderson was dead, so they're aware Shayne wasn't present and why. You'll have to go to the office tomorrow or Monday, get listed as his guardian with a change of address, but you'll take care of that, right?"

"Absolutely. Will I need copies of the foster parent stuff?"

"I imagine so. I'll make sure you get them. I'll call over to the junior high myself, tell them Shayne will be back Monday and that you'll come in to fill out all the paperwork."

"I owe you, big time. Thanks, cuz."

"Don't worry about it. Hey, while you're on the line, there's no funeral for Anderson. He didn't have any insurance, there wasn't any next of kin, so I had the funeral home cremate him."

Cremation made Lamont cringe, but it was the best option in this case. He wouldn't want the kid to endure a funeral on top of everything else.

"Thanks. So, I'm good, as far as school is concerned?"

"For now, you bet."

Matilda stirred her pea salad after he ended the call. "So, it's handled?"

"Yeah. Shayne, you'll go to school on Monday and I'll come along to fill out papers, all that junk."

At the Schusterman Center, Lamont's vitals were good. An unfamiliar doctor he'd never see again listened to his heart and lungs, thumped and poked his belly, stuck a finger up his rear to check his prostrate, and banged on his knees with a rubber mallet. The doc perused the sheaf of paper Lamont had filled out on his medical history.

"You pass," he said after a few moments. "I thought you looked familiar – Lamont Fortune, world champion saddle bronc rider for the last two years, right?"

"That's me." It amazed him whenever he was recognized. He preferred a low profile.

"And you're becoming a foster parent. That's admirable."

Lamont thought it was likely insane but didn't say so. He collected the kid and Matilda from the waiting area. They trekked to his next appointment where another doctor, this one a tall brunette who wore thick glasses but had a model's smile, performed the examination. She asked him dozens of questions, wanted to know about his personal life starting with his childhood, inquired about any anxieties he might have, and focused on the reasons he'd chosen to become a foster parent.

Once she learned about his parents' deaths and then heard about the tornado, Dr. Bella Barnes honed in on those events. Lamont described how his parents had died when the Cessna plane they were in crashed, leaving no survivors.

"Was it your parents' airplane?" she asked.

"No, they were with a friend of my dad's," he replied. Before she could frame the question, he added, "They were flying to Prescott, Arizona, to watch me perform in a rodeo there."

Back then, he'd ridden both bulls and saddle broncs, but later, he switched to just bucking broncs, although it wasn't any easier. The biggest difference was broncs don't have horns that could gore a cowboy, and bulls did.

That prompted a new objective for the inquiry. She wanted to know about his rodeo history, how he'd felt when his parents passed away, and his reaction to the tornado that destroyed his family home. She pried into his past relationships, so he had to mention Remy and their break-up.

"Why do you think that happened?" Dr. Barnes asked.

"We were too different, I guess. She was glitz and glamor. I'm more blood and guts."

Lamont thought it was a funny remark, but the doc didn't crack a smile. Nor did he reference how cold-hearted she'd said he was.

By the time she finished and made the determination that he was in good mental health, stable enough to become a foster parent, it was almost five o'clock. Lamont had a raging headache from the stress, and his stomach hurt. Whether lunch hadn't agreed with him or he was hungry, he didn't know, but he wasn't feeling good.

In the waiting room, Shayne jumped to his feet. "Man, I didn't think you were ever going to get finished. I got bored."

Matilda rose, her expression calm as a quiet pond. "It did take a long time. Did it go well?"

"Yeah," Lamont said. "I passed."

"What took so long?" Shayne asked.

"It wasn't an exam – it was an interrogation. Let's get out of here."

He piloted them through rush hour to Woodland Hills Mall. Lamont said little on the way, concentrating on winding through the heavy traffic. If his head stopped pounding and his stomach settled down, he'd be fine.

Once he parked and climbed out, Shayne rushed ahead. Matilda hung back and put her hand on his arm.

"Are you all right? You look sick."

Her concern moved him. He started to blow off her question, then admitted, "I got a bad headache, and my stomach's bothering me. Stress sometimes gets to me."

"If you'd rather head home, we can. I can explain it to Shayne."

Although Lamont would like nothing more, he didn't want to make another trip to Tulsa.

"I'll manage. I'll take something and probably feel better. We can always get a hotel room for the night if I don't."

"Lamont," she said. Her sweet tone made it an endearment. "If you feel that rotten, we should just go home."

She called his place home twice, and he wondered if that meant anything. Probably not.

"I don't want to come back tomorrow or Saturday. The kid needs more clothes and stuff, like school supplies. Anything left in that hovel he lived in won't be worth keeping."

She lifted one small hand and cupped his cheek, then laid it over his forehead. His mama used to do that, and the gesture brought a rush of appreciation.

"I don't have a fever. I'd know if I did. I'm all right."

"If you're not, promise you'll say something and not just tough it out."

Her dark eyes met his, and he shivered at the powerful emotion she invoked.

"I will, Tilly. Okay?"

Matilda nodded as Shayne doubled back.

"Hurry up, what's taking so long? I'm hungry."

Lamont summoned up a faint grin. "Then let's go find something to eat, buddy."

He would be fine, sooner or later. In the meantime, he was responsible for this kid and he wanted to do right by him.

CHAPTER FIVE

After washing down the over-the-counter pain reliever Matilda dug out of her purse with an ice-cold soda, before long, Lamont felt better. There were multiple food choices but they opted for a Chinese place, offering a buffet with a wide variety of dishes. He started with some egg drop soup, then ate some chicken chop suey as his stomach eased. A portion of fried rice and some beef scooped out of the beef and broccoli finished his meal. Mathilda ate sushi, which didn't surprise him, along with some Kung Pao Chicken and a shrimp dish. Shayne ate several egg rolls and rangoons, then had a serving of sweet and sour chicken.

"Where do you want to start?" Lamont asked after they left the restaurant. "I was thinking JC Penney's, maybe."

"What are we buying?" Shayne questioned.

"Jeans, maybe some khakis, t-shirts, button-down shirts, underwear, socks," he replied. "Maybe a jacket, I don't know. I'll get you some boots but not here – we'll go to a Western Wear store later for that. A backpack for school."

The boy's face brightened, and he grinned. "Okay. Can I go to the restroom first?"

"Sure, buddy."

As they waited, Matilda scrutinized him. "How do you feel? You don't look as ill."

If he didn't know better, he'd think she might actually care. "Better, thanks. I'll live. I'm a tough old cowboy, Tilly."

She laughed. "Handsome and cocky, too."

Surprise made him laugh out loud. "You think so?"

"With that gold hair, blue eyes, and that face, I know so."

He thought Matilda might have said more, but Shayne returned before she could. Instead, she smiled.

Two hours later, they exited the mall with multiple shopping bags. After he stowed them behind the truck seat, they climbed in and headed for home. Lamont fueled the truck at a big travel plaza on the way out of town, appreciative of the cool night breeze against his face. The last few days had been the busiest and longest since he'd been sick. By the time they rolled into his drive, he'd be more than ready for bed.

He grabbed a soda so he'd remain alert on the drive home and decided to take Route 66 back to Claremore. Shayne and Tilly wouldn't be able to see the sights along the way, but they could make another trip in the daylight. He debated whether to mention the Old Route 66 history, then decided he'd wait. From habit, he popped a CD into the stereo, and Lamont's favorite classic country music filled the cab with sound. Hank William's plaintive voice crooned the old, sad ballads. The tires whined as the truck ate up the miles toward home, providing additional accompaniment. If he'd been alone, Lamont would have been belting out the songs, more familiar to him than nursery rhymes. He'd grown up with Hank, Johnny Horton, Marty Robbins, Webb Pierce, and Johnny Cash as a soundtrack for his life. His dad had loved this music and Lamont knew most of the lyrics by heart.

Until the kid joined in singing *Kaw-Liga*, he'd thought Shayne had fallen asleep. Tickled that the boy knew the old song about the wooden Indian who never went anywhere, he sang, too. The music raised Lamont's spirits, and happiness spread through him, lessening his fatigue.

Shayne chimed in on *Say Hey Good Looking;* although he missed more than a few notes, he made up for it with enthusiasm. When the mood shifted from bright to plaintive, Matilda sang along to it, too, her voice a rich alto that blended with the music and resonated with emotion.

The song was Lamont's least favorite, *Cold, Cold Heart,* because of Remy's accusations that he didn't care and wasn't capable of love, but when Matilda belted it out, his heart beat so fast he thought he might pass out at the wheel. She owned the song, he thought, and her voice infused it with power. If he had ever owned a heart of ice, it melted. Lines from the lyrics struck him with profound meaning. If anyone ever needed to free a doubtful mind, it was Lamont. He possessed a lonesome past, and he'd been hiding from life. He'd gone through the motions, nothing more. Shayne's appearance in his life had propelled him out of his inner cave back into the real world. Lamont, who hadn't shed a tear since his folks died, had a tear trickling and tickling down his cheek. Something broken within him began to heal as Lamont listened to Tilly sing along with *Take These Chains From My Heart.*

He had no idea if she realized how much her singing had impacted him, but she stopped after that. They were coming into Claremore by then, and once he mustered control of his emotions, he said, "You have an amazing voice, Tilly."

"Thanks. It's been a long time since I sang," she said.

"I don't imagine there was much demand for ol' Hank in New York City."

Matilda laughed. "There's probably more than you'd think, but not among the people I knew. I grew up on that music."

"So did I. Hank Williams was my grandpa's favorite singer, and my dad liked anything vintage country." Lamont couldn't help but grin.

Well, knock him winding, but he had something in common with this citified gal. Lamont never dreamed she'd be familiar with vintage country or like Hank's tunes. He'd known she could bake fancy confections, cakes that were works of art but it surprised him how she could sing like a country music queen.

At his place, stars sparkled in a clear sky, and a full-bellied moon shone above. Lamont gazed upward for a moment, then headed toward the small side porch. "Shayne, go get your shower, buddy," he said. "You got the key?"

"Yeah, but do I gotta?"

"You bet. My old granny used to say: 'cleanliness is next to godliness.' Clean up, then go to bed. We got stuff to do tomorrow, too."

The kid grinned and dashed inside. Lamont fell in step behind him and then realized that Matilda stood staring at the sky. "Hey, Tilly, are you coming inside?"

She startled, then offered him a little smile. "I am in just a minute. The stars are so lovely. I haven't seen a night sky like this for years. I'd forgotten how beautiful it was. *There is one glory of the sun and another glory of the moon, and another glory of the stars: for one star differeth from another star in glory.*"

Lamont recognized the verse from the Bible. "From First Corinthians?" he guessed.

Matilda nodded. "Chapter 15, Verse 41."

"Don't you have stars in the city?" he asked. He remembered his one trip to the Big Apple and how the urban lights were so bright that the night sky was diminished.

"I always knew they were there, but it's hard to see them. Sometimes I try, but I can barely see the moon, let alone any stars."

Memories of the rooftop terrace at the hotel where he'd stayed returned, and Lamont sighed.

"All I could think about was the fact there were thousands more people in all the buildings around me than in Claremore," he said, without thinking. Standing on that hotel roof had made him feel very small and insignificant. That had been on his first night in New York, and he'd been overwhelmed. That had lessened over the next few days as he navigated the streets between the hotel in Midtown Manhattan and Madison Square Garden. "I really felt like a hick."

And although he'd scored well enough to take home a fair-sized prize, he'd been ready to head back to Oklahoma. His single bite of the Big Apple had been more than enough to last a lifetime.

Matilda paused her steps. "I didn't know you'd been to New York."

Another assumption, he thought and shrugged. "You never asked. I went once – that was enough for me."

"Why did you go?"

"Rodeo at the Garden."

"Madison Square Garden?" Her voice rose higher. "Really?"

"Yeah, for real and true." For a moment, he had a sudden, strange desire to kiss her but didn't. Heavy fatigue hung over him. So much for the songs and stars. He longed to lay down and sleep for a good ten hours, although he probably wouldn't.

Lamont stepped back and let her enter first. She continued through the kitchen, but he sat down on the couch and pulled off his boots. It had to be close to midnight by his reckoning but when he glanced at the clock, it wasn't even ten o'clock. He groaned. If he went to bed now and fell asleep, he'd wake up at 2 or 3 in the morning. Then he'd toss and turn in a futile effort to go back to sleep. He could watch some television, maybe one of the corny old sitcoms he enjoyed, but then he'd probably drift off on the couch. Lamont had done it many times.

"Hey, Lamont," Shayne said as he entered the den. "Good night."

Lamont reached out a tired hand and ruffled the kid's hair. "Night, Buddy. Did your aunt go to bed yet?"

"I think she's taking a shower."

Good. When she sang, she evoked emotions he usually

kept hidden. Her reaction to the stars had done the same. Lamont didn't like memories because too often they brought pain. If he focused too much on the past and all he'd lost, it would taint the present, so he lived day by day, his feelings repressed. Tilly – Matilda was too long and fussy of a name for the woman that touched his heart and soul – engaged him, and he liked her. He had almost kissed her but didn't dare. As much as he dreamed of having a family, he feared being hurt more.

Remy's rejection had wrecked him, not because he'd loved her so much but because she hit his self-esteem. In hindsight, Lamont doubted he had ever loved her but when she broke off their engagement, her harsh words had wounded his soul. She'd accused him of being cold and uncaring, said that he didn't like anyone but himself and that he would end up a lonely old man at the end of his life. He figured he probably would.

Now, he wasn't as sure. Shayne's presence changed everything, more so if he adopted the kid. Lamont was willing, but the idea also terrified him. He'd never been a parent and worried he might not manage the job. If he messed up and the kid ended up in the system, Lamont would hate himself for failing. If Tilly lived in Oklahoma, he might want to pursue a relationship, but she'd leave soon, and he'd be left lonely. She had a life in the city, and his was here. Soon as he got everything with the kid settled, Lamont had to hit the circuit.

He rubbed his bad knee, which twinged, and realized he lacked any enthusiasm to go. Three times, he'd won the title of National Saddle Bronc Champion. That alone brought a tremendous amount of money, more than he could spend in years. It also came with increasing wear and tear on his body. At 31, a lot of rodeo guys were quitting or at least thinking about hanging up their spurs. Since he was already late starting the season, Lamont wondered if he should take a year off. He could use that time to think about his future and focus on Shayne.

Maybe, he thought. He could either get up and head for his bedroom or pick up the remote control. Lamont hadn't decided yet which to do when Matilda came into the den.

She wore a long flannel nightgown in a pink paisley print. It covered her from neck to ankles, baggy enough to conceal any curves. Her feet were bare, and he could smell the fresh scent of her shampoo across the room.

"Lamont?" she said. "I didn't realize you were still in here."

"I am. I have a niece named Paisley. She'd like your granny gown."

Somehow, Lamont figured Tilly would sleep in something else, pajamas if not lace-trimmed lingerie, but the nightdress suited her.

A tiny grin flirted with her mouth. "It's comfy. How old is she?"

"Six. She likes pink too."

She hadn't expected him to be here. "What are you doing, anyhow?"

"I thought I'd make a cup of hot chocolate or herbal tea. Want one?"

Lamont couldn't remember when he'd drank hot chocolate but it would have been in childhood. "I don't need anything with caffeine. I have enough trouble sleeping sometimes."

He hadn't meant to tell her – that fact was one he seldom shared with anyone.

Matilda stepped closer. "The cocoa only has a little, but the tea has none. It should help you sleep."

Suspicious, he asked, "What's in it?"

"Chamomile, spearmint, some lemongrass. It tastes good. Do you want some or not?"

"I don't have anything like that here."

She laughed. "I got some when we bought groceries."

That impulse to kiss her had returned. Lamont replied to avoid acting on it. "All right, I'd try a cup."

"Then sit back down – I'll bring it to you."

Matilda put two steaming cups down on the coffee table and settled into one corner of the couch, her feet tucked underneath her. "I put just a little sugar in both," she told him. "It can be a tiny bit bitter without."

"Thank you." Lamont picked up a mug and smelled the tea before he took a sip. When he did, the taste surprised him. "That's not bad."

"You're welcome."

They sipped in comfortable silence for a few minutes. Maybe he was just tired, or the tea worked, but Lamont got drowsy. "I'm going to turn in soon," he told her. "Or I'll fall asleep here."

She nodded. "I'll make breakfast in the morning."

"Sounds good. I want to get the kid some boots and whatever school supplies he might need, but it won't take all day."

"Then I'll plan on something for dinner."

Lamont had to ask. "I know you're from Texas, but do you mean dinner at noon or supper?"

Matilda grinned. "I finally learned to say dinner in New York for the evening meal, but it took some time. I meant supper."

"All right. We can grab a bite out at noon or pick up something or make sandwiches." He stood, then stretched. His joints and back ached, an affliction that most rodeo riders suffered. After multiple injuries and years in the saddle, it happened.

She stepped forward and reached for their empty cups.

Lamont moved, and they bumped heads together, not hard enough to hurt.

"Whoops," he said. "I'm sorry, Tilly."

Matilda rubbed her forehead. "My fault, Lamont."

Her face was just below his, her lips pretty and pink, eyes shining, and he couldn't resist. Lamont leaned down and let his lips touch hers. It was a brief kiss, but when his mouth met hers, he shivered. A delicious sensation rocketed through him and surprised him.

"Oh, my," she breathed, faint as a shadow.

He would have quit if she hadn't said that but he had to give her a good, proper kiss and did. Lamont wrapped his arms around her and let his lips linger over hers. He tasted a hint of tea on her warm mouth. Her lips melted beneath his, soft and sweet. As he cradled her close, Matilda leaned into him. Her hands rested on his upper arms, and she gave back the kiss.

Lamont ended it, his breath quick and short. If he didn't walk out of this room now, he might not make it tonight. "Good night, Tilly."

He knew it was lame and inadequate. So many other words he could say crowded his mind, but shied away from his tongue.

Her face lit like a candle in the darkness. Matilda lifted one hand to touch his cheek and smoothed it over his bristles. "Night, Lamont."

With a graceful swoop, she grabbed the cups and dropped them in the sink on her way through the kitchen. She paused long enough to run a little water in each, then headed to the room where she was staying.

Lamont followed, the lingering scent of her shampoo and a hint of perfume filling his nose. He decided he'd shower come morning. Once he'd stretched out, he fell asleep. Rare for him, he slept through till early morning. It wasn't quite six when he woke, and the sun hadn't risen. After a shower, he made coffee and took it outside to the front porch. To the east, the sun crept up the sky, and Lamont watched. It'd been a while since he'd taken time to enjoy dawn, and he'd almost forgotten how beautiful it could be.

Although the morning air was cool enough to make him consider going inside for a jacket, he liked it. Tornadoes came most often when temperatures soared to unseasonable highs. Around 7:30, Shayne came out.

"Breakfast is ready," he said. "Hey, Lamont?"

"Yeah?"

"Aunt Tilly made pancakes, but they're really thin and flat. I don't think she knows how to make them, but don't say anything 'cause it might hurt her feelings."

Tickled the kid had picked up on the nickname he'd given her, Lamont nodded. "Okay, I won't. I appreciate her making breakfast."

Despite having spent the last five years with one of the rudest men he'd ever known and a poor example for a human being, Shayne had manners and was considerate. His concern for his aunt's feelings pleased Lamont.

The moment he saw the "pancakes," Lamont grinned. He recognized them from some of the fancy brunches he'd had in the Remy years. He leaned down and said to Shayne, "Those are crepes, not regular pancakes. They're supposed to be thin and flat."

Although he hadn't intended her to, Matilda heard him, but she smiled.

"They're French," she said. "Lamont's right – they are crepes. I've got some jam and some fruit you can eat with them."

Shayne wrinkled his nose. "What about peanut butter?"

"There's some in the cupboard," Lamont said. "Next one past the sink."

Over breakfast, he had Shayne write out his school schedule, and they talked about what supplies he might need. School would be out for the summer by the end of May. Lamont realized he couldn't head out on the rodeo circuit until school dismissed, another reason why he might skip this season.

"So you have Language Arts, honors math, science, social studies, PE, art, and computer technology?"

"Yeah."

"Honors math? I'm impressed."

Shayne shrugged. "It's just numbers."

He was humble, a good thing, Lamont thought. "Figure out what notebooks, folders, pens, pencils, and stuff you'll need. We'll get them today – along with some boots."

"Cowboy boots?"

"Sure."

"Awesome!" Shayne pumped his fist in the air and grinned. "When are we leaving?"

"Soon."

The trio loaded into his pickup truck, and they went to town.

Lamont figured it would be a quick, routine day, but as it turned out, it wasn't.

CHAPTER SIX

They entered town on Highway 88, which became Will Rogers Boulevard, traveling past the Will Rogers Memorial Museum. Once they had rounded up an appropriate amount of notebooks, wide-lined paper, ink pens, #2 pencils, and a backpack, they went to a Western Wear store. Boots were the priority on Lamont's mental to-do list. Once Shayne had picked out a pair of quality western boots in a large store downtown that smelled like good leather, they moved on to the school. Although Lamont knew where the junior high was located, he let Shayne provide directions so he would be familiar.

"I can't remember if my old backpack is in my locker or if I left it at the old house," Shayne said. "Can we go see?"

Lamont had planned on waiting until Monday, but the way the kid talked, there were things he might need in his pack. If it was in his locker, they could retrieve it, but he wasn't about to set foot in that rundown wreck Anderson had called home.

"Do you really need it?" he asked the boy, reluctant to face the school personnel today.

"I've got library books in it. If I left it at the house and I don't bring them back, you'll have to pay for them."

"I can do that, no problem."

"Yeah, but I want to read them. One of them is *Tuck Everlasting*.

Resolved that he'd buy Shayne a copy if the backpack wasn't at school, Lamont sighed and headed for Will Rogers Junior High School. He wished he had all the official paperwork, but if necessary, he could call his cousin or Ms. Wellington for verification.

Lamont hadn't visited a school in years, so the high level of security surprised him. He had to ask to be buzzed into the building and then sign a visitor's record sheet.

The school administrative assistant, Mrs. Childers, recognized Shayne and smiled.

"Hello," she said. "I didn't expect you to be here today. Do you need a tardy pass?"

Before Shayne could part his lips, Lamont took the lead. "I'm Lamont Fortune, and I have temporary custody of Shayne, working toward permanent custody and then adoption. He'll be in school on Monday, and I'll be coming in to take care of any paperwork, but right now, he needs to see if his backpack is in his locker. Can he go check?"

Mrs. Childers nodded. "Of course, but you'll have to wait here, Mr. Fortune."

"Sure." He sank into a chair to wait.

"You're one of our local celebrities," Mrs. Childers, who couldn't be much more than twenty-two or three, said. "National Saddle Bronc Champion for two years running."

"That's me." Lamont wished Tilly had come inside instead of opting to wait in the truck. She was probably better at small talk.

"You'll need to bring your custody paperwork with you Monday," the woman said. "I'll make copies for Shayne's file and add you to the list of who can pick him up and check him out. That's extremely important, and we won't give any information to anyone not on that list."

"Good deal."

Shayne returned with a ragged khaki backpack. Lamont took it and winced at the rank smell. It reeked of tobacco smoke and weed. He toted it at arm's length to the truck and placed it in the bed. "Get your library books," he told the kid. "We're gonna pitch that nasty thing first chance we get."

He let Shayne climb into the truck, sitting between him and Matilda. Lamont noticed she had her cell phone in her hand and said little.

"Did you miss me?" he joked.

She nodded. "I missed you both. What's up now?"

"Well, we can drive around so you can see more of the sights," he said. "We can stop at the store for a few more groceries, eat lunch, or just head home."

"Okay." Her quiet tone was the softest he'd heard from Matilda. He had to strain to hear her reply. "Supermarket's fine. We have sandwich stuff at the house."

Lamont caught the difference. She'd said 'home' twice, but now it was 'house.' He didn't mind eating a sandwich but since she suggested it, now he wanted to take them out to eat.

"We've got some good local restaurants, my treat."

Something was amiss because Matilda sighed and said, "Lamont, really, it's fine to have sandwiches at your place. I'm planning to make pizza for supper."

"Yay!" Shayne said. "I love pizza."

"All right," Lamont said and tried to sound gracious, not grumpy. "I like it too."

Matilda offered him a small smile. "Then we'll go to the supermarket, then head back."

At the store, Lamont sent Shayne ahead to pick out a few snacks, then turned to her.

"Everything okay, Tilly? You're awfully quiet."

She sighed. "It will be. Can I tell you later? Shayne will be back in a minute."

His stomach clenched. "Yeah, sure. Is it something bad?"

"I don't have a job any longer. I'll explain later, I promise."

Lamont had a dozen questions, but he kept them for now.

"All right. Let's get the shopping done."

His job seemed to be pushing the buggy around the store and paying at the checkout, but he didn't mind. After dumping the ragged backpack in the first trash can he saw, Lamont loaded the bags into the truck and headed home. Some of the local sights he had meant to show them, like the Will Rogers Memorial and the JM Davis Arms and Historical Museum and Belvidere, could wait.

After turkey sandwiches with tossed salad and a few chips on the side, Shayne withdrew to the front porch with his library books. Although Lamont had planned to show him around the forty acres that surrounded his home, he changed his mind. He put the food away while Tilly washed dishes. As soon as the last plate rested in the drainer, he cleared his throat.

"We need to talk."

Matilda nodded. She'd kept up with the conversation over lunch but had added little. "I suppose we do."

"It's a pretty day. Let's go to the back deck."

Lamont led the way and settled down in one of the chairs. One of these days, he figured he might get an above-ground swimming pool, although he doubted he'd use it often. He was more of a creek or lake swimmer if he wanted to splash in the water. Matilda took a seat across from him, twisting her hands together.

He got right to the main points. "First, how long are you staying?"

When her expression crumpled, Lamont got more specific. "Before you get riled up, you can stay as long as you need. I just want to know if you plan to leave soon or what."

She exhaled a long breath. "I hadn't decided, and now I don't know."

"Because of your job?"

"Yes."

"Want to tell me what happened?"

Matilda sighed. "I'm a cake baker, a master baker, cake artist, whatever you want to call it. I bake and decorate fancy cakes for special occasions, birthdays, weddings, anything."

"I saw that online," Lamont told her. "Looked like you're pretty good at it."

She shrugged. "Delphine, the woman who owns the bakery where I work, well, worked, hired me three or four years ago because I had a flair for decorating and creating cakes. Before that, I was a chef who sometimes made cakes. She called me earlier, when you and Shayne were inside the school, and told me she was terminating me."

Her tone was flat and too calm, Lamont thought. "Why?"

"Remember when you called me about Shayne?"

"Yeah, of course."

"And I booked a flight online while I was on the phone."

"I remember."

"I didn't think about work or calling Delphine or anything but Shayne. When my sister, his mom, died, Theodore called me, but that's all. He said there wasn't going to be any kind of service, and I don't know if that's true or he just didn't want me around. When I didn't hear anything more, I took some vacation days and went to Jacksonville. I thought maybe he'd let me have Shayne, but they had moved. I didn't know where and I kept looking. If you hadn't called me, I still wouldn't know."

Lamont listened, but his patience eroded fast. "I hope you're going somewhere with this."

"I am, trust me. I booked that flight, and the next day was my day off. I came and didn't think to tell Delphine anything, not until I was here. I didn't get ahold of her, but I left a message."

"Sounds fair enough."

Matilda made a sound halfway between a laugh and a sob. "It might have been, but I had a very special cake to create, an engagement party three-tiered confection for a celebrity. Cakes like that can take days to put together, but I wasn't there. I forgot all about it. Nobody at the bakery realized it until earlier today – when it was time to load up the cake to deliver out on Long Island."

Now he saw the problem. "And there wasn't one."

"Right, no cake. That meant huge problems because Delphine has built a reputation. When Bellissima found out the cake didn't get made, she threw a hissy fit."

"Bellissima, as in the singer and actress?"

Even a rodeo cowboy in rural Oklahoma had heard of the beautiful woman, famed for performances on Broadway and in Hollywood. Lamont didn't care much for her – he wasn't fond of the artsy way she sang, and he thought she was far too glitzy to be truly pretty.

"That's her. I doubt the news has hit the tabloids yet but she announced her engagement today to some Wall Street wizard today."

"Rich?"

Matilda shook her head. "Very."

She named the man, a well-known financier, one likely old enough to be the star's grandfather.

Lamont whistled. "That's pretty tall cotton."

"You might say so. Bellissima demanded that I be fired, and Delphine said she didn't have a choice, not if she wanted to keep selling pretty cakes to the rich and famous. I'm now unemployed."

"I'm sure sorry, Tilly," he told her. "But you'll be able to get another job, won't you?"

She laughed, but it had a wild sound. "Not in the City. If Delphine doesn't blacklist me, Bellissima will make sure everyone who is anyone knows what I did. I won't be able to get work as a cook, let alone a cake artist or chef."

As big as New York City was, there had to be a place for her, he thought, but maybe he was naive. "Surely there would be someplace."

"I doubt it, not even in Queens or Brooklyn," Matilda said. "I don't know what I'll do or where I'll end up."

"You can stay here while you figure it out," Lamont told her. "Shayne would like that."

So would he, but he wasn't going to admit that, not just yet.

"Thank you. I can stay for a few days, I suppose, but I can't just live off your generosity. I wouldn't feel right, Lamont."

"What did you do before you got into professional food gigs?"

Matilda buried her face in both hands for a few moments. "I waited tables back home in Marshall," she told him. "I was a waitress who sometimes helped out with the cooking in a little old diner, like something out of the 1950s."

That surprised him and brought questions. "Did you go to New York to be a chef, then?"

"No, Lamont," she replied, her voice breaking as she spoke. "I thought you might guess – I went to break into show business. I thought I could be a singer and that I was good enough to star on Broadway. Turns out, it takes a lot more than a good singing voice to make it. I didn't have what it takes."

He could imagine, at least a little. On Broadway, she would have been competing against the best of the best, many of them legacy actresses and actors from theatrical families. Tilly had beauty and a voice but not the wealth. Whether or not it was true, he'd heard dirty stories about how young actresses sometimes got their first break, and he hated the idea, especially if it involved Mathilda.

"You have more than it takes," he said and meant it. "You're way above that kind of show business life. It's worse than rodeo."

Matilda stared at him, her eyes huge in a pale face. For a moment, he feared he'd made her mad and that she was about to unleash her temper on him. If she did, it was all right. He could take it and she needed to vent. Instead, she issued a rich, deep burst of laughter that echoed from the deck to the woods behind the house.

"Lamont, you are really something. I'm at the lowest point of my life, I think, no job, I have to leave New York and give up my apartment, and I have no prospects, but you compliment me. Then you make me laugh. I don't know what I'll do, but at least, for now, you're here to cheer me up."

When it dawned on him that she meant it, he grinned. "I'll do my best, Tilly. And I'll help you any way I can."

"Nobody but you ever called me that," she said, shaking her head. "Now you have Shayne using it too. I didn't like it at first, but it's starting to grow on me."

"Maybe you can start over as Tilly. It might bring you better luck."

She nodded. "Maybe so. I guess I don't have to decide anything today."

When she stood up, so did he. Matilda took three steps forward until she was close enough to touch. "Babe, we'll figure something out."

"You make me believe that." Her voice was no more than a whisper, softer than the echo of tires over on the paved road. "I worried you might tell me to go, get out of here."

As far as he knew and for as long as he could remember, Lamont had never been that hateful or mean. "I wouldn't do that, especially not to the kid's aunt."

"I need to get the pizza dough started," she said and started to step around him. "Thanks for listening and being understanding."

"De nada."

He'd thought her to be cold, sophisticated, and urban, but right now, she wasn't any of those things. From the first time he talked with her on the phone, she spoke with Texas flavor but after just a couple of days, it had become more pronounced. In her faded blue jeans and a rose-colored blouse, he found her beautiful. Last night's kiss began as an accident, but this time, it was deliberate.

Lamont pulled her into his arms and lowered his mouth onto hers. He didn't get in a rush and let his lips linger over hers. It wasn't as much passionate as sweet and cherishing. Tilly didn't push him away or protest. Instead, she met his kiss. The world around them narrowed to a few small feet on the deck, his home and her nephew fading into the shadows. Nothing existed for a brief time except the two of them and this kiss.

He hadn't meant to become a foster parent, and now he was one. Although often lonely, Lamont hadn't been searching for a woman and definitely not one fresh from the Big Apple. He savored her, and after he removed his mouth from hers, Tilly didn't move. She stood, her head resting against his chest, and he realized he was smitten. He might have held her for five minutes or thirty — he had no idea, but when she stepped back, he missed holding her.

"I'll be in the kitchen," she told him, her voice more than a little breathless. Matilda let her fingers stray across his cheek and outlined his lips with her thumb. "You're a fine man, Lamont Fortune."

He watched her return inside, then sat down with his hands resting behind his head. A week ago, he lived alone and had been itching to get back on the rodeo circuit. In rapid sequence, he'd met the kid, refused to hand his old beater truck for free over to Teddy Anderson, the boy reached out, and he'd called Matilda. Then Anderson overdosed, Tilly arrived in Oklahoma, he gained custody, and his life shifted direction. The changes were still coming, and he wondered how it would all work out.

One way or another, Lamont thought.

Garth Brook's voice with the refrain of "Rodeo" interrupted his reverie, and he realized it was his ringtone, so he answered his phone, "Yeah, it's me."

His brother chuckled. "It's me, too, Lamont. What in tarnation are you up to? Lanelle thinks you've lost your mind or that you're sick."

"I ain't either one," Lamont told Logan. "I'm finally over that flu, although it was rough, and I'm not crazy."

"Then why aren't you out on the circuit?"

"I meant to be by now, but life threw me a curve."

"And you've taken on a kid."

"Yeah, his name is Shayne."

Logan whistled long and loud. "I hope to shout that you know what you're doing."

Lamont laughed. "Me too. I know you're gonna ask, but Shayne's aunt is here too."

"I heard – some New York City girl. When is she heading back east?"

"No idea, but she's from Texas."

"Do tell. Hey, I called because I thought I might come down and do a little fishing at Oolagah Lake tomorrow. Want to wet a line with me?"

Lamont considered it. They had no plans and he could use a day out on the water with his brother. "I'd love to."

"I'll bring the boat and be there in time for breakfast, brother."

"I'll be ready. Looking forward to it. You mind if I bring the kid?"

"Fine with me. See you in the morning, by 7 at the latest."

Lamont headed out to the shed to dig out his fishing rods

and gear. He found them and dug them out of a corner. A slight movement caught his attention, and he turned around. A large copperhead snake slithered out from the same area. Snakes of any kind gave Lamont the willies, but he reached for a hoe he'd seen leaning against the wall. In slow motion, he brought it down and severed the snake's head from the body. The serpent twitched and wiggled in its death throes, but he left. He'd come back later and remove it.

Shayne came around the house, and his face lit up when he saw the fishing poles.

"Are we goin' fishin'?"

"We are tomorrow," Lamont told him. "Stay out of the shed. I just killed a copperhead in there."

"Can I go see it?"

He sounded avid, not afraid.

"No," Lamont said. "And watch out. Where there's one, there are probably others."

He'd have to tell Tilly to be careful, too. It hadn't happened often, but he'd found a few snakes on the deck or close to the house. Last year he'd killed a copperhead curled up behind a flowerpot on the side porch. Back when he grew up here, when the old house still stood, they'd found an occasional snake in the cellar or blacksnakes in his mama's chicken coop.

"Go wash up for supper, Buddy," he told the kid.

Two large pizzas rested in the center of the table, each cut into generous slices. Lamont's most recent experiences with pizza had involved the cheap frozen version sold in supermarkets, slices sold in convenience stores, or a rare treat from a national chain. Tilly's pizzas resembled neither. The aroma made him start drooling, and both were the prettiest pizzas he'd ever seen. One had all meat, pepperoni, sausage, hamburger, and Canadian bacon. The other had sausage or hamburger with black olives, onions, mushrooms, and small bits of green pepper. Both were smothered with mozzarella cheese.

"Those look fantastic," he said.

Tilly, with a smudge of tomato sauce on one cheek, grinned. "I hope you like them. One's all meat, the other is my favorite – sausage with all the good veggies."

Shayne rushed in and skidded to a stop. "Wow, that looks great, Aunt Tilly."

He reached for a piece and she shot him a warning look, then clasped her hands together.

"We ask a blessing first," she told him.

Lamont had been two seconds from grabbing a slice, but now, he bowed his head and folded his hands.

Tilly spoke in a clear but low voice. "We thank you, Lord, for all you give, for the food we are about to eat, and for the lives we live. Bless our loved ones here and far away. Please send your blessings, Lord, today. Help us all to live our days with thankful hearts and loving ways, amen."

The simple grace brought back memories of the past, of his mama saying similar words over supper or a Sunday dinner. Lamont spoke an amen, too, out of old habit. He was out of practice with prayer, and he knew it.

"Let's eat," he said, and the memories blurred into the present.

CHAPTER SEVEN

He liked pizza – who didn't – but Tilly's version topped any he'd ever tasted. The dough tasted like good homemade bread, the sauce brimmed with flavor, and the pizza melted on his tongue. Although he preferred meat toppings, Lamont took a slice of the combination one to encourage Shayne to try the veggies. The mushrooms, black olives, onions, and green peppers complimented the sausage.

He savored a few bites and sighed with delight. When he glanced up, Tilly stared at him.

"It's good," he assured her. "There's just one thing, Tilly."

She wrinkled her forehead. "Is it too spicy? Or is it too much garlic?"

Lamont laughed. "No, not at all. It's perfect, but it's ruined me for any other pizza."

"Really?" Her smile shone bright.

"Yeah, really. I don't think I can go back to cheap pizza, not after this."

He probably would, but he wouldn't enjoy it. It might taste like cardboard after this.

"As long as I'm here, I'll make pizza for you," Matilda told him. "There should be some leftover for lunch tomorrow."

"We're going fishing!" Shayne cried as he grabbed a second piece.

Matilda's smile faded. "I didn't know that."

"Neither did I until my brother called," Lamont said. "You can come along if you want. Logan's coming down early tomorrow, bringing his boat so we can fish on Lake Oolagah."

"I don't know. Boats scare me. Shayne, do you know how to swim?"

"I sure do!"

"So do I," Lamont said. "If you want to go, I'll watch out for you. Why are you afraid of boats?"

"I had a bad experience at Toledo Bend when I was sixteen."

He knew Toledo Bend Reservoir, the largest manmade lake in the South, created by damming the Sabine River. Lamont had fished there and crossed over it many times on the way to rodeos. Boasting over a thousand miles of shoreline, it extended sixty-five miles from top to bottom. "I've been there. What happened?"

Matilda avoided meeting his eyes. "I don't like to talk about it, Lamont. It's still one of the scariest things that ever happened to me."

"Come on, tell me."

She sighed. "Oh, all right. I went with my friend Mandy's family on a weekend fishing trip. They had a cabin at Toledo Bend and a boat. I hadn't been around boats very much. I was sitting on the edge of the boat, goofing around, and I fell off into the lake. I can't swim very well, and I panicked. I thought I would drown."

Lamont winced. "That would be scary, but you didn't."

"True, but the experience made me skittish around boats."

"Were you wearing a life jacket?"

Matilda frowned. "No, one of us were."

"Nobody gets on a boat without one in my family," he told her. "Logan has plenty, so if you want to go, you wouldn't have to worry. We'll all be wearing one, and besides, if you got in trouble, I'd go in after you."

Her serious look faded. "I believe you would, Lamont."

"Of course, he would," Shayne cried. "Come with us,

Aunt Tilly."

"Maybe. How early is your brother coming?"

He'd neglected to mention the time. "For breakfast, if you don't mind. If you do, we'll grab sausage biscuits at a drive-through or something."

"I can make breakfast. I like to cook and besides, I feel like I'm doing my part around here when I do."

Lamont thought she did plenty more, but he grinned. "Thank you, Tilly. He said he'd be here by 7."

Shayne had wolfed down his supper and pushed back his chair. "Can I go see the dead snake now, Lamont?"

"It's not a good idea, Buddy," he replied. "There might be another one. I'll drag it out of there, and you can get a look before I toss it into the woods. I'll do that in just a few minutes."

The kid sighed long and deep. "Okay."

Shayne headed into the den to wait and turned on the television.

"Snake?" Matilda asked.

He might as well tell her now. "I killed a copperhead in the shed when I was getting out my fishing stuff."

"I don't like snakes!"

"Honey, I don't care for them myself, but as long as we keep our eyes open, it's not a problem."

She stood and stacked the dishes, then turned to put the leftover pizza in the fridge. "Do you think there are more?"

Lamont shrugged. "Probably, but don't get worked up over it. I might kill two snakes a year, if that."

Matilda shuddered and rubbed her arms. "That gives me the willies. I'll be afraid to set foot outside."

He moved closer and put one arm around her shoulders. "Don't be."

She leaned back against him, and he closed his eyes, enjoying the moment. "I'll try."

"As long as you're here, I'll watch out for you, Tilly. I don't plan to let anything happen to you and if you're worried about Shayne, don't. I'll take care of him."

Matilda turned around and rested her head against his chest. "I know."

Lamont had been set not to like her and hoped she would leave. Now, he wanted her to stay, but as far as he knew, she planned to go. Those kisses had ignited a fire within him, a flame beyond anything he'd ever felt with Remy. Although he couldn't find any words, he wrapped his arms around her and held her close.

Shayne hollered from the den. "Lamont, are you coming? I want to see the snake."

"I'll be there in a second, kid."

Lamont untangled from Matilda. "We won't be long. Want to watch some TV?"

She nodded. "I'll finish in here, then."

In the shed with Shayne at his heels, Lamont scooped up the dead snake along with the detached head using a shovel. He toted it to the edge of the woods and dumped it.

"Stay away from it," he warned the boy. "I've known there to be two snakes where there's one. I don't want you bitten, so let's not take any chances."

"Would it kill me if it bit me?"

It was a disturbing question, but Lamont could see how a boy who'd lost his mother, then his lame excuse for a stepfather, might ask it. "Probably not, although there's a few cases where a copperhead bite was fatal. It would make you very sick, though, and I'd have to haul you to the hospital. Promise me you'll leave it alone. Same for any other snakes you come across."

He knew very well how curious a boy could be since he'd been one once.

"I will, Lamont. Why's Aunt Tillie acting funny?"

For about two seconds, he considered fibbing but didn't. His parents had raised him with honesty, even when it was unpleasant, and he vowed to do the same with Shayne. "She lost her job in New York."

Shayne grinned. "Does that mean she's not going back?"

"Don't know yet, neither does she."

The kid gazed up at him with brown eyes like his aunt. "I kinda hope she stays. I like her."

Lamont ruffled the kid's hair. "Yeah? It's fine with me if that's what she decides. Let's go find something to watch before bedtime. We'll be up early in the morning."

Matilda sat on one end of the couch, feet tucked beneath her. Shayne sat at the other end while Lamont settled into his recliner. He reached for the remote, then wondered what to choose.

"What do y'all like to watch?"

"Movies," Shayne said. "Cool movies."

That really narrowed it down, and Lamont laughed. "What about you, Tilly?"

"I like vintage TV shows," she said, surprising him. "Ones from way before I was born. I used to watch some of them with my grandparents."

"I like those too," he replied and named some of his favorites. *"Beverly Hillbillies, Green Acres, MASH, Andy Griffith,* and my favorite, *Bonanza."*

"I could watch any of those," Matilda said with a smile. *"Or Family Affair, Bewitched, I Dream of Jeannie* and *Twilight Zone."*

"I watched most of those with Granny. I like them fine except for *Bewitched* because of Darrin Stephens."

"What's wrong with Darrin?"

"He never could accept his wife for who and what she was," Lamont explained. "Maybe he didn't know she was a witch when they said "I do," but after he did, he told her not to do witchcraft. Kinda hard for a witch, right?"

Tilly's smile widened. "I never thought about that, but yeah, you're right. Love means accepting someone for who they are, not trying to change them."

Lamont wondered if that included saddle bronc riders, but before he could figure out a way to ask, Shayne spoke up.

"Please," the kid said, drawing the word out long and slow. "Can't we watch something on Disney? Like *Avatar* or *The Sorcerer's Apprentice* or one of the *National Treasure* movies?"

"It's up to Lamont," Matilda said.

"Any of those are fine. I've got several streaming services," he replied. He'd rather it not be the Nicholas Cage movie because it was set in New York. It might make Tilly homesick for that urban life. He tried to consider what might be age-appropriate for Shayne but reminded himself that the boy had spent the last few years with Teddy Anderson. Lord only knew what he'd seen or watched.

They settled on *Avatar*. Once it ended, Lamont rose, yawning. "I'm beat. Let's go to bed. See y'all early for breakfast with my brother."

"Does it matter what I fix?" Matilda asked.

"Anything you want, sugar. I have no doubt it will be good."

Although he set an alarm, Lamont overslept. He shut it off when it blared, thinking he'd roll out of bed, but he didn't. By the time he woke, he had caught the aroma of coffee and more. As he sat on the edge of the bed, rubbing his face to wake up, he saw Logan pull into the drive with his vintage 15-foot aluminum boat with a brand new Evinrude engine.

Lamont scrambled into his clothes, tugged on his boots, and made it to the front door before Logan had time to knock.

"Come in, brother," he said.

Logan grasped him in a bear hug and then punched his

shoulder. "You're lookin' good, Buddy. The way Lanelle talks, I thought you'd be pale and skinny, dragging one foot in the grave."

"Lanelle exaggerates," Lamont told him. "Come on, meet Shayne and Tilly."

His brother lifted one eyebrow. "Her name's Tilly? That sounds like an old lady's name."

"She's anything but, and her name's Matilda. I just call her Tilly."

Lamont led his brother through the living room toward the kitchen. Behind him, Logan said, "So you like her?"

He did, very much, but he wasn't ready to admit that to his brother. "You sound like we're still in junior high."

Shayne burst into the dining area from the kitchen. "I *am* in junior high."

Both men laughed. Lamont said, "This is Shayne Sawyer. Shayne, this is my big brother, Logan."

He gestured for the kid to remove his hat, which he did. Then Shayne offered his hand.

Logan shook it. "It's nice to meet you. I heard a lot about you."

Matilda approached with the coffee pot. "Cups are on the table if you want some coffee. The food's ready, too."

He thought she'd never looked prettier. Although her hair wasn't that long, she'd scooped it up and clipped it to the back of her head. If she wore any make-up, Lamont couldn't tell. Her jeans fit nicely, and the vivid scarlet blouse with three quarter ruffled sleeves favored her coloring. "Tilly, meet my brother, Logan Fortune. Logan, this is Matilda Mannheim. She's Shayne's aunt."

"Hello," she said. "Go ahead and sit down. I'll bring breakfast to the table."

She delivered a platter of biscuits, a bowl of sausage cream gravy, and another of scrambled eggs.

Lamont inhaled and grinned. "This looks great!"

"Thanks." She took her seat and extended her hands. Lamont grasped hers and accepted Shayne's. Logan glanced around the table and tried to hide a smile when she asked the blessing.

"Amen," Logan said. "Good to hear some prayer in your house, Buddy."

"Not my idea," Lamont mumbled as he filled his plate.

"I thought you called me 'Buddy'," Shayne said. "I'm confused."

"I do, but that's what they called me when I was a kid, too," Lamont said.

Shayne's face glowed with delight. "So, you named me after you. That's cool."

"Glad you like it," Lamont muttered around a mouthful of eggs. Accustomed to being in control of his life, he felt like he rode a rollercoaster. A week ago, he was a bachelor living his life, trying to figure out when to find a rodeo. Now he had a kid in his charge, a woman in his kitchen, and his brother grinning, making assumptions Lamont didn't want to examine. For a moment, he wanted to throw down his fork, leave the house, and take off at top speed in his truck. He could drive fast and furious until his mind cleared.

Not a possibility, he thought and remained. Lamont ladled gravy over an open-faced biscuit and tasted it. He'd never had any as good, not in a restaurant and not even his mama's. The moment of panic passed, and he realized he liked exactly where he was and who he was with.

"That was a fine breakfast, honey," he told Tilly when they'd finished. "I won't be hungry till supper."

She laughed. "I made some sandwiches you can take if you want, bologna and cheese. They're sacked up in the fridge."

"That was very nice," Logan said. "Hey, kid, let's go get the fishing stuff loaded in my truck."

Lamont sent a silent look of gratitude in his brother's direction. Once Logan and Shayne were outside, he moved closer to Tilly. "Are you coming with us?"

Matilda shook her head. "I don't want to push my way into boys' day out. I thought I'd stay here."

He frowned, disappointed. "Come with us."

"I don't know, Lamont."

On a whim, he sang a few lines from a folk song about if she'd get a line, he'd grab a pole, something like that.

Her lips curved into a smile. "You're tempting me, Lamont Fortune."

"That's because I'd like it if you would come. There's room in the boat, and you haven't seen Lake Oolagah."

"I told you I'm scared of boats."

"You did. Logan has life jackets for all of us, and if anything happens, which it won't, I'll be there to keep you safe. I promise."

Lamont used one finger to outline an invisible heart on his chest and crossed it.

She took one step forward and put her hands on his arms. "I might if you'll promise me we'll go to church tomorrow."

"Church?" The word had the effect of ice water pouring over his head. "I don't do church."

"I do, though, and I want Shayne to have it. I doubt his stepdad ever took him."

"Probably not."

"So will we?"

He tried to think. He could take to any one of a dozen or more churches in Claremore, big churches where they'd insist they fill out visitor cards and make introductions. Or he could haul her and the boy over to the little church he attended as a child. If he had to get a dose of religion, he'd rather it be there.

"Do you really want to go?"

"I do, Lamont."

He would regret this, he knew he would, but he sighed. "All right, we'll go to church tomorrow."

Matilda stood on her tiptoes so she could kiss him. It was light and fleeting, but his lips tingled, and he pulled her closer. He kissed her back, a lingering kiss.

"Thank you," she said. He didn't know if she meant for church or the kiss.

"Let's go fishing," he said.

"Give me five minutes."

He waited while she cleared away the kitchen, put up leftovers, and loaded the dishwasher he seldom used. Matilda packed the sandwiches into a soft-sided cooler and reached for his hand. Lamont accepted it, and they headed out to the truck. Logan drove a club cab so he let Shayne right up front and climbed into the second seat with Tilly.

In half an hour, they were at the lake, and in forty-five minutes, they were on the water. Logan anchored the boat, and they began fishing in one of his favorite spots. It wasn't long until Logan began hauling in both crappie and bass.

Lamont felt a tug on his line and landed a large bass, but the best moment came when Shayne brought in his first fish, an impressive bass. Lamont helped the kid reel it in because it put up a fight.

"That's at least five pounds, probably seven," Logan said. "Good catch."

"We'll eat fish tonight," Lamont said.

Shayne grinned. "I like fishing. This is fun."

By late afternoon, they'd long since eaten their sandwiches and had a good catch, so Logan called it a day. They put the fish on ice bought at a small store near the lake. At home, Logan and Lamont cleaned the fish while Shayne went to clean up. Matilda headed to the kitchen to gather ingredients to fry fish.

Once alone, Logan nudged Lamont. "I like your Tilly."

"She's not mine," Lamont replied, although maybe one day she might be.

Logan shook his head. "Whatever. When are you heading out on the circuit? It's almost May, and you've missed a lot of rodeos already."

His decision had been made in a contemplative moment on the lake. "I ain't going this year, Logan."

His brother's mouth dropped open with shock. "Seriously?"

"Yeah, for real. It's too late to start this season and besides, I have enough money and nothing left to prove in the arena."

After a few moments of dumbstruck silence, Logan said, "Wow. I think you finally got some sense. There's more to life than rodeo, and we worry about you getting hurt."

"We?"

"Me and Lanelle," Logan stated. "You've been injured so many times over the years. Besides, you're getting old to ride broncs."

Although he knew it, Lamont laughed. "I don't have one foot in the grave just yet, bro."

"Most rodeo people quit in their thirties, and you're there. Is it because of Shayne and his aunt?"

Lamont chose his words with care. "The kid, Tilly, and it's time. I don't want to keep riding until I end up crippled or in a wheelchair."

"It's a wise decision. What will you do, though? Get a job?"

Hard to imagine himself in a suit and tie at a desk or punching the time clock at a factory. "I don't know. First, I want to get some horses out here. I might raise some rough stock for rodeo."

"That's a good option. You could always see if Davy needs

a deputy."

Lamont laughed. "Law enforcement doesn't have much appeal, and it takes some experience or education. I have neither, and the same goes for being an analyst and accountant."

Unlike his brother and sister, Lamont hadn't gone to college. Instead, he'd continued with rodeo even after his parents died. He hadn't had much reason to do anything else.

Logan had worked for the past 11 years as an analyst and accountant for one of the major oil companies headquartered in Bartlesville, but it wasn't a career Lamont would enjoy.

With the fish gutted, scaled, and fileted, they had finished. Logan slapped him on the shoulder with one smelly fish hand. "You'll figure it out."

Matilda coated the fish with a blend of cornmeal, a little flour, onion powder, a hint of garlic powder, a dash of cayenne, and some lemon pepper, then fried it. She served it with oven-baked fries, pinto beans from a can that she'd seasoned, and cornbread.

Logan stayed to eat with them, and the conversation was almost as good as the food.

It was a good meal to follow a great day. Maybe now life would settle into a new routine and Lamont could enjoy it.

CHAPTER EIGHT

The small white clapboard church sat nestled among a few tall trees on a dirt road less than three miles from Lamont's place. He'd grown up attending the Pioneer Faith Church, so it was as familiar to him as old photos from a family album. He could recall the last two times he set foot within the sanctuary – Lanelle's wedding and his parents' double funeral. He liked his brother-in-law fine but had little in common with a university math professor from Kansas.

He'd dragged out his Western-cut suit jacket, a soft charcoal gray with black leather yokes on each side of the upper chest, paired with black jeans. Beneath it, Lamont wore a white-on-white Western shirt with pearl snaps and his favorite string tie. He wore his least worn cowboy hat, a black felt one with a snakeskin hat band. Although Lamont didn't tell Matilda, he'd killed the rattler and skinned it for this purpose.

When she emerged from the bedroom in a dress, he was glad he made the effort. Tilly wore a dress with a sleeveless black sweater top attached to a skirt in a red, white, and black patchwork print. It fell below her knees, modest but attractive.

"You look nice," he said and realized the word was inadequate.

Matilda blushed. "Thank you. You and Shayne are both quite handsome in your Sunday best."

The kid wore black jeans with a long-sleeved plaid shirt and the new boots.

"Buddy, you look sharp," Lamont told him. Already tall

for twelve, he realized for the first time that Shayne would soon become a teenager and then a man. In all the fluster and flurry of gaining temporary custody, he hadn't paid attention to the kid's birthday. He'd have to check to make sure he didn't miss it.

Shayne rewarded him with a grin. "I don't remember much about church. What's it like?"

"If it hasn't changed, they start with singing, then move on to preaching," Lamont answered. "I suppose there's still Sunday School first."

The boy wrinkled up his nose. "Do I hafta to go to that?"

"We won't get there early enough today," Lamont told him.

"But you should go after this," Matilda said. "It'll be fun. They probably have a youth group, too, with activities. I don't suppose you have a Bible."

Shayne shook his head, and Lamont wondered where his might be. Probably dust-covered on a shelf somewhere. He hadn't used it in years.

"I found yours," Matilda said, as if she could divine his thoughts.

He accepted the book from her hands. "Where was it?"

Her eyes narrowed. "It was in one of the drawers in that chest under the front room windows, the one with the half-dead plants on top."

"Thanks. I suppose I should water them more often. Lanelle, my sister, brought those. She said they would help clean the air or something. I don't have much of a green thumb."

"They're all easy to grow," Tilly said and listed them. "Two aloe vera plants, two cactus plants, and a money tree. As long as I'm here, I'll take care of them for you."

"I appreciate it," he said, although he didn't care if the plants flourished or died. "Are we ready to roll?"

Tilly smiled. "Sure, whenever you are. Do you always get

grumpy when you go to church?"

"I'm not cranky," he said, then realized he was a little. "I haven't been to church in a long time, so I'm a bit nervous. I think my sister's wedding would be the next to last time I was there."

"How long ago was that?"

Lamont had to think. "Ten or twelve years. After that, it was my parents' funeral, and that was six years ago."

Because he'd rather not revisit those memories, he picked up his keys. "Let's go."

By the time he parked the truck under a tree, Lamont had some serious apprehensions. Would the pastor – as far as he knew, it was the same minister who had served here for the last thirty years – chastise him for his absence? Would the congregation figure he had to be a big sinner since he did rodeo? His stomach tightened, and the scrambled eggs he'd eaten earlier threatened to come back up his throat. When he hesitated at the foot of the concrete steps leading to the main entrance, Matilda took his hand in hers.

"Lamont, let's go find a pew. I don't want to be late."

Neither did he. He wanted to reverse direction and bail on the church experience.

"I don't know if I'm ready for this," he mumbled.

Inside, those gathered began singing an old familiar song, "Power In The Blood." It had been his mom's favorite hymn. The words washed over him and brought anguish. Lamont hadn't heard it since they laid his parents to rest from this very church. Matilda added her voice as they walked into the sanctuary, lifting the refrain high.

"There is power, power, wonder working power in the Blood of the Lamb," she sang. "There is power, power, wonder working power in the Blood of the Lamb."

Her voice brought life to the old words. As she led them down the aisle to an empty pew about halfway down, tears rained down his face. Without thinking, he brushed them away and joined in the song as the second verse began, "Would you be whiter, much whiter than snow?"

Matilda didn't miss a note as she found a hymnal, opened it to the song and handed it to Shayne. Lamont sang along, his heart aching and eyes leaking, as the congregation followed it with "The Old Rugged Cross" and "Blessed Assurance."

Lamont sank onto the pew with relief when the praise worship ended, and the preaching began. Brother Alec Cartwright stepped to the pulpit, older now than Lamont remembered, but his voice hadn't changed at all as he read out Scripture in a booming voice that had always reminded Lamont of Johnny Cash. Then, he began his sermon, based on Matthew 17:20, comparing faith to a mustard seed. Lamont's mind wandered as Brother Alec expounded on the theme. His emotions were in a tangle, and if it hadn't been for Tilly and the kid, he would have bolted.

He hadn't expected to experience a sense of homecoming, but he did. Memories assailed him, precious but with the power to wound. Guilt reared an ugly presence, too. He'd been raised in church, *this* church, and he'd believed. *Maybe I should have been here all the time. Maybe I wouldn't have been so lonely or got as busted up in the arena if I had.*

Lamont recalled he'd never brought Remy here. When he'd suggested it, she had rejected the idea, mocking the small church as too redneck for her tastes. Her family worshipped at a mega church in Dallas on rare occasions. During the time they dated and were engaged, Remy had never attended. He'd figured he was done with church for good after losing his folks, and the homeplace was devasted by that tornado. Maybe he'd been a little too stiff-necked about church, he thought.

His daddy had always claimed Lamont was as stubborn as a mule, and he was. Part of his soul rebelled against it all, unwilling to admit he might have been wrong. As his thoughts flew within his head like birds before a storm, his uneasy stomach churned. Lamont glanced around, trying to plot an escape route if he had to go puke, but didn't see one. Matilda sat beside him with Shayne at the end. On his other side, a couple he didn't recognize were firmly placed. If he left, it would create a stir through the entire church and turn attention to him, the last thing he wanted. So he remained in place, hoping his guts would calm down, and waited for the service to end. When the collection plate was passed, he tossed a twenty into it from his billfold. The closing song was "Amazing Grace," and this time, he didn't sing. Tears clogged his throat, and he concentrated on not weeping.

Lamont held back as the pews emptied. If he had his way, he would be the last man out of the building. Maybe then everyone would have gone home or to Sunday dinner. Matilda turned to him as the crowds thinned.

"Are you all right?" she asked. "You look upset."

"Stomach's bothering me," he said in a low tone.

Her dark brown eyes scanned over him then she laid one small hand on his belly. "Lord, calm Lamont's stomach," she said. "Take away any discomfort or pain. Let him relax here in Your house and give him peace."

The simple gesture floored him. No one had prayed over him in years, but a dim memory of his mother speaking similar words returned. Lamont put one hand over hers. "Thank you, Tilly."

"You're welcome. Let's go. You'll feel better with some fresh air."

He'd be fine as long as none of the folks he'd known his whole life spoke to him. Lamont didn't think he could stand any conversation. Before he exited the pew, though, Miss Marcy Ellis saw him. She smiled.

"Well, Lamont Fortune, you grew up right nice," she told him. She had to be eighty years old or more by now. "It's good to see you here in church. We've missed you."

Had they? He found that hard to believe. He figured it was more out of sight, out of mind.

"It's been a long time," he said, uncertain what else to say.

"It has, but you've been busy out winning rodeo titles, I hear," she said. "I keep up. Sometimes, one of my grandsons will take me to the rodeo if it's not too far away."

"That's very nice of him."

"Oh, yes, it is," Miss Marcy told him. She patted him on the arm and moved on toward the exit. Behind her, a tall, lean old man approached Lamont.

"I don't reckon you'll remember me," the man said in a gruff voice grown high with age.

"Bud Bartlett," Lamont said, surprising himself. "Yes, sir, I do."

"Well, now, that's something. Your daddy bought your first pony from me, a little paint horse."

Pinto Bean had been his name. "I remember," Lamont said. "He was a fine pony."

"Got you a good start," Mr. Bartlett replied. "I still raise a few horses, got a couple ponies if you're looking for this young man here. Is he your boy?"

"I'm fixing to adopt him," he said. He'd thought about a horse for himself and maybe one for Shayne. "I might come over and see what you have. I'm looking to get one for myself, maybe a mount for the boy."

"I've got 'em whenever you're ready. Are you going to try your hand at roping or another event? Don't need a horse to ride broncs."

"That's right, but I'm hanging up my spurs," Lamont said. He had forgotten he'd told no one but his brother until Shayne gasped, and Tilly stared wide-eyed at him. "I'm retired now."

He offered Tilly his arm, and after a brief hesitation, she

accepted it. They walked out together with Shayne on the left. At the door, Brother Alec shook hands and exchanged greetings as church members filed outside.

"Brother Alec," Lamont said and offered the pastor his hand.

"I'll be! It's Lamont Fortune. Son, you've been in my thoughts and prayers often. It's great to see you here with your family."

Reluctant to explain the reality, he didn't, but Matilda stepped forward.

"Hi, I'm Matilda Mannheim," she said. "And the young man is my nephew, Shayne Sawyer. Lamont has temporary foster custody after Shayne's stepfather passed away, but he plans to adopt him."

To Lamont, that seemed like too much information.

Brother Alec held Matilda's hand. "Bless him for that," he said. "Lamont seems to be a fine young man, though I've not seen him in years. He was raised right, though, with good parents. I'm happy to have you all in church and hope you'll be back next week."

Lamont nodded and moved on, heading for the parking lot in a hurry. His stomach had eased, and now he was hungry. If he didn't return for another decade, it might be too soon.

"I like this church," Matilda said as they got into his truck. "It's traditional, and everyone is so friendly. I didn't know you weren't planning to rodeo anymore."

He shrugged. "I've been thinking a lot about it but I decided for sure yesterday. I told Logan, and I was planning to tell you."

She nodded. "It's not really my business, but it is Shayne's. I'm glad you won't be going, though. I was worried you might drag him on the road all summer."

"I wouldn't have had much choice," he said. "It wouldn't

have been the best thing, though. Did you have something in mind for dinner?"

"No, but I can make something at the house if you want. How's your stomach?"

His nausea had eased once they'd left the sanctuary and after Tilly had prayed.

"Better. I was thinking maybe we'd grab some take-out fried chicken and head over to the Blue Whale at Catoosa. They've got picnic tables, and it's an awesome place, an old roadside attraction from the Route 66 glory days."

"Cool!" Shayne cried.

"How far is it?"

"Ten miles, maybe. It won't take fifteen minutes to get there. Why?"

"No reason, just Shayne goes back to school tomorrow so I wanted to make sure we're home in plenty of time for him to get ready."

Lamont laughed. "He's going to school, not on vacation, Tilly. All he'll need is a bath and get his school stuff together."

She relaxed and offered him a smile. "All right, let's go see the Blue Whale and eat some chicken."

With a bucket of fried chicken, some potato wedges, coleslaw, and hot rolls, they headed to Catoosa, home of the legendary Blue Whale. The sun shone, and temperatures shot up into the low 90s. A light southern breeze kept it from feeling too sticky or humid. Lamont settled down at a picnic table near the whale and its surrounding moat of water. He savored the wind and the shade from a nearby tree.

The crispy chicken had plenty of flavor. He polished off three pieces, a thigh, a drum, and a small breast along with the sides. As his emotional upheaval from church faded, Lamont allowed a deep and favorable serenity to take hold. He made small talk with Tilly and Shayne. When Shayne headed off to enter the mouth of the whale, walk through, and visit the tail, he linked his fingers through Tilly's. "It's a great day."

"I'm enjoying it." She stretched and leaned against his shoulder. "I like your church."

Lamont said nothing. It had been his church once, but not anymore. He didn't really have a church now or any faith left. This morning had been a stroll down memory lane and had affected him more than he wanted to admit. He ignored a yearning in his soul for God and focused on the woman beside him.

One question burned in his heart, so he asked it. "Do you plan to go back to the city?"

Her sharp intake of breath warned him he might not like the answer. "I have to go get my things from the apartment, Lamont. After that, probably not. If I can start over here, I'd like that."

She told him two things. Tilly would make a trip to pack up her possessions, then return and stay. "What all you have to get?"

"Most of my clothes, although they're not much, but there are some pictures and sentimental things I can't give up."

As a man who once lost everything he owned when a tornado destroyed his home, Lamont lacked the same attachment to possessions. He'd salvaged a few things from his boyhood, and Lanelle had reprinted many photos for him, but he'd learned to live in the moment. Memories mattered. He didn't have to own the objects to have them in his mind and heart. Matilda, though, wouldn't understand that.

He sighed long and loud. "When are you planning to go?"

"I don't know," she said, glancing over at Shayne, still exploring the whale. "I want to be here for him to go back to school, to help provide some stability and all that. I thought maybe you two could go with me, maybe after school's out for the summer."

That idea struck him with the force of a thrown rock. Lamont thought he might rather take a beating than return to the Big Apple. Worse, though, was the idea Tilly would be absent from him. "I don't know about that," he said. "I wasn't overfond of the place when I was there."

Matilda ruffled her fingers through his blond curls in back, where it had grown out. "I know. You told me. But Shayne should see it, don't you think? Just so he would be able to visualize New York City. I never could, not until I went."

The fragrance from her shampoo wafted into his nose, and he thought she might be wearing a lavender scent. That distracted him. "Still didn't turn out the way you expected, though."

"That's true, but…"

She didn't finish the sentence because Shayne rushed up. "There's turtles in the water. It's so cool. Come see, Lamont."

He exchanged a look with Matilda. She pulled away with a nod. "All right, kid, I'll come see."

Dozens of turtles moved through the murky depths. Long before his time, people were allowed in the water here, and a pair of aging, rusted slides remained.

"Wish I could go for a swim," Shayne said.

Lamont shook his head. "That water's probably filthy, and they haven't allowed swimming in years. It was a major roadside attraction back in the glory days of Route 66, The Mother Road."

"I think I've heard of that," the boy said. "But why is it so famous?"

"First highway that ran from Chicago to Los Angeles," Lamont told him. "Back in the 1930s, it's the road most Okies took heading for California after the Dust Bowl wiped out their crops and farms. Then it became the main highway in the 1940s, 1950s, heck, even 1960s to go across the country. There are songs and shows and all kinds of stuff about Route 66. The old road is gone, now, most of it except for bits and pieces like this one."

Matilda joined them and sang a line from the famous song about the highway.

Lamont grinned. "Sing some more, Tilly."

She laughed. "That's about all I remember."

"If you want, we can run over to Foyil to the Totem Pole Park," Lamont said. "It's only about ten miles east of Claremore. Sometime, I'll take you over to Miami to see the Coleman Theater, eat hamburgers at an old-time drive-in, and over to Afton to see a vintage service station."

"Let's go!" Shayne cried.

"I'd like to see all that someday," Matilda said. "But Shayne has school tomorrow, so we probably should head back."

Lamont didn't want the day to end, probably any more than Shayne did, but he heard the voice of reason. "True. We'll have plenty of days to explore Oklahoma. School will let out in a month or so. We can go then."

He'd also remembered he had made an appointment with a family attorney in Claremore to talk about adopting the kid. It would be a busy week, he thought and realized it hadn't been seven days yet since Anderson overdosed.

It had been Saturday, a week past, when Anderson came to look at the truck and Monday when the kid showed up at his door, upset. He'd picked Matilda up late Tuesday, met with his cousin Sheriff David Wills and the social worker Wednesday, and endured a home inspection and two doctors' appointments on Thursday. They'd visited Shayne's school on Friday and gone fishing yesterday, then church today.

Slow your roll, Lamont, he thought. *A lot's happened and life is moving faster than the speed of light.* He still had to adjust to having a foster son, sort out his feelings about Tilly, and wrap his head around his decision to quit rodeo.

This would be the week to get things in order and settle down. Sooner or later, Matilda would disrupt it with a trip back to New York, but that could wait until she insisted. Maybe after school let out for the summer, he mused, maybe.

For now, he figured he would head home, find a baseball game on television, and sleep until time for a simple sandwich supper.

No more complications, no more worries, just time to recharge and relax.

CHAPTER NINE

He drove home on autopilot, holding the old truck to the road with skill and familiarity. By the time they rolled through Claremore, he'd become sleepy and more than ready for a nap. Lamont had enjoyed the day, but he needed to prepare to start the week.

As they rolled into his drive, Shayne asked, "So, will I ride the bus tomorrow or what?"

Lamont wanted to groan. He should have talked to the school about transportation when he was there, but didn't. Besides, he had to deliver copies of the custody paperwork. "I'll take you on your first day back. After that, we can look into the bus if you want."

The boy turned toward him. "I'd rather not ride it if I don't have to, Lamont."

Surprised, he said. "Okay, but why not?"

Shayne shrugged. "Some of the kids rag on me. They try to pick fights or make fun."

Recalling how cruel children could be and remembering what a ragamuffin Shayne had been before coming to live with him, Lamont understood. "I can drive you to school. It's no biggie, kid. You'll just have to get around early so we can get there in time."

"I can do that, no problem."

He found a St. Louis Cardinals game on television so Lamont flopped onto the couch in the den to watch. He left the side door open with the screen up to catch the breeze. It didn't take long to get sleepy, and he dozed, the sound of the game audible in the background. Lamont dreamed about rodeo. Everything seemed true to life, the smell of hot dust in the arena and livestock, the roar of the crowd, and the heavy thud as a bronc rider got tossed into the gate.

Lamont woke with the resounding crash echoing in his head and realized the sound was real. As he slept, dark clouds had gathered overhead as a weather system moved into the area. Thunder echoed, loud and fierce, as he sat up and rubbed his face. Although he hadn't slept long, he'd slept deep, which left him groggy.

Voices roused him more. Shayne and Tilly stood on the deck, faces upturned to the sky. Grumbling, he headed through the kitchen and out through the sliding glass door onto the deck.

"What are y'all doing out here?"

"It's about to storm," Tilly told him.

"Is it going to be a big one?" Shayne asked, a frown wrinkling his forehead.

Lamont sat down on the rustic bench and shrugged. "No idea. I didn't even know it was supposed to rain, let alone storm."

"There's storm warnings out," Tilly said. "And a tornado watch until 3 a.m."

His chest tightened. Lamont hated storms, and if he was honest, they scared him a little. Thunderstorms were fine, but tornadoes were different. Although he hadn't been at home when a twister wiped out the original farmhouse, the aftermath had been sobering. Not only did the storm break the old house into scattered debris, but he also found odd things when cleaning up, stuff like a suitcoat wrapped around a broken jar of grape jelly, a few pictures within the pages of rain-bloated books, and his dad's pocket watch within the broken remains of a dresser.

He'd noticed that once he found something that might be salvageable if he walked in outward spirals, he would discover items from the same room. Yet, other items might be scattered across the field or even located at a neighbor's place miles away.

"There's gonna be a tornado?" Shayne asked, eyes wide.

Lamont shook his head. "Hopefully not. A watch just means it's possible. A warning is more serious because it means one's been spotted in the sky or on radar. If that happens, we go to the storm shelter."

Tilly wrapped her arms around her torso and hugged herself. The temperature had dropped probably twenty degrees as the storm hit. "Where exactly is it? Is there a basement or what?"

"No." The cellar underneath the original house had been crammed full of wreckage. If he'd been home and had taken shelter there, it was likely that the house would have come down on him. "It's made from steel-reinforced concrete. It's right behind the garage and shop. You can't see it from here, but it's there. It's above ground, by the way, which they say is safer."

"I hope we don't need it," Tilly said.

"Me, too," Lamont replied. "But it's there if we ever do."

He persuaded Shayne to take his bath and go to bed because school loomed in the morning. Lamont couldn't sleep, though, not with the possibility of more storms and tornadoes. Although he owned a weather radio that would broadcast any warnings, he preferred to monitor the weather himself. On occasion, he slept through his alarm clock, and he always worried he might sleep through a warning.

Lamont set up his weather command post in the den after changing into comfortable faded sweats and an old T-shirt. He wiggled into a comfortable position on the couch and turned the television audio down low. His nap would help him from falling asleep, but he also brewed a cup of dark roast coffee. He sipped from it, trying to keep his mind on the late-night programming with a colorful weather map in the corner. Sometimes, a weathercaster broke in with live reports, but so far, no storm action was taking place near Oklahoma City or around Enid.

Until she walked into the room, swathed in her ankle-length flannel nightgown, he'd thought Tilly had retired. He noticed she wore slippers this time and that a frown line creased her forehead.

"Lamont?"

"Right here. What are you doing up?"

"I couldn't sleep, wondering about the weather," she replied and sank down next to him on the couch. "I haven't thought about tornadoes in years, but they freak me out."

"I doubt there's gonna be one, not tonight," he told her. "There could be, but it's not very likely. There's been some weather west of here, but the storms appear to be weakening as they move in this direction. Still, I want to be sure, so I'm staying up."

Matilda tucked her feet beneath her and moved closer. "I'll keep you company."

"Thanks," he said and meant it. "I hope the kid's asleep, though. He's got school."

"He is," Tilly told him. "Isn't that appointment with a family lawyer tomorrow too?"

Lamont drew in a deep breath. "Yeah, at nine in Claremore. I'm nervous about it."

"Why?"

"Getting approved as a temporary foster parent was harder than I thought. I have a feeling this will be more involved, too."

"Would you like me to come with you?"

Relief swept through his body. "I really would, thanks."

"Then I will."

Lamont put an arm around her, and they pretended to watch the movie while waiting for weather updates. Their conversation remained light, but he enjoyed every moment.

When the tornado watch was cancelled around midnight, they both headed for bed.

Although he would have happily spent money on a fast-food breakfast, Lamont woke to find Tilly had made bacon, egg, and cheese biscuits. They were tastier than any he'd ever eaten and washed down with coffee, made a fine breakfast.

Shayne seemed muted as he ate, then gathered his backpack. For the meeting with an attorney, Lamont donned khaki pants and a dark green Henley. Tilly wore jeans and a pastel print blouse.

Since Shayne would exit the truck, he took the passenger seat by the window, and Matilda rode beside Lamont. Although he had plenty on his mind, he became very aware of the lavender scent she wore. He rolled down the window a little so the fresh air would prevent distraction. After last night's storms, the breeze that wafted into the truck combined freshness with coolness.

At the junior high, Lamont pulled into the drop-off lane.

"Have a great day, buddy," he told Shayne. "Don't forget to drop off those papers at the office."

"I won't. You'll be here to pick me up after school, right?"

"I will," Lamont promised.

With more than an hour until his appointment with the family law attorney, Lamont drove around Claremore, showing Matilda more of the sights. He considered stopping for coffee, but he'd already had more than he needed. Too much caffeine made him fidget or caused frequent bathroom breaks. He didn't want either today.

Right before nine, he pulled up to the compact brick building a few blocks from downtown. If Lamont remembered, it had once been an ice cream store or a restaurant.

"Let's do this," he told Matilda. "I hope this guy, Ronnie Upton, is a good attorney."

She nodded and grasped his hand. "I'll say a prayer."

It couldn't hurt, so he agreed. Then they exited his truck and walked into the office.

A reception counter sat across from the main entrance, and behind it, a short corridor led to offices, maybe a conference room. The older woman seated at a computer glanced up.

"Good morning. I'm guessing you're Lamont Fortune, first appointment today."

"That's me," he said.

"Ronnie said to take you on back." She eyed Matilda with curiosity.

"This is Matilda Mannheim," Lamont told her. "She's with me."

From the name, he expected a man, hopefully, a seasoned lawyer, someone in a three-piece suit with a tie. Maybe he'd be a little bald or a bit overweight, but if he knew law, Lamont would be fine.

They entered the office, decorated in shades of ivory and mauve. Behind the large desk, a woman stood and greeted them.

"Come in and have a seat. I'm Ronnie Upton."

Startled, Lamont sank into one of the two chairs, aware that Tilly sat beside him. She reached for his hand and held it.

He tried not to stare, but he failed. Rather than a middle-aged attorney, Ronnie Upton had long, dark red hair that streamed past her shoulders. Instead of a suit, she wore a pin-striped dress with one side white and the other black. It fit her body and accented her curves. She wore pearls around her neck and matching earrings. To him, she appeared more like a fashion model than a lawyer and he hoped she knew her business.

"Tell me about the child you want to adopt," Ronnie Upton told them after they all were seated. "I have a few notes but I want to hear the story from you."

Lamont nodded and sketched out Shayne's story, from visiting with his stepdad to look at an old truck he had for sale to

Anderson's overdose and Shayne's plea for help.

"I have emergency custody as a foster parent now," Lamont explained. "I believe it's temporary pending either becoming a full-time foster parent or adoption. Sheriff Wells – he's my cousin – and Donna Wellington, the social worker, can provide confirmation."

"I have Ms. Wellington's report and notes here," Ronnie told him. "I also have copies of all the official paperwork. Before I agree to represent you, however, I have several questions. The first one is, why do you want to adopt this child? By your own admission, you didn't even know him until recently."

"That's right. I like Shayne," he told her. "I want to help him and give him a home base. He had a rough go with his late stepfather, and I think I can be a mentor, even a parent to him if I get the chance."

"I understand that, but why?"

Lamont struggled to find the words to express how he felt. "Even though we haven't been acquainted for very long, I think we've become friends. That seems like a good foundation. I think if you asked him, he'd tell you the same."

She nodded, tapping a pen against the desk. "I definitely will be speaking to Shayne to hear how he feels about the adoption. We also need to talk about your suitability to adopt a child."

"I figured you would. Go ahead, ask whatever you want."

He hadn't meant to sound defiant, but maybe it came out harsher than he intended because she frowned.

"I intend to," she stated. "First, I know you're Lamont Fortune, three-time and current PRCA National Saddle Bronc champion. You're somewhat of a celebrity around town because of that. However, that doesn't guarantee an income and I need to prove you have a regular occupation."

It didn't seem like the moment to announce he had retired.

"I own property, and I have bank accounts with plenty of money," he told her. "I'm considering raising rough stock to sell to rodeos."

"Are you currently involved in rodeo? Because if not, I'll need immediate documentation of another livelihood."

"I am," he said, aware that his planned retirement had ended before it began. If he needed to ride another season so he could adopt Shayne, he would. "I got a late start because I came down with the flu."

"Do you consider rodeo arenas a good place to raise a child?"

That was a loaded question if he ever heard one. "That depends on the parent and the supervision," he replied.

"Will you travel on the circuit with Shayne, or is there someone at home who can be depended on for care?"

Tilly spoke up. "I'll be there if needed. I'm Shayne's aunt, Matilda Mannheim."

Ronnie Upton turned both barrels of her invisible shotgun on Tilly. "Do you live in the home?"

Lamont sighed. "Right now, she does, if that matters. And we're not married if that does, too."

The attorney put down her pen and began fashioning paper clips into a chain. "Your marital status doesn't. From Ms. Wellington's initial findings, your home provides adequate space for the child, that you can provide for him, that you have no criminal record, and that you passed both physical and mental examinations. She also noted the presence of Ms. Mannheim."

Then why are you asking, Shayne thought.

"So, do you plan to accept me as a client or not?" Sometimes, a man just had to cut through the nonsense.

"I'm leaning that way," Upton replied. "Whether I do or not, you need to be aware that there will be an in-depth home study made, that you'll need to attend 27 hours of pre-service training, and submit to another background check with fingerprints. Are you willing to do all those things?"

"I am," Lamont told her. "I'll do whatever it takes."

"This question is for Ms. Mannheim – if you're the child's aunt, why aren't you adopting him?"

"My current address is in New York City," Tilly replied, head lifted high and proud. "There's no space in my small studio apartment. I am considering relocating to Oklahoma, and I'm originally from Texas."

After three grueling hours, a mountain of paperwork, and much discussion, Ronnie – which it turned out was a nickname for Veronica – Upton agreed to represent Lamont in his bid to adopt Shayne. An appointment was set up so that she could talk to Shayne and another for a home study. Lamont provided references and after a moment, so did Matilda. He signed up to begin the pre-service courses and arranged to be fingerprinted for the background check. If – and it was a big if – everything went well, he might be able to adopt Shayne in six months.

It was past noon when they finished and headed to his truck. Once behind the wheel, Lamont paused. He released a long, slow breath. "Well, that was a short retirement."

Although it wasn't necessary, she scooted across the seat beside him. "How soon will you need to rodeo?"

He shrugged. "Probably as soon as I can. If not before, I'll ride in the annual Will Rogers Stampede PRCA Rodeo here in Claremore. It's over Memorial Day weekend. I need to get back on a horse and soon. I'm probably out of shape."

"Don't you have a horse?"

"No, because I was never home in the season to take care of one. I'll call Bud Bartlett and see if he's got anything I practice ride. Saddle bronc riders compete on rough stock, not our own mounts. I probably should see if it's not too late to compete in the Pioneer Days Rodeo at Guymon the first weekend of May. It's got some of the biggest purses in the business. I can always ride at The Cowboy Coliseum in Fort Worth, too."

Lamont was thinking aloud and realized it. "I'll get it figured out – are you ready for lunch?"

"Yes, I'm hungry."

"Are you up for chili? There's a local place that has the absolute best anywhere."

Matilda's lips curved into a smile. "I'm willing to try it, but remember, you haven't tasted mine."

"If you fix it, I'll try it."

"I'll hold to you that."

As it turned out, she liked the chili fine, and Lamont enjoyed the meal with her. They didn't hurry and lingered over lunch until it was almost time to pick up Shayne. On the way back to school, they stopped long enough that she bought some hamburger, buns, mushrooms, and Swiss cheese.

"That's for supper, right?"

"Of course," she told him.

Neither of them said anything to Shayne about meeting with the attorney until after supper. Lamont gave him time to share about his day, which, according to Shayne, had been awesome. Despite his brief absence, he hadn't missed out on too many lessons, although he had some make-up homework to finish.

Lamont waited until supper was over and the kitchen restored before he brought up the subject. He condensed it as much as possible but made sure Shayne understood the three most important parts – he had to talk to the attorney, if everything went according to plan, he'd be adopted in six months, and that Lamont had to return to the rodeo circuit.

Shayne grinned. "Can I come too?"

"It'll depend on if you have school or not," Lamont replied. "Maybe. Did you go with Teddy Anderson?"

The smile wilted. "Not much, no. He wouldn't take me, and if I went, I had to stay in the camper most of the time, or he'd leave me with some woman to watch like I was a baby."

Anger flared. "That won't happen if I take you. One, I don't have a camper or trailer. Two, I won't palm you off on anybody."

"Unless it's me," Matilda said with a smile.

"That's right," Lamont said. "Are you gonna come?"

"I'd like to, at least, to some of the rodeos. If Shayne's still in school, I can stay here with him."

Her simple statement filled him with sudden joy. Lamont had never figured she would want to go to the rodeo, thinking New York, not Texas. He would like to have her there, watching from the sidelines, ready to cheer for him. He wouldn't even mind if she was on hand to kiss any bruises or care if he got bucked off.

She planned to return to New York to gather her belongings soon. Lamont had almost decided he would go, too, with Tilly and Shayne if they would drive, not fly. If he competed this season, he probably couldn't. Lamont hated change so he didn't ask, not tonight. So far, the evil of the day had been sufficient. He wasn't going to seek out anything more.

CHAPTER TEN

He stayed up late, working out everything he needed to get in order for the home study until he had a headache and his eyes hurt. He also registered for his first two rodeos of the season. Lamont should have been wearing the glasses he had for close work like this but hadn't. The specs were new within the last year, and he didn't like to think his vision had changed. Lamont was also vain enough to hate the way he looked when he wore them, so most of the time, he didn't.

Since he knew Bud Bartlett would be up early, Lamont called him during breakfast. He explained what he needed, and the old farmer agreed.

"Sure, come over anytime. Bring your gear. You can ride any of my horses whenever you want, Lamont. I don't have any broncs, though, but I could probably arrange it where you could ride some if you want."

"I might," he replied. "Thanks. I'll come by after I drop the kid at school."

"I'll be here."

Although he invited Tilly to come along, she declined. Lamont had noticed she'd been quieter than usual and that breakfast had been cereal served with milk.

"Are you sure?" he asked before he headed out. "I can come back after I drop off Shayne if you need more time."

Matilda shook her head. Until she blushed, he hadn't realized how pale she seemed.

"Thanks, Lamont, but no. I'm not feeling very well."

That brought him three steps back into the kitchen. "Are you sick?"

She didn't look at him as she offered a tiny half-smile. "It's my girl time," she told him.

That didn't make sense until she added, "My girl time of the *month.*"

Lamont nodded. He had a sister, so he understood. "I might not be back for lunch but I will for sure by supper. Is there anything I can bring you from town?"

"I can't think of anything. Thanks, Lamont. There's plenty of sandwich stuff for lunch, and I'll make something delicious for supper, I promise."

"I can pick up something…"

"Don't. I want to cook. I love it."

"Okay." He had an urge to kiss her, just a light little peck on the forehead or cheek, but he didn't. Maybe she wouldn't welcome it right now.

"Lamont," she said, and he faced her. She stood on tiptoe and brushed her mouth across his. "I'm really fine."

"I know," he replied and did. "I just…well, I don't know. I'll see you later."

Riding a horse was second nature, but it had been several months. Lamont saddled up the buckskin quarter horse Bud Bartlett offered and rode most of the morning. He savored the feel of a good mount beneath him and reveled in the fresh spring air. As much as Lamont loved riding, he wasn't as eager to ride saddle broncs, although he would.

"So, you're not giving it up just yet?" Bartlett asked him after Lamont had finished for the day.

"I can't, according to the lawyer I've hired to help get Shayne adopted," he told the older man. "It seems being a bronc rider is better than not doing anything."

"You ought to have plenty of money, three times national

champion," Bud observed. "Two of those three times in the last couple years."

"I do, but I guess it's not enough just to have it in the bank. I planned on maybe raising some rough stock, but that'll have to wait. I'd get a job if I could, but I don't know what I'd do. I've never worked, been rodeoing since I was a kid."

"Take it to the Lord," Bartlett suggested.

Lamont remembered he knew the man through church, although he'd been a friend of Lamont's dad, too. Tilly would probably tell him the same. He couldn't come up with an answer, so he nodded. "I'd better take off."

"Come back whenever you want and bring the boy."

"I will," Lamont said and meant it. "I do want to buy a horse or two, something for the kid to ride, too, but it'll be down the road a bit."

"See you in church on Sunday."

After a long pause, Lamont said, "I'll be there."

Since Bartlett lived southwest of Claremore along the Verdigris River and Lamont's place was north, he traveled through town on his way home. Although he wondered how Tilly felt and thought about going home to see, Lamont decided to grab lunch. After the light breakfast, he craved food, but he didn't want to spoil his appetite for supper. He decided to grab a roast beef sandwich and then ate it in the park. His truck provided privacy, and he called Lanelle.

"Hey, sis," he said when she answered the phone. "How's life up in Kansas?"

"Fine and dandy," Lanelle said. "I'm so glad you decided to hang up your spurs."

Lamont laid his head against the steering wheel for a moment. "Well, there's a change in plan about that."

She sputtered her protest, but he explained why after updating her on the adoption process.

"That doesn't seem fair, Lamont."

"Bureaucracy and rules," he told her. "I'll figure out some other livelihood before next year. Hey, I have a question for you."

"Ask."

"If a lady is having her, uh, girl time, what could a friend get that would make her feel better?" He used the same phrase Tilly had, and his sister understood.

"Flowers," Lanelle said without hesitation. "Pick Tilly up a nice bouquet."

Lamont sighed. "Won't that give her the wrong idea?"

"Which would be what, exactly? Logan said you're smitten with her."

Her tone made him feel about thirteen, in the throes of his first crush.

"I like her, yeah."

"Then get flowers – not roses, but something pretty."

"I wouldn't know a lily from a carnation."

"It's spring – how about sweet peas and peonies? Any florist should have both and put them together in a pretty bouquet. What's her favorite color?"

Like he would know. "Maybe pink."

"Get white peonies if they have them and pink sweet peas. If they don't have white, get dark pink peonies."

Then she giggled, and he figured he probably blushed bright red. Thank goodness no one was around to see.

"Sure, and then I'll stop by the jewelers to pick out a diamond ring," he said.

Lanelle laughed. "Whoa, cowboy, not just yet..."

Then, as he anticipated, she cackled and said a line from their favorite movie growing up, *The Wizard of Oz*, "All in good time, my pretty, all in good time."

Lamont roared with mirth. "Watch out, sis," he gasped. "Or I'll send those flying monkeys."

They both lost it, and the shared laughter over the miles moved him more than he wanted to admit.

"Keep in touch," Lanelle told him. "If you rodeo up this way, let me know, and I'll be there."

"Will do, sis. Love you."

He made a stop at the sheriff's office to let his cousin know what he'd learned about the adoption process. Davy – Sheriff David Wills to everyone else – shook his head.

"Puts you between a rock and a hard place, Lamont. Are you sure this kid is worth the hassle?"

"Definitely," he replied. *And so is Tilly.*

Lamont's last errand before he maneuvered the truck into the parent pickup line at school was a stop at a florist shop. He chose the oldest one in town where the current third-generation owner might remember him from church.

"Why, Lamont Fortune," the woman said when he entered. "It was so good to see you back in church. What can I help you with?"

"I need a bouquet, Miss Ava," he told her. She acted like he'd missed a few months of church, not years. "Something pretty, maybe some peonies and sweet peas."

She put together a bouquet with the biggest white peonies Lamont had ever seen, blooms with a sweet fragrance that filled his nose paired with dainty pink sweet peas and trimmed with greenery. Miss Ava held it up for his approval, and he nodded.

"That's perfect and very pretty."

She winked. "I'm guessing it's for the young lady who was with you at church. She should like it."

When he picked up Shayne, the kid eyed the bouquet on the seat as if it were a ticking bomb. "What's that?"

"Flowers for your auntie. She wasn't feeling very well this morning."

Shayne frowned. "She's okay, though, right?"

"Tilly's fine. I just wanted to do something nice."

Lamont, remembering his sister's response to that time of the month when she still lived at home, half-expected to find Matilda in bed, curled up with a heating pad. With a finger to his lips to avoid disturbing her, he and Shayne entered the side door into the den.

Matilda, dressed in baggy sweat pants and a stretched-out t-shirt, leaned against the kitchen counter and perused a recipe on her phone. She glanced up with a smile.

"I wasn't sure when you'd be home," she said. "I'm glad to see you both. How was school?"

"Good," Shayne said. "But I got homework again."

"Then you'd better get started," Lamont said as he approached Tilly. He held the flowers behind his back. "How are you, honey?"

She turned to him. "I'm all right, much better, thanks for asking."

Lamont presented the bouquet. "I picked these up, thought they might brighten up your day."

Matilda took the bouquet and buried her face against the blooms. "Ohhh! You didn't have to do that, but I'm glad you did. I love flowers and never get them. They smell wonderful, and you're so sweet, Lamont. Thank you!"

Not once had his mom ever called him sweet before, and that had been when he was six or seven. "You're welcome, Tilly. What's for supper? It smells good."

"Chuck roast with potatoes, carrots, onions, and mushrooms," she told him. "I'll make gravy, and I have some bread rising now to go with it."

"Come take a break if you have time," Lamont said.

She rooted through the cabinets.

"If you're looking for a vase, I don't have any."

Matilda pulled out a glass pitcher. "This will work. Let me

put the posies in water, then I'll sit down with you. There's fresh iced tea if you want some."

"I do, thanks."

She arranged the bouquet with nimble fingers, then placed it on the table where they ate. Tilly brought two glasses of tea to the den and sat down beside Lamont.

"How did riding go?"

"It went," he said with a half grin. "I'm out of shape and practice. I'm stiff now, and I'll be sore tomorrow, but I have to catch up fast. I registered for a couple rodeos late last night."

"How soon do you compete?"

"First rodeo's in Guymon in two weeks, first weekend in May," he told her. "Then the Will Rogers Stampede over Memorial Day here, in Claremore. Will you be there?"

"I want to be, Lamont."

What she didn't mention was her planned trip to New York to pick up her possessions. Neither did he. Lamont avoided the possibility by refusing to talk about it. If – well, he guessed *when* she went, he would miss her.

Although it hadn't been his intention, and he'd started out not liking her, Lamont realized he had become fond of Tilly. He ached for her to stay so they could pursue something more than the friendship that had sprung up like spring grass after a rain.

He rubbed his throbbing right knee. Since an injury years ago, it troubled Lamont. Riding today had brought back the pain.

"You're hurting," Tilly said. "Do you want something ibuprofen or something?"

"I'll take some before long," he said.

"I'll get them now."

Before he could tell her not to bother, Matilda headed into the kitchen and brought back several tablets.

Lamont washed them down with sweet tea. Tilly massaged his knee with a gentle touch. He shivered, not just because it felt good but it created an electricity between them. He ached to kiss her, but he held back.

"Does that help?"

"It does," he said. If he was going to move forward with what might be a relationship, his first since the disaster with Remy, they had to talk. He had questions that must be asked. "Tilly, can I ask you something?"

Her hand kneaded his knee with a light touch. "Of course."

"Do you have someone back in New York? I know you're divorced, but were you dating anyone?"

Matilda drew a deep breath and released it. "No, I haven't been, not since the divorce. Some of my friends – my gal pals – set me up with a few dates, but nothing ever clicked. It wasn't anything more than a quick cup of coffee or an afternoon at an art gallery. Are you?"

Relief shot through him like a sharp breeze. "No, ma'am. I will tell you before someone else does that I was engaged awhile back to Remy Carter, but it didn't work out."

Her hand stilled on his knee. "How long ago?"

"It's been two years since I called it off," Lamont said, remembering.

"What happened?"

Although he'd rather not reply, he did. "It's more what didn't," he said, with honesty. "I met her at a rodeo in Fort Worth. She's from an oil rich family, but she likes cowboys, so she decided she wanted me. Remy started showing up at every rodeo, and so we went out a few times. Her family would like to see her settled down, and when she gets married, she comes into a fair-sized trust fund. It took me a while to figure out that our relationship was more about that than each other. We were too different – she's glitzy and full of glamor, and I'm just an old cowboy, country to the bone. After the tornado, I built this house, but she hated it. Said it was too small and tacky."

"You won't ever get me to live in this cracker box. Let Daddy build us a real house, a big one with a swimming pool, and hire a staff," Remy had told him. *"I can't live in this terrible cowpoke country anyway. I hate Claremore, I don't like Will Rogers, and Oklahoma is awful."*

"I like your house," Matilda said. "Is that why you broke up?"

Lamont shrugged. "I figure it's part of it. I got busted up in a rodeo down in Laredo. Tore my knee ligament again, dislocated a shoulder, and had a concussion. It wasn't the worst that I've ever got hurt, but it put me in the hospital for a few days. Logan came down, and Lanelle called me every day I was in the hospital. Remy didn't."

Tilly's mouth drooped open with surprise. "She wasn't there?"

He shook his head. "Nope, it was right before some big black-tie gala in Dallas, a star-studded for charity where millions of dollars are raised. Champagne flows like a flooding river, and there's dining and dancing. You probably know more about such events than I do. Remy didn't like to miss any of them and she got a new designer dress each time. She'd flown to Paris to get a gown for that one, and she wasn't about to miss it. She got mad at me for being hurt because that meant she had to find another escort. I lay in that hospital bed, hurting so bad, and she called me up, cussing and fuming because I told her I couldn't go. Then she told me I had a cold, cold heart, that I was selfish, and that I don't care for anyone but me."

"What a spoiled, self-centered woman," Tilly cried. "My only experience with such big events is as part of a catering team or to deliver a cake. If I were your fiancée, I would have been with you, no matter what. I'd be there now if you were hurt, and I hope you don't get injured."

Lamont grinned. "You've shown me more tenderness than

she ever did, Tilly, and that's a fact. Soon as I felt like it, I went to see her and told her I was done. There wasn't any love between us, and I realized that. Some other oil baron's son took her to the gala, and as far as I know, she never looked back. I'm glad, now."

Her dark brown eyes met his gaze, bright with tears.

"You deserve so much more," Tilly told him. "And you're far from selfish or cold-hearted."

His wounded spirit, scarred from losing his parents, his failure to have a relationship, the loss of his home, and his many injuries, skipped a beat as he looked back at her. Maybe he did have a right to more, maybe not but Lamont wanted Tilly in his life. He'd known her for a short time, but he had no doubts.

Without words, Lamont took her into his arms and kissed her, slow and sweet. He drank in her signature lavender fragrance and held her close until Shayne yelled their names. The interruption shattered the moment.

"Someone's coming down the drive," he hollered. "I think it might be your brother."

With a groan, Lamont released Matilda and stood, knee aching.

If it was Logan, there had to be a reason he'd driven down from Bartlesville on a weekday. "Better set another place at the table," he told Tilly as he headed toward the front door.

He opened it before Logan could knock. "Look what the cat dragged down," he said. "What's up?"

Logan wore a deep frown and had his six-year-old daughter by the hand. Teagan's face was red, and her eyes puffy, like she'd been crying for a long time. She clutched a rag doll.

"Can you keep Paisley for a day or two? Tatum was in a car wreck, and she's in the hospital. It was closer to come here then drive all the way to Pittsburg to Lanelle's."

Without any hesitation, Lamont responded. "Of course, Logan. Bring her inside. She can sleep in the room between

Shayne and Tilly's, the one with the pink curtains."

"Let me get her suitcase," Logan said, face sober. "Thanks, Lamont."

Paisley stepped inside, and Lamont swooped her up into his arms. "Hey, there, baby girl," he said, using Logan's nickname for his daughter. "It's good to see you. You've grown since Christmas."

She burst into tears, put her arms around his neck, and buried her face against his shoulder.

Lamont had no idea what to do so he patted her back and said what he hoped were comforting, cheerful words. The little girl clung tighter than a possum, which surprised him.

For the first time in years, he said a silent prayer, this one for Tatum, for his niece, and for his brother, asking the Lord that all would be okay.

CHAPTER ELEVEN

As soon as Logan toted his daughter's pink suitcase decorated with colorful butterflies inside, he turned around to head back to Bartlesville.

"Stay long enough to eat a bite," Lamont said. He could see how tense his brother was from the way he hunched his shoulders tight. "Otherwise, you probably won't eat, or you'll grab something awful from a vending machine."

"I shouldn't," Logan said. "But I did want to talk to you before all this happened. Lanelle called me and said you're out of retirement. That didn't last long."

"Did she tell you why?"

"Yeah, part of the adoption. Isn't there anything else you could do?"

Lamont spread his hands out wide. "I don't know what, Logan. I thought before this came out of the blue that I might raise rough stock here, but that won't happen now until next year, at least."

Logan took a seat at the table. Paisley, face washed and calmer, sat beside him.

Everything tasted delicious. Lamont savored the tender roast and fixings. Conversation was scant, with Tatum's injury hanging over them like a storm cloud. He'd taken time to give Matilda the bare details before supper.

"That was good, but I gotta get back," Logan said when he'd finished. "No one's called from the hospital, so I guess no news is good for now."

"I'll pray for your wife," Tilly told him. "We all will."

Although Paisley begged to go home with her daddy, Matilda distracted her with a cookie and the offer to help in the kitchen.

Lamont walked out with his brother and, at his truck, asked, "How hurt is Tatum?"

Logan sighed and covered his face with his hands. "She's in serious condition. Broken ribs, a broken leg, and traumatic brain injury. They were talking about surgery tomorrow, maybe. That's why I brought Paisley down. Tatum's parents moved to Florida two years ago. I haven't even told them yet. Thank you for letting my kid stay."

"*De nada*, bro," Lamont replied. "Take care driving home, and keep me updated. If you need me, holler, and I'll be there in an hour."

"I might do that," Logan said. "I'm a mess, Lamont."

"We'll take care of Paisley, don't worry."

Lamont hugged Logan, then watched as he drove away and prayed his brother's journey would be safe. Driving distracted was never wise but it couldn't be helped in this situation.

After treating Paisley to a bubble bath, Matilda read to her from her phone, then tucked her into bed after kneeling with the little girl to pray. Lamont listened, marveling as Tilly nurtured his niece. After a career in New York and without any children of her own, Matilda appeared to have an instinct for taking care of kids.

Lamont settled into his recliner in the den but didn't even turn on the television. Right now, he couldn't focus on a program or even a ballgame. Shayne found him there after he'd showered and put on his pajamas.

"Am I going to school in the morning?" the kid asked.

"Sure, why wouldn't you?"

Shayne shrugged. "I didn't know if you might be going

over to Bartlesville to be with your brother or something."

Lamont brought his feet to the floor. "I will if Logan asks me to, but right now, I should be here. If I do go, your aunt's here to mind you and Paisley."

"Is her mom gonna die like mine did?"

It wrenched Lamont's heart to remember that's how the kid lost his mom.

"I don't know, Shayne. I hope not." He couldn't promise what might not be.

"Okay. Good night then, Lamont."

"Night, Buddy."

Eyes closed, Lamont considered going to bed, although it was early. Matilda joined him, still dressed, and sat down on the couch across from his chair.

"Paisley's in bed, and I think she's asleep," she told him. "I met Shayne, and he's going to bed, too. Did Logan tell you any more about his wife?"

"A little, but it ain't good," Lamont told her and shared the details. "Broken bones heal – I know that all too well – but traumatic brain injuries are serious. I've never had one, but I've known bronc riders who did. Tatum's going to have a long road to recovery."

He didn't add "if she makes it," but the thought hovered in the shadows.

Matilda wrapped her arms around her torso and rubbed her arms as if she were cold.

"I feel terrible for Logan and poor little Paisley," she said. "And for Tatum, even though I don't know her."

"I think you'd like her," Lamont told her. "I've known her for probably twenty years. Logan started dating her when they were really young – I think she was fourteen. They were together all through high school. Logan had a scholarship to Rogers State at Bartlesville so that's where they both went to college. He's worked as an accountant and financial analyst since he graduated. Tatum is a special education teacher and active in their church."

When he thought about Tatum, memories flooded Lamont's mind. She'd been Logan's best friend first, then girlfriend. His brother took her to prom and they'd taken their photos at the homeplace, Logan in a light blue tux with a dark blue tie and cummerbund, Tatum in a gorgeous blue dress. Her blonde curls had cascaded down her back and over her shoulders. Their wedding at the Frank Phillips Historic Home in Bartlesville was lovely. Lamont had been the best man.

"When my folks died, Tatum made most of the funeral arrangements, chose the flowers and songs, and all that. I couldn't do it. Logan and Lanelle helped her, but it was mostly Tatum. They'd only been married for about two years, then."

"How long have they been married now?"

"Eight years," Lamont told her. "Lanelle got married twelve years ago. She's the oldest."

There had been a phrase his grandmother had often used, 'a goose walking over your grave' to describe a momentary cold chill. Lamont had one now and shuddered. Time moved too quickly, he thought. A dozen years since Lanelle married Pete, eight since Logan and Tatum tied the knot, six years since Paisley was born, three years since the tornado took out the old house, and two years since his engagement ended.

Life didn't stop and wait, he reflected. It continued, and you had to do your best to keep up with the pace. He would turn 32 on his next birthday, in November. His brother and sister had spouses and families. Lamont had champion belt buckles. They had a foundation in church, and his had become shaky in his absence. Things were changing, and he resolved to do his best to catch up.

"You probably should get some sleep," Matilda told him.

"Tomorrow's likely to be a long day."

It would be, no matter what happened. He would drive the kid to school, come back, check with Logan if he hadn't heard anything, and investigate more rodeos for the season. On Thursday, after school, Shayne had an appointment to talk with the attorney. If necessary, he'd head up to Bartlesville. If not, it still wouldn't be a regular day. Paisley would need attention and care. Although he loved his little niece, Lamont had no clue what to do with a little girl. He understood Shayne because he'd been a boy, too.

At Matilda's suggestion, Lamont stopped at a discount store to buy a few age-appropriate books for a girl. He also picked out a pink and purple tea party set, complete with cups and a teapot he thought Paisley would like, and then chose a stuffed tiger. Then he filled every item on Tilly's list, including chicken nuggets, peanut butter, bananas, and chocolate milk.

He made a visit to the sheriff's office to tell Davy about Tatum and learned that Paisley was required to ride in a booster seat.

"You'll need an extended cab pickup or a car with a backseat to accommodate it," Sheriff Wills told him. "It won't work in your old truck, Lamont. Let me know about Tatum, too. I'll call Suzy-Q and get a prayer line started."

"I appreciate it," Lamont said and stood up. "I'll catch you later, and I'll let you know if I get any news."

"Leaving already? I thought if you hung around, I could grab some lunch with you."

"I'd like that, but not today. I've got a truck to buy."

Davy hooted. "You're not serious."

"I ain't jokin'," Lamont told him. He had money in the bank, and with a larger truck, one with a club cab, he could haul four, maybe five passengers. Even if Paisley went home tomorrow, he liked knowing he'd have space for her and a car seat. If – make that when – Tilly went back to New York, it would be a more comfortable ride because there was no way he would fly.

Once he made up his mind, he wasn't one to dither. Lamont drove to several local used car lots and found the truck he would buy at the third. The silver metallic Toyota Tundra had a club cab with graphite gray leather seats. He drove it around town, then out to his place. It ran well, and the tires were good.

At his house, he honked the horn, and Matilda peered out. Lamont rolled down the window and waved. "Come here a minute, honey."

"Whose truck is that?" she asked.

"It's fixin' to be mine," he told her. "Baby girl needs a booster seat, and this truck has plenty of room for one. Ride back with me, and I'll pick one up, then you can drive my old truck home."

She put her hands on her hips above her snug gray jeans and stared at him. "You're going to buy a truck, just like that?"

"Yeah, I can afford it. Being saddle bronc champion two years in a row comes with good money."

"It must. All right, give me a minute, and we'll come."

On the way back to the car lot, Lamont buckled his niece into a rear seat. It would serve until he bought the truck and picked up a booster seat. Since it was required, he would buy that first, then the truck.

Lamont offered to buy lunch for the ladies. Paisley rode in the new seat with him, still in the back. They dined on chicken chunks, wedge fries, and hot rolls. He bought cookies for dessert. Afterward, Tilly drove his faithful old truck home, but Lamont lingered in town so he could pick up Shayne. His niece stayed with him.

Paisley sang along with the radio, laughed at his lame jokes, and chattered. For now, she wasn't upset about her mother, and Lamont hoped that wouldn't change. Although Shayne had been a stranger to her until last night, Paisley had taken a shine to him. Although it was a few hours till school would dismiss, Lamont went inside to check out the kid since he wouldn't know the new truck.

"Is everything okay?" Shayne asked.

"So far, so good," Lamont told him. "I checked you out early so you could see the truck."

"I've seen your...oh, wait, did you get a different one?"

"Yes and no. I'm keeping my old pickup, but I bought one today with more room. I think you'll like it."

Using the key fob, Lamont made the horn honk, and the lights flash. Shayne laughed, then climbed into the front passenger seat once Paisley was buckled into her booster.

"This is awesome," Shayne told him, running his hands over the leather. "Do you have to make payments?"

"Nope, it's bought and paid for," Lamont said, grinning at the boy's expression. When the dealer had learned he was paying in full, he had smiled, too.

Exhilarated with his new purchase, it had been a good day. He had almost forgotten the terrible reason that Paisley was with him. When his cell phone rang as he headed out Highway 88 toward home, he remembered and stiffened, shoulders tense. Lamont pulled into a church parking lot, parked, and stepped outside to take the call.

"How's it goin'?" he asked.

"Bad," Logan said. Lamont could hear the anguish in his voice. "Can you come?"

"Sure, as soon as I drop the kids at home, I'll head that way," he told his brother. "I just picked up Shayne from school. Did Tatum have surgery?"

"Yeah, but there were complications. I'll fill you in when you get here. I need you, Lamont. I can't deal with this on my own."

"I'm coming, bro. I'll be there."

"Don't say anything to Paisley yet, please."

Lamont promised he wouldn't. He pushed the new truck to top speed to reach home but said nothing to either child. At the house, he pulled Tilly into the den and told her.

"I gotta go," he told her. "I'm sorry to leave you with the kids, but Logan is really upset. All he said is that there were complications so I don't have any idea the extent of them."

"Don't worry about me or the children," Tilly said. "Let me fix you a sandwich or something to take with you."

"Okay, thanks. I'll leave the Tundra here for you – it's got the booster seat for Paisley, and Shayne has to get to school. He also has that meeting with Ronnie Upton Thursday after school. If I'm not back, will you take him?"

Matilda nodded. "Of course I will. That's tomorrow. What do I tell Shayne and Paisley?"

Lamont ran a hand through his hair. "I don't know. Just that I went to be with Logan, for now, I guess. I'll call you when I know anything, good or bad."

"Please do, and I'll call you if anything happens. Maybe I'll just call to hear your voice."

That gave him a brief moment of joy, but it faded fast in the face of his brother's trouble.

He gathered a few clothes, some toiletries, and some over the counter meds in a duffle bag. Although he had his debit card, Lamont also took some cash from his rat hole stash. Tilly made him several thick sandwiches, his favorite bologna and cheese, ham salad, and turkey. She wrapped up some homemade cookies, too. Lamont had no idea when he might feel like eating. His nerves had a sharp edge, like a well-honed knife blade, and his belly hurt.

Lamont hollered for Shayne, and when the boy came into

the kitchen, trailed by Paisley, he said, "Hey, I'm gonna run up and spend some time with Logan. I think he's a little bit lonely. Mind your aunt and if you need to talk to me, she'll call me. Paisley, give me a kiss for your daddy."

The little girl, sober-faced now, kissed his cheek when he leaned down. Shayne hugged him tight, then stepped back. "I'll look out for everything while you're gone," the kid told him.

Matilda put her arms around him and held him close. "Take care of yourself, Lamont," she said in a soft voice. "If you need anything, let me know. I'll come to Bartlesville, too, and bring the kids if that's warranted. If I don't hear from you, I'll come hunt you down, you hear?"

She sounded more Texas than she ever had, and he loved it. "I do, honey."

"Kiss me, then go."

Lamont obliged her. He delivered a long kiss, cherishing her mouth with his. He kept her in his arms for a long moment, lingering over her scent and the warmth of her, then released her.

"Goodbye, honey," he told her. "I'll be back as soon as I can."

"Be careful, Lamont," Tilly replied. "I'll be praying for your family – and for you."

Although many people had told him the same over the years, her promise meant more.

"I probably need it," he said, more than a little gruff. He knew that he did. "I'll call you when I get up there."

Matilda cupped one hand against his cheek and nodded.

Lamont couldn't look back. If he did, he might lose his resolve to go. He walked out to the truck, his duffle bag in hand, and climbed inside. He hit the road, the stereo blasting tunes from Steve Earle, Lyle Lovett, and the two Johnnys, Cash and Horton. Lamont turned onto 88 North with a squeal from his tires, then switched to 75 at Ramona. He rocketed the old truck into Bartlesville in less than an hour.

Guessing, he would have thought it had to be five or six o'clock in the evening, but it was just after three when he rolled into town and headed for the hospital. The large multi-story building centered in a sprawling medical complex wasn't hard to locate. Lamont found a place to park and hiked inside, then called Logan.

"I'm here," he said. "Tell me where to find you."

"I'll come meet you," Logan replied. "You just about need a trail of breadcrumbs to find anything in this place. Tell me where you are."

Within five minutes, Lamont saw his brother and met him. He enveloped Logan in a hug, noting how haggard his brother appeared.

"Thanks for coming. I don't think I could have handled this alone much longer."

"No problem. Do you want to get some coffee or something? Tilly sent some sandwiches and cookies."

Logan rubbed his belly. "I don't think I can eat. Let's go up to the neurotrauma ICU waiting area. I don't want to be too far if the staff needs me for anything."

They settled into a corner and huddled as Logan outlined his wife's condition.

"Tatum suffered a TBI, that's a traumatic brain injury, in the wreck. That's the worst, most serious thing. The broken bones would heal, but this is bad, Lamont, it's terrible. They tried surgery to relieve the pressure and to drain off fluid, but her brain's swelling. This sounds so awful, but the doc took out part of her skull to give her brain space, but she's non-responsive. She's on a ventilator and hasn't woken up at all since they brought her here. The damage…"

Logan paused and swallowed a sob before he continued. "The damage is extensive. If she lives – and I guess that's a big if right now – Tatum is likely to be paralyzed and suffer permanent brain damage. She won't ever recover to the way she was. I don't care what she'll need, though. If she lives, I'll make sure she gets. I can deal with Tatum in a wheelchair or even bedbound. But, the chances are not good. On top of everything else, the swelling hasn't gone down, and she's picked up an infection. Tatum has a fever and she's weak, getting weaker."

Lamont's stomach fisted into a hard knot. "Is she in a coma?"

His brother nodded. "Yeah, and they don't think it's very likely she'll come out of it. She wouldn't be alive now without the ventilator and the other machines. Earlier, right before I called you, the doctor came in and told me that if she has 'prolonged survival without meaningful recovery, they'll want to pull the plug by Saturday."

Logan buried his face in his hands and wept, his body shaking with the force of his sobs. Lamont sat beside him, one hand on his brother's back, uncertain what to say or do.

He had no idea.

CHAPTER TWELVE

Lamont ached for his brother's anguish but at the same time, anger rose within his soul. He'd taken a few baby steps toward trusting God but now the Lord had walloped Logan with something so terrible, so intense that Lamont's spark of faith faded. Just as he'd wondered how a loving God could take his parents, then the homeplace, and leave him abandoned by his heartless fiancée, Lamont puzzled why He'd take a healthy, vivacious young woman from her family. Unless a miracle happened, Logan would lose his wife and Paisley, her mother. He should be searching for words of comfort but wanted to rage.

He could imagine standing up and trashing the room. Tossing chairs in every direction or shredding magazines wouldn't change anything, however, so Lamont remained beside Logan.

His brother recovered his emotions first. "I'm sorry," Logan said, scrubbing his face with both hands. "It's just hard to accept. I mean, Tuesday morning, everything was fine. We had breakfast, she dropped Paisley at school, and I went to work. It was just a normal day, Buddy, nothing different. I kissed Tatum when I left, just a quick kiss. I asked her if she wanted me to pick up something for supper, and she told me no, that she'd grill some chicken."

To stay grounded, Lamont did his best to focus and shed his anger. "What time did the wreck happen?"

"During the noon hour. Most of the time, she ate lunch at school, but on Tuesday, one of her friends, another teacher, needed to drop off her car for service. Tatum went to pick her up, but when she merged onto 75, a loaded semi-truck switched lanes and hit her. The impact pushed her into the back of another eighteen-wheeler."

Lamont shuddered. "Thank God Paisley wasn't with her," he said, without thinking.

"I'd be losing them both," Logan said, rubbing his forehead with his three middle fingers. "I feel like death warmed over."

Their mother had sometimes used the phrase, most often, to one of the kids if they were under the weather. A sharp pang of grief sliced through Lamont. Most of the time, he tried not to think about his parents because it brought home the loss. With a new loss looming large, though, he couldn't help but remember his mom and dad.

"Is your head hurting?" he asked. "I've got over-the-counter pain relievers if you want some."

"Yeah, it is. I'll take them, thanks."

With change scrounged from his pockets, Lamont bought a cold soda so Logan could wash the tablets down. "Have you slept at all?"

"I don't think so, maybe dozed once or twice," Logan replied.

"You ought to try to grab a nap. You aren't helping Tatum by wearing yourself out, and Paisley's gonna need you."

"I'll try," Logan groaned. "If I do fall asleep, wake me if anyone comes in or has something new about Tatum."

"Will do," Lamont said.

He watched as his brother settled onto one of the couches. In less than five minutes, Logan slept, snoring softly. Logan sat back, overwhelmed with a simmering stew of emotion.

When his cell rang, he answered. "Hello."

"Did you get there?" It was Tilly.

"I did, honey, and I meant to call. Logan's a mess, and the

news, well, it's the worst."

Lamont explained Tatum's condition and the sad anticipated outcome.

"Oh, I am so sorry to hear that," Matilda told him. "Nothing new here. Oh, the lawyer called to make sure Shayne will be at the appointment tomorrow. I told her he would but that you're out of town and why."

"What did she say?"

"That it's understandable but if you're going to be away long, check in with her."

He sighed. "I will. I hope it's not going to affect the adoption. Kids okay?"

"It shouldn't, and they're fine, Lamont. You've only been gone a few hours."

It seemed longer. "I miss you," he told her. "And the kid, too."

Matilda paused, then said, "Lamont, I miss you, too. I guess I'm getting used to having you around. I won't keep you, but call me, okay?"

"I will, Tilly."

Lamont didn't want to hang up. The sound of her voice connected him to his life and to her. Although he lacked the words to explain it, he craved the life they had built in such a short time. Until Shayne and his aunt entered his life, he'd failed to realize how lonely he had been.

Logan slept, and Lamont paced up and down the length of the room. He noted every detail, from the color of the curtains – light brown – or the blue cushions on the standard furniture. A few others huddled in other areas of the waiting space, their faces as drawn and anxious as Logan's. People spoke in hushed voices, and sometimes, they wept. Some were camping here, awaiting recovery or resolution. Those had blankets and sleeping bags, pillows, and backpacks strewn about.

In the corridor, the swish of wheels echoed as gurneys and wheelchairs passed. The PA system announced codes and other information. Although he'd never been in this facility until now, Lamont knew medical centers. He had spent more time as a patient than he liked to remember.

Although he wasn't hungry, he dug out one of the sandwiches Tilly had packed and ate it. It remained cool from the ice pack she'd tucked in beside the food. He nibbled on an oatmeal raisin cookie she'd baked and marveled at how well she could cook. Sometimes, he had trouble imagining her as a baker or chef in an urban setting, although he knew she had been. His early impressions that she was a highfalutin, silly city woman had faded fast as he became more acquainted. Despite her New York City years, she seemed far more Texas than Times Square.

Logan roused just after six. He sat up, bleary-eyed, and sighed.

"I didn't think I'd really sleep," he said. "You should have woken me up."

Lamont shook his head. "You needed some rest, and nothing's happened."

His brother nodded. "I need to go back and see Tatum. I haven't for several hours. Shift change is at 7, and they'll want us all to leave for a little while then. Come with me, Lamont."

The last thing Lamont wanted to do was to see his sister-in-law on a ventilator with tubes and lines. He'd rather remember her laughing and smiling, her blonde curls dancing as she walked, but he couldn't refuse. "All right."

First, they had to speak to a nurse through a glass window and ask permission. Once they secured it, they waited to be buzzed back. A required stop at a hand washing station was necessary, and they scrubbed with antibacterial soap. Masks were also mandatory so Lamont slipped one over his nose and mouth, then followed Logan to the cubicle where Tatum lay.

There were two straight-back chairs near the single window. Lamont sank into one as Logan approached the bed. Tatum was unrecognizable. Her head was swathed in bandages from the recent surgery. A vent tube between her lips vied with at least three IVs connected to her. What he could see of her face appeared bruised and somewhat swollen. He'd known she wouldn't look like herself, but she resembled a broken doll, fragile and in pieces.

Logan clenched his hands on the bed rail, tears in his eyes. He leaned over and planted a butterfly kiss on the single open spot on one cheek. Then he lifted his wife's slack right hand and held it between his. "Hey, sweetheart, I'm here. I love you so much. Lamont's here, too."

Prompted, he said, "Hey, Tatum."

Could she hear him, Lamont wondered? His grandmother had always claimed hearing was the last sense to go. Although he wanted to believe that Tatum could, he doubted it. It seemed like she had already taken the first steps on a journey from which there would be no return. He'd awakened more than once in a similar cubicle, and the place made him antsy. Lamont wanted to rush out of the room, away from here, to where he could let the wind blow away the medical aromas. He longed for the warmth of the sun on his shoulders, but he steeled himself to stay for Logan's sake.

When they left, they remained silent as he followed Logan out into the hallway.

"What now?" he asked.

"I don't know. We'll come back after shift change," his brother said. "I usually go to the chapel or cafeteria."

"I could use a cup of coffee," Lamont said.

They sat in the almost empty cafeteria and sipped black coffee. It tasted old to Lamont but he drank it for the caffeine. He coaxed Logan to eat part of a salad and some warmed-up soup.

Lamont ate another of Tilly's sandwiches, aware they wouldn't last much longer without some refrigeration.

As he considered whether he should call Tilly, Lamont heard the unmistakable sound of someone wearing high-heel boots approaching the cafeteria. He recognized the gait and sat up straight before the woman came into view. Wearing boots, a denim skirt and jacket, and a soft blue blouse, Lanelle strode into the dining area. She stopped and looked around so Lamont waved.

"We're over here," he called. Lamont stood when she reached them and opened his arms for a hug. He inhaled her signature White Shoulders perfume, one their mother had also preferred. "I didn't know you were coming, but I'm glad you're here."

"I could have been here sooner," Lanelle said. "I wouldn't know about Tatum now, except I tried to call Lamont and got Matilda."

Logan stumbled to his feet to greet his sister, knocking over a chair in the process. "There's not much you can do."

"I can be here," she told him, voice firm and lips tight. "You look awful, Logan."

He sank back into a chair. "I've been better. Where's your kiddos?"

"At the hotel with Bradley," she said. "Depending on what happens, they'll probably go home in the morning. I'm here for as long as I need to be. Tell me about Tatum."

Logan did, then went to get a cup of coffee.

In his absence, Lamont turned to his sister.

"When did you call me and why?"

"Around suppertime," Lanelle said. "I wanted to try to convince you not to rodeo this year. When I didn't get your cell, I called your landline, and Matilda answered."

Most of the time, Lamont forgot about the home phone.

He'd installed it when he built the house in a nostalgic moment, unwilling to lose the phone number the family had since before he was born. "And she told you."

"Yes, she did," his sister said. "Why didn't one of you let me know?"

"I ought to have," Lamont replied. "I guess I thought Logan might have called. After he brought Paisley last night, today was busy. I bought a truck, and then Logan needed me here, so I came."

"That's what Matilda told me, so Bradley brought us down. Lamont, do you think Tatum's going to recover?"

The question hit like a slap in the face. He drew a long breath, held it, then exhaled. "To be honest, no, I don't believe she will. Logan told you her condition, but he didn't say anything about the fact they'll want to turn off life support by this weekend if she doesn't improve."

Lanelle gasped. "Oh, dear Lord."

"Logan told me that even if she did recover from the injuries, it's doubtful she would be able to walk or talk. She suffered brain damage, and now she's fighting an infection."

She shook her head back and forth in slow motion. "That's awful. I'll keep praying, and you should, too."

Lamont lacked the energy to argue. "You know I don't, not anymore." First prayer he'd said in years had been his brief, silent one when he first heard about the accident.

Her eyes met his without blinking. "You should. Are you staying tonight?"

He shrugged. "I'm planning on it. I'd best call Tilly, though, and make sure it's all good at home."

"If you need to go, I'll be here."

"I know," Lamont told her and put his hand over hers. "That's a good thing. Logan needs us both."

Mentioning home reminded him he wanted to call Tilly,

so when Logan led Lanelle back to the ICU waiting area, Lamont stepped outside into a courtyard to call. He inhaled the cool evening air with pleasure, savoring the clean scent after being cooped up in the hospital for hours. A light breeze touched his face as he sank onto a bench.

"Hey, honey," he said when she answered.

"Hi, Lamont," she replied. "I hoped you would call. Your sister did."

"I know – she's here. Thanks for filling her in. How's the kids?"

When she hesitated, he knew something was up.

"They're fine," Matilda reassured him. "But Paisley has been crying for her mama and daddy. I distracted her with storybooks and watching an old movie. Shayne's upset because it's brought back losing his mom. He's worried about talking to the lawyer, but I told him it'll be okay."

Lamont leaned his chin on his hand. "He needs to chill out. All she wants to do is ask if he's good with the adoption."

"He wants it so much he's afraid he'll mess it up."

"Is he still awake?"

"No, he went to bed early."

"I'll call in the morning, before school, and I'll talk to him," Lamont told her. "If I need to, I can run home. I'm only an hour away."

That hour, though, was one to get there, another to return, and time spent at home. If anything happened with Tatum's condition in his absence, he would be guilt-stricken.

"Talk to him on the phone first," Matilda advised.

Her voice flowed into his ears like a healing balm. Just listening to her eased something in his soul. "Tell me where you're at right now so I can imagine it."

Tilly laughed. "I'm sitting on the sofa in the den, shoes off and feet tucked under me. Both kids are in bed, and I turned off the TV, so it's quiet. I'm drinking a cup of herbal tea, and until you called, I was praying."

Lamont imagined the scene and longed to be beside her. "I'd rather be there than here."

"I know." Her gentle tone dropped lower. "Are you okay?"

That she asked meant everything. "Yeah, I'm all right."

"Try to get some sleep tonight. I know that's asking the near impossible."

"I'll do my best, honey, and I'll call in the morning."

"Good night, Lamont. Take care."

Before he could summon up words to tell her the same, she ended the call.

In the waiting room, time stagnated. Minutes became hours, and the hours didn't seem to pass at all. At the later time, fewer people remained, and he figured they'd gone home. Logan sat on the end of a couch, feet flat on the floor, and stared at nothing.

Lanelle fidgeted and flipped through magazines without reading a word.

Visitors could go back in pairs, so Lamont remained while Logan ushered Lanelle back to see Tatum. His sister returned, wiping away tears.

Logan emerged, one hand clamped to his midsection. "I need to go find a restroom," he said and exited.

"He's got a bellyache," Lanelle told Lamont. "And it's no wonder. I couldn't stand to see Tatum like that. Her vitals are poor – her temperature is up, her heart and pulse rates are down. I'm not sure she'll last long enough to have to worry about turning off the life support."

"That might be for the best," he responded, and his sister nodded.

"I don't know if Logan can live with a decision like that," Lanelle said. She folded her hands and bowed her head to pray.

Lamont shut his eyes and tried to sleep but couldn't.
It would be a long, hard night.

CHAPTER THIRTEEN

In the wee hours of the morning, unable to sleep or relax, Lamont left the waiting room and wandered. At that hour, the halls loomed empty, lights dimmed, and activity light. Nurses in soft-soled shoes made rounds, their occasional voices muted. He roamed like a nocturnal animal, rambling like an opossum, aimless as a mouse, and as wakeful as an owl. If it hadn't been so late, he might have called Tilly but if she slept, he wouldn't want to disturb her.

After his boots covered what seemed like miles of tile, he came to the chapel. Lamont hesitated, then entered. He reached up to remove his hat, then remembered he hadn't worn it inside. It remained on the seat of his truck in the parking lot. A combination of wooden chairs and benches filled the space, all facing a large cross on the wall. He sank onto a bench, unsure why he'd come here.

In the hushed chapel, he found a sense of peace, something he hadn't expected. In the waiting room and even in the cafeteria, he'd been anxious, so uneasy he had trouble remaining still. Here, however, he relaxed and let the silence fill his emptiness. Although Lamont was the only person present, he didn't feel alone.

Although he didn't set out to pray, never put his palms together, or bowed his head, Lamont talked to God. A door shut out any sounds from the corridor and provided privacy, so he spoke aloud in a rough whisper.

"God, You and me have been on the outs for a long time,"

he said. "It's my fault, probably, more than Yours, but I didn't like the things that happened. I couldn't figure out why you'd take my parents or let a tornado destroy the only place I ever knew as home. As long as I could remember, I wanted to get married and raise a family, but when I had a woman, it turned out she wasn't the right one. I used to think You'd watch over me when I rode and wore a cross around my neck. But after getting busted up more times than I can count, having broken bones, concussions, and about every kind of hurt a man can get, I decided You didn't care. Jonah ran from You, and so did I. I don't know how I feel right now, although Tilly got me in church last Sunday, but if You can hear me, if You help people, help Logan now. He's fixing to lose his wife, Paisley will lose her mama, and that's gonna hurt. If Tatum's time has come, then let her go, bring her home or whatever You do. If there's any help left, give me a hand with the kid. I want to do right by Shayne. I'd like to have Tilly in my life. She touches my heart in a deep way, and if she went back to New York, I'd miss her something awful. I don't want to rodeo anymore, but I don't see any other way. If there is one, point it out to me so I can't miss it. Might take an angel with a flaming sword in hand. If You hear me, if You help us right now, I won't forget. If I wasn't desperate, I wouldn't be sitting here at three o'clock in the morning, yapping out loud. I need to go back and sit with my brother, maybe get some sleep."

He didn't end with amen, and Lamont didn't really consider it a prayer, although his heavy spirit lightened after he'd said his piece. When he returned to the waiting room, he found Logan sprawled out on one of the couches, a pillow tucked beneath his head and a light blanket over his body.

Lanelle put a finger to her lips and he nodded, understanding she didn't want Logan to wake. Lamont sat down, put his head back, and shut his eyes. He cleared his mind, and although he didn't think he would, he slept until his sister roused him.

"It's almost time for shift change," she said. "We need to clear out as soon as Logan comes back from visiting Tatum."

He rubbed his face and nodded. "Yeah, okay. Is Bradley coming by?"

"He was already here, then took the kids home. I guess we can get something to eat downstairs."

Unsure if he could stomach the on-site cafeteria again, Lamont stood up. "I can go bring back something, too. Might be good for us all to have a change of scenery if you both want to go, too."

"It might," Lanelle said. "Where'd you go last night for so long?"

"I wandered the halls, mostly, and ended up in the chapel," Lamont replied. "I'm going out to the truck to call the house. I need to talk to Tilly. I'll be back, or y'all can meet me there."

Matilda answered on the fourth ring, about the time Lamont was about to hang up.

"Hello, Lamont. I'm sorry it took me so long. I was mopping up a mess."

In the background, he heard both Shayne and Paisley, but he couldn't tell if they squabbled or giggled. "No problem," he said. "Nothing's changed here."

"I hope you at least got some rest," Tilly told him.

"Not much but I did go to the chapel during the night." Once said, Lamont had no idea why he mentioned it. "Does Shayne still need to talk to me?"

"Definitely," she told him.

"Hey, kid," Lamont said when he had Shayne on the phone. "How's it going?"

"When are you coming back?"

"Soon as I can," he replied. "After school, you've got that appointment to talk to Ronnie Upton, the adoption attorney."

Shayne's voice shifted into a whine. "I don't wanna."

Lamont counted to ten silently. "Kid, you have to – it's part of the adoption process. All she wants to know is how you feel about being adopted. You're old enough to have a say in it, and she'll have to tell the court that you want this. She might also ask if you like me – "

"Well, heck, yes, I do, Lamont."

A grin teased his lips as he answered. "I'd hope to shout. Anyhow, she might want to make sure you have a decent place to sleep, that I feed you, all that stuff. It won't take long and even if I wasn't up here, she has to talk to you alone. Can you do it?"

"Yeah, sure. I thought it'd be more than that."

Hopefully, it wasn't. "So, you're good to go?"

"Of course," Shayne answered. "Hey, Lamont?"

"Is Paisley's mom gonna die?"

He cringed and hoped the little girl wasn't within earshot. "She might," he said, choosing his answer with care. Lamont didn't want to mislead the boy or offer false hope. "But don't say anything about it to Paisley, okay?"

"I won't. Aunt Tilly's braiding her hair, in case you wondered."

"I did, and thanks."

There wasn't time to do more than tell Matilda bye because she had to take Shayne to school. "I'll call this evening to see how it all went," Lamont told her.

Although he hadn't thought Logan would agree to leave the hospital, he did so they loaded into Lamont's truck, the brothers flanking their sister in the middle. After a quick fast-food breakfast, Logan asked if they could run by his house.

"I really need to shower, shave, and put on clean clothes," he told them. "It won't take long."

"Sure, it's not a problem."

He'd been to his brother's house on Osage Avenue many

times, most recently at Christmas. The two-story brick house sat in a settled neighborhood with a spacious yard, a sun porch, and a deck in back surrounded by a privacy fence. Lamont and Lanelle sat out on the deck while Logan took care of his business.

The lack of Tatum's physical presence loomed large, and Lamont wondered how his brother would adjust to life without his wife. The late April sunshine warmed his bones and he tipped back a deck chair, eyes closed.

"It's a pretty place," Lanelle said.

"Too much town for me," Lamont replied. "There was a time when I wouldn't have thought Logan would be content with houses on every side, streetlights shining in the windows at night, and neighbors in all directions."

His sister laughed. "His tastes changed."

"That came with Tatum," Lamont said.

He could never be a number cruncher like Logan or live in a neighborhood. It wouldn't have been upscale enough to suit Remy, but he figured Tilly might like it. It would be an improvement over Manhattan, anyway.

When Logan emerged, clean and in fresh clothing, his mood had improved but that didn't last. Before the truck left the driveway, he received a phone call. His face changed expression and paled. "I'm on my way," he said. "We gotta get back, Lamont."

"What's wrong?" Lanelle asked.

"Tatum's condition is worsening," Logan told them. "Her body's weak and having trouble fighting off the infection. The damage to her brain is complicating that. They're not sure how long she can last."

His voice cracked with emotion as he spoke, and then he added in a lower tone, "If it wasn't for the vent and life support, she'd be gone already."

The brief span of semi-normalcy vanished. At the medical

center, Logan rushed back to see Tatum while the others remained in the waiting area. He returned, tears wet on his cheeks, and said, "I don't think it will be long, tomorrow maybe."

Someone had to be practical. "Did you ever call Tatum's folks?"

Logan collapsed onto the couch. "No, I didn't. I haven't even called her brother in Missouri. I don't know how I'll manage to tell them."

Lanelle spoke. "I will, Logan, if you want."

By Friday morning, Tatum's parents, her brother and his wife, and her closest cousins joined the vigil. Lamont and Lanelle remained at Logan's side although each hour that passed, Lamont became increasingly uneasy. He hated the environment and he did not go back past the first time to visit Tatum. Lamont would rather remember her as she had been, and when Tatum's mother suggested that they bring Paisley to see her mother, he rejected the idea.

Although Tatum's mother cried when Logan agreed that wasn't going to happen, it was the right decision. So was Logan's choice to have the funeral in Claremore, not Bartlesville. Tatum would be laid to rest in the same small cemetery where their parents had been buried, and the funeral would take place at the Pioneer Faith Church.

"I thought you'd have it where you got married," Tatum's mother cried.

Their vows had been said at the Frank Phillips home, not a church, although they'd attended a mega church. Logan had seldom taken his family to services there. When possible, Logan brought his wife and daughter to their childhood church. "I want to bring her back home," he said with quiet dignity.

Tatum slipped from life late on Friday night. At the last, all the artificial devices were removed, and she died with her husband holding her hand. Logan stood on one side of the bed, and her parents on the other. Lanelle and Lamont huddled at the foot of the bed. Lanelle cried and prayed.

Lamont recalled his conversation with God in the chapel and said a silent thanks that the Lord had let his sister-in-law go home. Although most of the medical staff had urged intervention if necessary, there had been one doctor who suggested Tatum could be kept alive indefinitely in a long-term care facility. To Lamont, that equaled a living death, and he vowed if he ever got injured so much that he was in the same situation, he wanted to die with dignity. He resolved to visit an attorney if necessary to ensure it.

Bradley drove down to take Lanelle home for now. "I'll be back for the visitation and funeral," she told her brothers, weeping as she hugged them. "Call me if you need anything, you hear?"

Tatum's parents rented a car and drove to Claremore with plans to book a hotel.

When everything was over, and they left the medical center, Lamont turned to his brother, worried. Logan's hands trembled, and he walked with the slow gait of an elderly man. "Where to? Do you want me to take you home or what?"

Logan shook his head. "No. I can't stay there. I'll stop to get some things, but I want to go home with you, Lamont. I need to see Paisley. Oh, sweet Jesus, I have to tell her, and I don't know how to find the words. Can I stay at your place?"

"My house is your house," Lamont said. "It's our home place."

A faint, sickly grin emerged on his brother's lips. "Thanks, Buddy."

Despite the time, Lamont called Tilly from Logan's house, sitting in the silent living room while his brother packed. "Hey," he said, his voice soft. "It's me. Tatum passed and we're coming home, me and Logan. I'm sorry if I woke you."

"I wasn't asleep," Matilda said. "Will you want something to eat when you get here?"

"Naw, don't go to any fuss, honey. I don't think Logan's hungry and I'll scratch around and find something. I just wanted to let you know. I didn't want you to think someone was breaking in or something."

She yawned. "I wouldn't. Is Logan coming to take Paisley home?"

"No, he's coming to stay for a bit. He doesn't want to be here in this empty house."

"That's understandable," she told him.

The last thing he wanted was to treat Matilda like a domestic, but Lamont had one request. "I'm giving my brother my bed. If you wouldn't mind, can you put clean sheets on it?"

"I don't, and I will, Lamont. Drive safely."

"You can count on it, honey. I'll see you soon."

They left Bartlesville around one in the morning with Logan's bags tucked into the truck bed. The luggage included a garment bag that Lamont figured had clothing for Tatum but he didn't ask. Logan hadn't said more than a few words since leaving the hospital, which concerned Lamont.

"Hey, do you want to stop for something to eat or coffee?"

Logan hadn't eaten more than a few bites in days. "No, thanks. I don't think I can get anything down."

"Sure," Lamont told him. His empty stomach protested but he could wait. "If you change your mind, holler at me."

In the dim light from the dashboard, Logan nodded and lapsed into silence for the remainder of the ride. The tires hummed against the pavement as the wind whined against the windshield. It made a lonesome sound. Already worn out, Lamont struggled to stay alert and turned on the radio. He fumbled to find a station through static, and when he heard Dolly Parton's familiar voice uplifted in a traditional hymn, he turned up the sound. He might not have been to church much in recent years, but Lamont still loved country music and liked Dolly. Besides, the words might bring comfort to his brother.

Rain began falling when they were about halfway to Lamont's place, and he slowed down a little. Until then, he'd been driving too fast in his rush to get home. It was after two by the time he eased the truck down the driveway to his house, lights off so they wouldn't rouse anyone asleep.

A single lamp burned in the window, the light spilling out like a warm welcome. If it hadn't been for Tilly, the house would have loomed dark, and Lamont was thankful for her presence. He grabbed his brother's luggage from the truck and headed for the front door, fumbling for his key.

Logan followed. Tatum was the one who died, but his brother resembled a ghost, pale and seeming almost disoriented. He shuffled, putting one foot before the other with what seemed like an effort.

Lamont inserted the key, but before he could turn it in the lock, the door swung open and Lamont all but fell into the living room. Matilda stepped back to give him space.

"Hi," she said in a soft voice. "I'm glad you're back."

Lamont halted. "Thanks. I didn't expect you to wait up."

In answer, she put her arms around him in a hug. Lamont held her close, comforted by her action. He ached to kiss her, but it would be poor taste in front of his brother, who'd just lost his wife. He brushed her cheek in a gentle caress before he stepped back.

"I wouldn't have been able to sleep," she replied.

He put Logan's bags down in his bedroom.

"My heart aches for you and Paisley," Matilda said to Logan. "I've been praying for you."

Logan nodded, then slumped into a chair and buried his face in both hands.

Lamont exchanged a long glance with Matilda and thrust his hands in his pockets. An appetizing aroma filled his nose, and he turned to her. "Something smells good."

"It's chicken tortilla soup," she told him. "I made it earlier, after supper. It's in the slow cooker if you want some."

His stomach rumbled with emptiness, and he nodded. "Yeah, I do. I'm starving."

She prepared a bowl of the hearty soup, sprinkled shredded cheese on top, and added a few crushed tortilla chips. Matilda brought it to him at the table.

Lamont stirred it, noting it included both black and red beans, corn tortilla strips, chicken, tomatoes, onions, and enough seasoning to provide heat but without a burn. He lifted the spoon to his mouth and tasted. "That's delicious. Thanks, Tilly. I would have fixed a bologna sandwich or something, but this is better."

"I'm glad you like it," she told him. "I thought you might need some comfort food."

Silence from the living room worried Lamont. He wondered if Logan had fallen asleep or if he brooded. His brother had every reason to do so, but he had to shake off his grief long enough to make arrangements for Tatum, lay her to rest, and find a new beginning.

Lamont didn't realize Logan had joined them until he spoke.

"I could use a bowl of that," his brother said, voice husky.

Tilly flashed a smile. "Sit down, and I'll get you one."

The brothers ate and made small talk. Neither mentioned Tatum. After a few minutes, Tilly yawned. "If you want another helping, it's in the slow cooker on low. Leave it – it'll be fine until morning. I'm heading to bed. Good night."

Logan glanced up and nodded.

Lamont reached out and caught her hand as she passed. "Night, honey. Thanks."

She leaned down and kissed his forehead. "No problem. I'll see you in the morning."

He held her hand a moment longer, then released her.

When they'd finished, Logan headed for the bedroom. Lamont lingered, first stacking their bowls in the sink, then washing them. Despite the fact it was early morning and his body ached with exhaustion, he stepped out onto the deck for a few moments. The rain had stopped, and the air cooled his overheated face. All the clouds had moved to the west, and on the eastern horizon, the first faint light of dawn brought the promise of a new day.

If Lamont still prayed on a regular basis, he would have bowed his head. Despite his recent conversation with God, his heart remained like a stone. Curious why God had taken a young woman from her family, his admiration for the beauty of the breaking day faded. Too tired to think very hard, he headed for the den so he could flop down on the couch for a few hours.

Two pillows rested on one end, a light blanket at the other. *Tilly,* he thought, *this had to be Tilly's doing.* "Bless her," he said, aloud. Matilda Mannheim nurtured, he thought, and lent her gentle spirit to everything she did. He cared about her and depended on her more each day.

If something happened to her, Lamont realized he would take it hard, maybe almost as bad as Logan. Risking his heart seemed worse than taking a chance on his body every time he rode a bucking bronc.

If their conversation hadn't been interrupted after that long kiss when Logan showed up with his daughter and dire news, Lamont thought they might have taken a leap into a relationship. He'd been gone the last four days, but it seemed like he had been away for a month.

Lamont feared he'd never go to sleep, not with his mind twirling in multiple directions, but once he shut his eyes, fatigue claimed him, and he slept.

CHAPTER FOURTEEN

Lamont woke to the sound of voices in the kitchen and sat up with a crick in his neck. Groggy from too little rest, he listened and tried to make sense out of what he heard. Shayne spoke with the intensity of a boy who didn't want to be quiet on Saturday morning, and Tilly responded with quiet calm.

"Hey," he called. "What's the deal?"

Shayne rushed into the den. "I told Aunt Tilly to wake you up, but she wouldn't."

Matilda trailed her nephew. "Because he didn't get much sleep last night," she told Shayne. "Neither did Logan."

"You didn't either," Lamont said. "Is my brother still asleep?"

She nodded. "I think so. He hasn't been out of the bedroom yet. Paisley is awake, but she hasn't realized he's here."

Lamont groaned. Once she did, things would get intense.

"Let's hope he gets up soon, then. I need coffee."

Tilly brought a cup, and he sipped it, savoring the flavor and sighing as the caffeine rushed through his body.

"Why'd you want to wake me?" Lamont asked Shayne.

"I want to know what happened," the kid replied. "Did Paisley's mother die?"

After glancing around in case his niece had arrived without notice, Lamont nodded. "Yeah, she did. It's going to be hard for her."

Shayne put his head down. "It was for me. Is she gonna stay here for a while?"

"Looks like it," Lamont told him. "Logan, too."

Shayne grinned. "We'll be like a real family."

Touched, Lamont ruffled the boy's hair. "We *are* a real family, kid."

Or they would be once the adoption was complete. He realized that once Tatum's condition worsened, he hadn't heard how Thursday's meeting went. Lamont opened his lips to ask, but Logan shuffled into the den. He wore the same clothes he'd worn to travel.

"Good morning," Lamont greeted him.

"I wish it was," Logan replied. "My in-laws are on the way over, and I need to tell Paisley before they do, but I don't know how. I don't know what to say."

"We'll figure it out," Lamont told him with more confidence than he felt. Sharing news of a loss, especially a parent, would be difficult. He'd been an adult when he learned their parents had died, but it hadn't been easy to hear. Telling had to be a hundred times harder.

Matilda sank down beside him on the sofa. "The Lord will help, Logan."

"I wish He'd hurry up, then," he said.

Shayne sat down on the floor at Lamont's feet. "It's too late," he whispered. "She's coming."

Logan, already pale, lost all color in his face. His knees trembled so Lamont stood to stand beside him for support and also to catch his brother if he went down.

Paisley sashayed into the room, a frown on her face. Her bare feet made no sound as she came closer, her rag doll clenched tight in one hand. She wore a knee-length pink polka-dotted nightgown with a unicorn surrounded by flowers. So innocent and adorable, Lamont thought, but her world was about to implode.

"Daddy!" she cried and halted. "Daddy, you came back."

Logan sank to his knees, and his daughter rushed to him. "I did, baby girl."

"Where's Mommy? I want Mommy."

The simple words ripped Lamont's heart into shreds.

"Mommy's gone," Logan said in a voice so sharp it could have shattered glass. "She died last night."

Paisley's face crumpled, and tears flowed down her cheeks. "No!" she screamed. "No, no, no. I want Mommy!"

At six, Paisley knew what death meant. Last year, the old dog Logan had for many years had died. He'd been upset, and so had Paisley.

Logan swayed on his knees and opened his arms to his daughter. "I want her too, baby girl," he said. "God needed her more than we did, I guess."

A terrible cry, something between a scream and a wail, burst out of the little girl's mouth. She threw herself into her daddy's arms, and Logan held her tight, rocking back and forth. He wept, too.

Watching, Lamont shed tears, too. Tilly stepped beside him, and he put his arm around her, grateful for her presence. Shayne joined them, and Lamont pulled him close as well. He wanted to say words of comfort, but he couldn't find anything to say. Matilda, though, did.

"To everything, there is a season," she quoted from Ecclesiastes. "And a time to every purpose under the heavens, a time to be born and a time to die."

As she continued reciting the familiar verses, Lamont cried. Those were the words that Lanelle had said to him after he returned home because their parents died in that plane crash. Earlier than that, their dad had said the same when his grandpa and then his grandmother passed away. That quote from the Bible had been a balm to the wounds of his grief, and he hoped it would be the same for both Logan and his daughter.

"Lord, help them," he prayed without speaking. "Give them strength and peace."

Following, Lamont marveled that he had said a prayer after his long, dry spell.

An hour later, his house brimmed full of people, gathered in the den and spilled into the kitchen as well as out onto the deck. Logan had showered, shaved, and changed into clean jeans and a chambray shirt. Matilda had helped Paisley dress and had braided her hair. Lanelle, along with her husband and two children, Samuel and Grace, had arrived. At eight and ten, the kids were ill at ease under the sad circumstances. Tatum's parents had driven out from a local hotel. Jeff and Janis Browning perched on the edge of one of the two couches, anxious and unfriendly.

Everyone else held a cup of coffee or a glass of tea that Matilda had provided but they had refused. Lamont figured they remained unhappy that Logan had rejected their ideas for the funeral. Besides, they were grieving too. He remembered how his mom had always said everyone handles loss in their own way. On arrival, they had tried to swoop Paisley into their embrace, but the little girl clung to Logan like a possum.

After caravanning to the funeral parlor and making arrangements, the same cast of characters, along with Pastor Cartwright and a few other church members, returned to the house. Matilda had remained home with the kids, including Paisley, and had put together brunch in their absence. She presented platters of bacon and sausage, a scrambled egg casserole with cheese and ham, biscuits, scones, and cinnamon rolls. Tilly set out a meat and cheese platter that the pastor had delivered. Most of the guests swarmed the food, but Lamont drew Tilly out of the kitchen and into the small adjacent laundry room.

"Baby, you didn't have to do all that," he told her. "I know you're worn out, too."

"I didn't mind," she told him. "People have to eat, and I

like to stay busy."

"I appreciate it, but you're gonna work yourself to a frazzle. They can fend for themselves at lunch and supper. Don't go making another big meal, Tilly."

"I was going to bake a ham and…"

Lamont interrupted her with a kiss. "Not today, you're not. You were up until all hours last night same as me. These next few days will be crazy busy and hard. We need to get a little rest while we can."

"What about a dinner for after the funeral? When is it?"

"Visitation is tomorrow afternoon at the funeral home, and the service will be at 11 a.m. Monday at the church. The ladies will put a dinner together for afterward so you won't have to do a thing. Okay?"

She lowered her dark eyes and nodded. "I suppose so. I just feel like I should do something – you're letting me stay here."

"You're here for Shayne." Lamont tilted her face upward. "I want you here, honey. You don't have to earn your keep."

Her sigh echoed between them. "I probably should get a hotel anyway. I didn't intend to stay this long."

Lamont bit down on a few hot words. The last thing he needed right now would be for Tilly to run away. "Something's wrong, and it's eating on you. Tell me."

Tilly forced a smile, but it resembled a grimace. "Nothing, Lamont. It's just that your house is full, and I'm taking up space…"

"Matilda," he said. If he knew her middle name, he'd use it. "What is it?"

Her bottom lip quivered. "You're not going to quit, are you?"

"Never."

"I feel like I'm in the way," she told him. "I'm taking up a bedroom that one of your relatives could use. I'm not part of the family. Besides, I said I'd stay a few days, and it's been weeks."

"I don't mind how long you stay, honey. You talked about maybe relocating here, and I would be glad if you did. You're Shayne's aunt."

She brushed a fallen lock of hair away from her face. "That's not all. I brought you bad luck."

Confused, Lamont shook his head. "What are you talkin' about?"

"You called me about Shayne and his stepfather overdosed. He died. Then I come here, and you're stuck adopting him, or he'll go to a foster home. There was a snake in the shed and then your sister-in-law was in a terrible traffic wreck. Now she's passed away. Your niece has been here – and that's no problem, she's a sweetheart – but your brother is staying now, too. You've had to go back to busting saddle broncs, and I'm worried you'll get hurt."

Lamont listened to her rapid spew of words. He didn't agree with anything she said. The idea that she might leave upset him. He counted on her, and more than that, he needed her. Call it smitten or whatever. He thought he might be falling in love with her. If she wasn't around, he would be devastated.

After gathering his words into something that might make sense, he said, "I don't believe in bad luck. Things happen – it's called life. I'm not stuck adopting Shayne. I want to and I wouldn't do it if I didn't. I like the kid a lot. Even if Teddy Anderson hadn't died, I still planned to get him out of that home, whatever it took. We've always had a snake or two on the place. You had nothing to do with what happened to Tatum."

"Lamont…"

He put a finger over her lips and continued. "There's room here for everyone who needs to be here. I don't mind bunking in the den. I might get hurt, that's true, going back on the rodeo circuit, but that's nothing you asked me to do. That's the attorney's idea. Quit talking about leaving, will you?"

Tilly gazed up at him. "Why?"

He came close to growling in his frustration. "I like having you here, Tilly. Maybe you haven't noticed, but I'm sweet on you, woman."

To prove his point, Lamont pulled her into his arms and kissed her. It wasn't slow but urgent. He wanted her to realize how he felt and to trust that wasn't going to change. Her tense muscles relaxed, and she rested her hands on his shoulders. After the kiss, he cuddled her close until he realized tears trailed down her face.

"What's wrong now?" he asked.

Matilda smiled through the tears. "Nothing. I was rude at first, and I shouldn't have been, not to you. But I was afraid. On top of that, I believe you, Lamont, and I…well, I think I l-l.."

Her voice trailed away, but he pursued it. "You think you what?"

He had a feeling she'd been about to say she thought she loved him, and if so, Lamont wanted to hear it.

"I care about you a lot."

"Good to know," he told her. "Then you'll stay?"

"Yes, for a while anyway. Some time, I do have to get my stuff from New York."

"We'll figure that out down the road. Let's get out of here."

"Where?"

"I'm taking you out for a late lunch in Tulsa, just you and me."

Lamont expected she would argue, but she didn't. Instead, she smiled at him, stood on her toes to brush a kiss across his mouth, and nodded. "All right, let me get my purse."

He hunted down his sister and told her he'd been gone for a bit. "Stay as long as you want," he told her. "We'll be back by six or so. I'll bring some chicken or pizzas or something. If you or

Logan need me, call."

Lanelle grinned. "Getting Tilly out of here is a good idea, Lamont. Take your time."

"I plan to," he replied. He pulled his brother out of a conversation with his in-laws and handed him the keys to his new truck. "It's the Toyota Tundra parked out there. Use it if you want or need to go anywhere. There's a booster seat for Paisley. I'm hauling Tilly off to Tulsa, but we won't be too long."

A tiny smile touched Logan's lips. "Since when did you buy a new truck?"

"Since last week, I don't know what day. It all runs together."

"I don't plan on going anywhere, but I can drive your old truck if I do."

"Naw, take the Tundra. Call me if you need me, man."

Ten minutes later, Lamont drove away with Tilly beside him in the truck. She rested one hand on his thigh, and every time he glanced at her, she wore a smile. That sweet expression took his breath away, and he savored each one. Moments together without Shayne or someone else had been scant, so he enjoyed this time alone with Tilly.

Despite the last few days when he'd been in Bartlesville with Logan, no awkwardness existed between them. As he rocketed down the highway into Tulsa, Lamont rolled the window enough for fresh air to blow into his face.

"What would you like?" he asked her as they got into town. "Mexican, steak, barbecue, French cuisine, Asian, Italian, classic diner or Irish pub?"

Matilda tossed her head back. "You pick, Lamont."

"I want to treat you," he replied. "I like it all. You're the foodie, not me."

Her laugh echoed through the cab, merry and bright as sunshine. "I'm a chef and a baker, not a foodie," she giggled. "Let me guess your favorite. You're a cowboy, so maybe steak?"

"I like a good steak," he told her. "But no, that's not my favorite."

Tilly guessed barbecue, burgers, and diner food, but Lamont shook his head.

"I give up," she told him.

"Thai," he said and grinned. "I tried some last year out on the circuit and loved it. If you like it too, I know a little place where we can go."

"I love it!"

Over Kao Pad Tom Yum with shrimp for Tilly and Noodle Rad Na with beef for Lamont, they talked and tasted. She shared a few little stories about Shayne during Lamont's absence and one when he was very small.

"He could mimic cartoon voices by the time he was three," Matilda told him. "He could sound like Scooby Doo or Mickey Mouse or Bugs Bunny. Melissa thought it was the cutest thing."

Lamont noted all were classic cartoons and liked that. "Can he still do them?"

Matilda shrugged. "I don't know. I haven't heard, but then I wasn't around him for a few years."

"Living with Teddy Anderson was likely enough to ruin anyone's sense of fun," Lamont commented. "I guess he kept Shayne cut off from you."

She swallowed a bite and nodded. "Yes, he did. My dad died when I was a little girl, but my mom lived until not long before Lissy died. Our grandmother didn't pass until last year, but I had no idea where Shayne was, and neither did she."

"That ain't right," Lamont said. "At least he'll have family now."

After sipping water, Tilly nodded. "I suppose he will. I'm glad. Paisley started calling me 'Aunt Tilly' because Shayne does."

"I like that," he replied. "You're part of it too, honey."

Whether or not she agreed, he couldn't tell. She stirred the last bit of her food, then laid down the fork. "I'm stuffed," she told him. "It was scrumptious, though."

"If we head for the house, maybe you can catch a nap," Lamont said.

Tilly stifled a yawn. "I'd like that. I am tired."

So was he. He left a generous tip and paid for the meal, then headed toward Claremore.

Most of the crowd had cleared out in their absence. Lanelle left a note explaining her family had taken Shayne to their local hotel so he could swim with her children but that they would be back for supper. Logan sprawled in the recliner in the den, staring at a movie he didn't appear to be watching.

"You're back," he said. "It's been quiet most of the afternoon. Jeff and Janis took Paisley with them. They offered to buy her a new dress for Tatum's funeral, and they said Ethan, Tatum's brother, is coming in from Missouri. Janis said they would bring Paisley home after dinner."

Lamont sat down. "All right. I brought home two buckets of fried chicken and all the fixings for anyone who wants to eat."

His brother nodded. "I might grab a leg or a wing later. I'm not hungry, though."

Once Matilda had put the food they'd brought in the oven to keep warm, she joined the brothers. She settled onto the couch beside Lamont and yawned. So far, she hadn't attempted to nap, and now there probably wasn't time. She laid her head against his shoulder, and within minutes, she slept. Her warm breath wafted against his arm, and Lamont liked the sense of intimacy. As he inhaled the soft lavender scent she wore, a wave of affection filled him. He leaned over and planted a kiss on her forehead.

"I like your Tilly," Logan said.

"So do I, but she's not mine, not just yet."

"If you want her to be, don't wait. Life is short," his brother returned. "I just found that out in a big way."

Lamont nodded. "Yeah, I know."

"If the family doesn't scare her off, don't let her head back to New York City."

The last thing Lamont wanted was for her to go, and he told Logan so, adding, "I thought about going with her, but I can't now, not if I'm back on the circuit."

Logan sat up in the recliner. "Is that something you really want, going back to rodeo?"

"No, I was happy when I thought I'd hung up my spurs," Lamont answered with honesty. "The only reason I'm going back to it is because of the kid. To adopt him, the lawyer thinks I need some kind of income or business."

"I have an idea about that," Logan said. "It came to me, sitting here today."

"What is it?"

His brother shrugged. "I'll fill you in when I get it all figured out. Tell me one thing, though – how would you feel if I moved back to the homeplace?"

Lamont stared at Logan. "It's yours, too, but I think my house is a little small."

"I have a notion about that, too. Would me and Paisley be welcome?"

He didn't have to ponder it. "You know you are, Logan. What are you thinking about?"

"Let me get through these next few days first. Then I'll fill you in."

"All right," Lamont said and sighed as Tilly stirred. "I can wait."

CHAPTER FIFTEEN

The next few days were a wild blur of emotion, events, and exhaustion. On Sunday, Lamont rose early to attend church without the misgivings he'd had before. Tilly wore a dress he hadn't seen before, a turquoise-blue cotton dress with pink flowers, maybe peonies, sprinkled over the fabric. The full skirt swirled around her legs, and it matched the snap-button Western shirt Lamont wore. She rode in the front seat of his new truck beside him while his brother, niece, and Shayne filled the back seat. At Pioneer Faith Church, they took up a pew.

Lanelle's family joined them and sat behind. Tatum's folks were in the back pew along with their son, who had arrived. This week, Logan, not Lamont, was the focus of attention because everyone had heard about his loss. After the songs and sermon, Pastor Cartwright offered a prayer for Tatum and the family. As most of the congregation gathered around Logan, offering condolences, Lamont moved through the crowd to talk to Bud Bartlett.

"I'd like to come over and ride this week," he told the other man. "It won't be until Wednesday. My sister-in-law's funeral is tomorrow, then they're doing a home study at my place, part of the adoption process. I leave Friday to head over to Guymon for the Pioneer Days Rodeo, so I gotta get some horse time somewhere."

"Come out whenever you can," Bud told him. "I'll get a buddy to bring over a bucking bronc you can ride. If you're still interested in buying a horse or two, I got several you can look at."

"I'd like that," Lamont said.

"So would I," Logan added as he stepped next to his brother. "I might come out with Lamont."

"Glad to have you, and I'm right sorry about your wife," Bud stated.

"Thanks," Logan replied. "Lamont, let's get out of here."

Since Tatum's visitation would be held that afternoon, they had decided not to go home after church. Instead, they gathered at a local restaurant. Lamont had suggested it so Tilly wouldn't have to cook for many people, although she'd been willing. After dinner, they went to the funeral home for visitation from two until four p.m.

Lamont's stomach balled into a fist. He dreaded seeing Tatum. He'd failed to convince Logan to have a closed casket. His last sight of Tatum had been sad, something he'd rather not remember. Too many times, he'd paid his respects and been upset at the viewing when the person laid out no longer resembled the deceased. He loitered near the back of the room at the funeral home until Tilly took his hand.

"I'll go with you," she said, voice soft. "Logan's up there, and he's about to bring Paisley to see her mom. I bet he could use moral support."

He nodded and encased her small hand within his. It might be childish, but he wanted to squinch his eyes shut. Instead, he stepped beside his brother and looked. No visible signs of her accident or injuries remained. Tatum's hair had been curled around her face and she wore a soft rose formal gown. If Lamont remembered, it had been the one she'd bought for their honeymoon cruise, the only one they had ever taken. With her eyes closed, she appeared asleep and at peace. Relieved, he exhaled a slow breath.

"She looks as pretty as ever," he told Logan, who nodded.

After that, the afternoon passed. Lamont shook hands and

accepted condolences. He exchanged hugs with people he hadn't spoken to in years and endured the visitation. Afterward, they headed home, the mood somber and sad.

At the funeral, there was standing room only at the church. Tatum's casket, now closed, sat at the front while Brother Alec read the Scriptures that Logan chose and talked about her. When it came time for the music, the elderly pianist played the notes of *On Eagle's Wings,* but the congregation provided the only vocals. Not everyone sang and most of those who did sang at low volume until Matilda lifted her voice.

Lamont knew she could sing. He'd heard her in his truck, but now, she used her voice with power and the sweetness of her faith. The song, based on Psalm 91, had once been a favorite but after his folks' funeral, he had pushed it away, like everything else related to the Lord. Listening now, tears fell down his cheeks, and he didn't bother to wipe them away.

I want to believe, he thought. *I want to have the faith I once had. I want to trust. Lead me back, Lord, please.*

He had no doubt, like in the chapel, that this time he prayed.

The closing hymn was *Lead Me Lord,* which matched Lamont's thoughts.

As one of the pallbearers, he helped carry the casket to the adjacent cemetery, where a brief prayer ended the service. As everyone headed back to the church for dinner, Lamont lingered. He didn't feel like eating, and if he could, he would just go home.

Matilda linked her arm through his. "What's the matter?"

"I don't feel so good."

"Are you sick?"

"Naw."

"Do you want to go home?"

"I can't," he told her. "Any other time, yeah, I might, but I have to be here. It's been one heck of a day."

"I know," she said, surprising him. "It's a hard day for everyone."

He shook his head. "Gonna be a long, hard week too."

Between Tilly's sympathy, her comforting hands, and some lemon-lime soda, Lamont felt better. He managed to eat a little bit, mostly to be polite. There was turkey and ham, stuffing and mashed potatoes, homemade hot rolls, plus more pies and cakes than he could count.

Afterward, Tatum's parents prepared to head back to Florida and her brother home to Missouri. Lanelle and Bradley came to the house long enough to say goodbye, their kids chasing around the yard with Shayne.

"Call if you need anything," his sister said. "We have to leave now so we can drop Logan off at his house."

That was the first Lamont had heard his brother planned to go. "I didn't know he was leaving, too."

"I'll be back late tomorrow, me and Paisley," Logan said, joining them. "I need to get some more clothes for both of us. I need my car here. Besides, you have that home study tomorrow, and I figured we'd just confuse the social worker or whoever does that."

"True," Lamont replied. "I hadn't thought about that. But you're coming back, right?"

He realized he wanted Logan to return.

"Yeah, we'll be here by suppertime at the latest. I still got that idea I want to run by you."

"I'm looking forward to that. Y'all be careful."

As much as Lamont longed to kick back and relax, he couldn't. He prowled the house, checking off each item on the home study form. Then he brought his important papers box and put in on the table so he'd have everything ready to display. Thanks to Matilda, the house had never been cleaner. His cupboards and fridge were stocked, all his firearms were locked in the safe, and as far as Lamont could tell, everything was in order.

On Tuesday morning, he dropped Shayne off at the junior high and came home to wait. The home study team, including Ms. Wellington, the county social worker, Ronnie, his attorney, a state-level social worker, an adoption specialist, and his cousin, Sheriff Wills, arrived on time. They spent the next three hours inspecting the house more thoroughly than the first time, walking the grounds to make sure that the deck was properly railed, and going over the paperwork.

Lamont answered more questions than he could have ever imagined, provided the proper documents, and explained why he wanted to adopt Shayne. Matilda told them that she was there to help with her nephew, but she wasn't a permanent resident of the home.

He raised his eyebrows at that and made a note to talk to her later. If she meant it, it would upset him but he hoped it was just said to satisfy the picky home study team.

The only sticky point was his income. It was debated whether or not riding rodeo could be considered a steady income, and despite his bank balances, which Lamont provided, there were questions about his ability to provide support. He was also reminded that he had to complete state mandated training as well.

"You're provisionally approved, meaning your home fits the criteria, and so do you," Mrs. Waterhouse, the state-level social worker, told him. "We'll set the date for the adoption hearing but I would suggest, if at all possible, you find a steady source of income prior to that. I don't think it will stop the adoption from taking place but it would make your petition more solid."

"I'll do my best," Lamont told them, wondering just what he would do. Should he consider a job at a discount store, a factory or what? He had no idea, but he would try.

Relief swamped him once the team departed. He sat down in the living room and sighed.

"I'm glad that's done. I'm not looking forward to those classes or trying to find a job."

"It'll work out," Matilda said with far more confidence than he felt. "The Lord will help."

"I hope so," Lamont muttered. Then, he gazed at her. "I prayed yesterday at the funeral. First time in years, Tilly."

A smile lit her face like sunshine through the clouds on a rainy day. "That's wonderful, Lamont."

"That ain't all." He told her about the night he spoke with God at the hospital chapel.

"And He's helped you."

"Yeah, probably. I don't think I could have made it through this without some help, Tilly. If you weren't here, it would be a lot worse."

She stood behind his chair and stroked his hair. "I'm glad my presence helps."

That reminded him of what she'd said during the home study. "Did you mean what you said earlier?"

"What's that?"

"That you're a temporary resident, that you're not planning to stay. I thought you'd changed your mind on that."

"I hope to stay, Lamont, but I wasn't sure they'd want to hear that."

He sat up straight, then stood and faced her. "Are you gonna leave and go back?"

If she did, she would take his heart with her.

Matilda shrugged. "There's nothing to go back for, Lamont. When I go, it'll just be to get my stuff. I need to find a reason to be here, though, something besides Shayne."

Lamont put his arms around her. "There's me, honey. I want you to stay."

Her brown eyes met his. "I'd like that, but I need to make a life for myself."

He didn't know what to think, whether it was good or bad, that she wanted her own life. If it could merge with his, Lamont didn't mind. He considered asking for an explanation but refrained. Right now, he didn't want to know if she planned to move to Claremore or even Tulsa.

Instead, he asked her, "Do you need anything from town? It won't be long till I go pick up the kid."

"If you don't mind, would you pick up some fresh chicken breasts? I thought I'd make nuggets for supper because Paisley likes them."

"I can grab a bag in the frozen foods case if you want."

Matilda frowned at him, then laughed. "I can make some that are ten times better than those overprocessed, tasteless hunks of chicken, Lamont. It's no trouble."

"If you say so," he replied. "Want to come with?"

"I'm going to stir up some brownies, or I would."

In town, he went to the supermarket first. After he selected the chicken breasts, Lamont noticed the bakery counter. There were cakes for sale, some already decorated, and mockups for cakes that could be ordered for special occasions. Maybe Tilly could do that, he thought, and then rejected the notion. These were simple designs made from kits. Lamont remembered the cakes and confections he'd seen online when he first looked her up and realized this would never do. It would be like asking him to operate a pony ring when he had the expertise and experience to ride saddle broncs or raise them.

At the junior high, Shayne dashed out to the truck. "How'd it go?"

"We passed," Lamont said. He'd told the kid about the home study and what it meant.

"Whoo-hoo!" His glad cry echoed through the truck.

"How soon will you adopt me?"

"When they set a date," he told Shayne. He didn't mention the continuing question over his occupation. "Originally, the lawyer said it could take six months. That would put it in October or November."

"Before Christmas?"

"I hope so," Lamont said. A stab of grief struck him. The past few years, the Fortunes had gathered at Logan's house for the holiday. With Tatum gone, that wasn't likely to happen. Maybe they could head up to Lanelle's, he thought, or he could host it at his place. As long as the family celebration didn't come to an end, he'd be good with whatever happened.

His mind drifted while Shayne spoke, and then he realized he'd been asked a question.

"So can I?"

"Can you what?" Lamont replied. He figured the boy was asking permission to do something, play baseball, go with friends somewhere, go fishing or whatever. The possibilities were endless.

"May I call you 'Dad'?"

The simple question blew Lamont away. He'd never thought about becoming a father. Even when engaged to Remy, the possibility of a child never entered his mind. She had been too preoccupied with her figure, her fortune, and her social circle, and he'd been busy holding his saddle bronc championship title. He thought for a moment he might shed a tear or two but nodded.

"I'd be proud if you do," he told the boy. "Son."

Shayne beamed, and although he was driving, Lamont took one arm and wrapped it around the boy's neck in a hug.

At home, Shayne rushed in ahead of him and told Matilda, "Dad said Uncle Logan and Paisley will be back in time for supper."

Tilly raised one eyebrow, but she smiled. "Yes, they should

be here any time. Do you have homework?"

The kid shrugged. "Just some vocab."

"Better finish it up," she suggested.

"Sure," he said. "I'll do it in my room."

Once he'd gone, Tilly turned to Lamont. "Dad?"

"He asked if he could call me that," he said, more than a little humbled. "I didn't see any reason why not."

"I'm glad," she replied. "He's never had a dad before. You have a good heart, Lamont Fortune."

That compliment prompted him to bend down and kiss the back of her neck. "I try, Tilly. That's it."

"That's all anyone can do," she told him.

Logan rolled into the driveway around six thirty, driving his four door Lincoln sedan from the last year the company made anything besides SUVs. The seat beside Logan and the backseat next to Paisley held bags and boxes. Lamont headed outside to greet him and to help carry the stuff inside.

"There's more in the trunk," his brother told him. "I hope we're not crowding you too much, Lamont."

"You're not," Lamont said, but as he eyed the pile of stuff, he wondered. A feeling that his house might become more than a little cluttered rose, but he ignored it. At least the home study was done.

"I can take the couch in the den so you can have your bed back," Logan told him.

"No, it's fine. Maybe we'll switch in a few days. Besides, I'll be gone Friday and Saturday to the rodeo at Guymon."

As they carried in the load, Logan asked, "That's the first one?"

"Yeah. Next one after that will be the Will Rogers Stampede here in Claremore over Memorial Day."

Paisley dashed into the house and to the bedroom she'd been using. Lamont noticed she sucked her thumb, an old habit but didn't mention it.

"What's after that?"

Lamont held up open hands. "I have no idea, but I have to get cracking and get registered at more rodeos."

"Why don't you hold off for now?"

He put down a load in his bedroom and sighed. "I'd love to but I have to show I have an income for this adoption. I don't want to get disqualified or have a judge decide against me if I don't."

"Do you trust me?"

"Yeah, you know I do. What are you talking about?"

"I told you, I have an idea. Give me a day or two to put it together, and I'll tell you."

Any urge to argue faded when Lamont reminded himself that they'd buried his brother's wife yesterday. "All right. Let's go eat supper. I'm tired, and we're going out to Bud's tomorrow. I gotta practice riding a little."

"I'll come with," Logan said. "I could use the distraction."

"I imagine you can. How was home?"

Head down, his brother sighed. "It sucked, Lamont. It really sucked. I ain't going back for a while, if ever."

That made sense, and Lamont understood. Logan would likely sell the house, purchase something smaller, and start over. Maybe he'd consider staying within the same school district for Paisley's sake, or perhaps he'd move to a different part of Bartlesville. Then, a thought caught him, and he asked, "Doesn't Paisley have school?"

"She would but her principal and classroom teacher agreed she can finish out the year by keeping up her work, doing it at home," Logan told him. "I've got this week's work now. I'll take it back on Monday and pick up the next week's homework then. There's only a few weeks left this year anyway."

Shayne overheard as they entered the kitchen space and

spoke up. "Man, I wish I could do that!"

"Not happening," Lamont told him. "Let's eat."

When Matilda held out her hand to him, he took it, and they all joined hands as she asked a simple blessing.

The past week had been rocky, and Lamont hoped that things would improve, one day at a time.

CHAPTER SIXTEEN

With two days left until he'd compete at the Pioneer Days Rodeo in Guymon, Lamont dug out his saddles and gear before heading over to Bud Bartlett's spread. He brought his halters and reins, including one of the colorful braided nylon reins he'd used last season. Lamont donned his leather protective vest, too.

"Does old Bud have any broncs to practice with?" Logan asked.

"He said he'd have a friend bring one over," Lamont told him. "The other time I came over to his place, I just rode. Figured it's a good idea to ride a bronc before I'm in the arena."

"I'd think so. I'll ride, but I ain't mounting any rough stock, not today anyway."

In his teens, Logan rodeoed too but he'd quit long ago.

"You can be my pickup man today."

Bud met them at the corral, where a chestnut quarter horse danced back and forth in one of the chutes, edgy.

"This is Firestone," he told them. "My friend brought her over early. She's not too experienced, but she's got some spirit."

Lamont grinned. "Just what I need."

He spent a few minutes getting acquainted with the mare, added a halter, and then put his saddle on her back. He adjusted his stirrups to suit him and climbed on. Logan held the horse until Bud released the gate. Firestone knew her business well and began bucking immediately. Lamont held the reins, one hand uplifted, and yelled. "Yee-haw!"

It was glorious right up until the horse pitched him off

into the dirt. Lamont landed hard, but Logan did his job. Then Lamont got up to ride again. He rode until both he and the horse wearied, then rode around Bud's property with Logan.

"How's your head?" Logan asked.

Firestone had tossed him straight out of the chute once, and Lamont had whacked his head against the gate. He rubbed his right temple and winced. "A little sore, but it's not bad. Probably gonna bruise, though."

"Tilly's not gonna like that."

He laughed. "I doubt it, but she'll have to get used to the fact I'll get banged up. It's gonna happen."

"You'll be gone more than you'll be home, won't you?"

"If I ride in enough rodeos, yeah," Lamont said. "I don't figure I can catch up enough this late to have any shot at holding my title, but as long as I earn some money to please the court, I guess it's all good."

They worked in tandem, unsaddling the horses and putting his tack back in the truck. "Will she travel with you, her and the kid?"

Lamont shrugged. "I don't know. Maybe. I'm still afraid she'll take off to the city. She has to get her stuff sometime, and I worry that she might not come back."

"Maybe you ought not go."

Although his brother's tone was casual, Lamont thought there was something more than the simple words indicated. "What do you mean?"

"I told you I've got an idea. Are you ready to hear it?"

"Sure. How about I buy you a bowl of chili in town, and we'll talk about it."

Seated in the same restaurant where he'd brought Tilly, Lamont dipped his spoon into his chili, then paused while Logan asked a blessing. "Tell me."

"Fortune Brothers Rough Stock Company," Logan said.

"We can raise rodeo stock. We both grew up on the place, although you're more familiar than I am now. I can take care of the financial stuff, keep the books, and all that."

Lamont savored a bite and swallowed. "I thought about doing that myself. Are you talking about being a silent partner or what?"

Logan laughed. "No, bro. I don't want to go back to my job or to Bartlesville. That part of my life seems over. I'm thinking I'll live here, and we'll build up the company on the home place."

A spicy morsel caught in Lamont's throat, and he choked. "I think the idea is sound, but are you planning to stay at my house?"

"I should tell you I am and watch your reaction," Logan told him with a light laugh. "No, it's not big enough. I figured maybe buying a mobile home and bringing it in. Paisley and I will live in it. The place is going to need a lot – a better barn, some corrals with bucking chutes, and the fences around the eighty acres need to be in top shape. We can't afford any escaped stock."

The more Lamont thought about it, the more he liked it, but he had to ask, "Whose money are we using for these improvements?"

"Yours and mine. I have some savings. When I sell the house, that will be more and there ought to be some fair life insurance. I want to keep some back for Paisley's education someday, but I don't mind sinking the rest into the place. What do you think?"

"Let's do it," Lamont said. "It'll take a little bit to get everything in place. We'll also need some sturdy horse trailers, rigs to pull them, some hands to deliver the stock to rodeos, and some pickup men."

"We'll get whatever we need," Lamont's brain spun with the possibilities and details. "And we can do some of that, at first, anyway. When are you giving notice at the oil company?"

For the first time since his wife died, Logan grinned, ear to ear. "I already did."

Anticipation rose in Lamont. It had been years since his life brimmed so full. Despite his success and back-to-back championship titles, he had plodded a lonely path in recent years. His bout with flu had brought that home, those long days when he lay sick, miserable, and alone. If he had been open to prayer, he might have asked the Lord for someone to share his life, but he hadn't been, not then.

Now he had a kid, a soon to be adopted son, a woman he wanted to keep by his side, and a brother who proposed a business partnership, one that would provide what Lamont needed. He hated that Tatum had died but the future had become something he looked forward to living.

Lamont lifted his glass of iced tea and took a long sip. "My cup runneth over," he said.

He knew his brother would remember their old catchphrase for being happy, and Logan did. "It's about time, little brother," he replied. "It's about time."

For the next few days, Lamont had to focus on the rodeo. Committed to ride, he would be part of both the one at Guymon and the upcoming Will Rogers Stampede Rodeo over Memorial Day weekend.

"We can get started next week," he told Logan.

His brother promised to work up a written business proposal and plan, something Lamont could show both his attorney and the court. Lamont's brain worked overtime on ideas, things to buy, stuff to do, and more.

They lingered at the restaurant well into the afternoon, then stopped by a farm store to browse. On the way out of town, they picked up Shayne from school. At home, Paisley sat at the dining table, finishing up some worksheets. Shayne joined her and completed his math homework before supper.

Despite being dirty and dusty, Lamont came up behind Tilly and lifted her up, then swung her around.

"I guess you had a good day," she said, with a smile.

"Yeah, sure did," he told her. He would fill in the details of their plan later, probably after Guymon.

She lifted her hand to touch his forehead. "What happened? You've got a bruise and a knot."

"The horse tossed me against the gate."

"It must hurt. Are you okay?"

It did, although he hadn't really paid any attention to it until now. "I'm good. It's just a little bump, honey. Do I have time for a shower?"

Tilly served a bacon cheeseburger pie, thick with meat and rich with cheese. Lamont savored his portion and enjoyed the brownies she'd made for dessert. Sometimes, he almost forgot she'd been a fancy New York chef, then a baker for the rich and famous. She'd never fit in at a discount or grocery in-store bakery, but maybe she could make cakes in Oklahoma. *If she stayed,* he prayed, *and I hope that she does.*

After supper, Lamont sat on the deck with Matilda. They watched the sunset, vivid with bright oranges and golden yellows, and then he asked, "Are you coming with me to Guymon, honey? I'd like it if you and Shayne were there."

"I thought I would," she said. "How far is it?"

"Guymon's in the Oklahoma panhandle, a good five, six hours from here. I'm competing both Friday night and Saturday, so we'll have to stay. I can get a hotel for all of us – a room for me and Logan to share, another for you, Shayne and Paisley. I'd best get it reserved, though, or there won't be any left."

"Okay," she told him. "I want to be there. What time will we have to leave?"

"Friday morning," he replied. "I'll have to pull Shayne out of school, but it's just for a day. There's always a parade and a carnival, too."

Although they could have all squeezed into the Toyota, they took both trucks. Lamont had his saddles and tack loaded into his vintage Chevy. Matilda rode shotgun with him. Logan drove the newer truck with the kids. Their luggage rode with them.

Since they left before 7 a.m., traffic was light most of the way. Lamont was in high spirits, happy to have time to spend with Tilly, and eager to compete. Midway there, they stopped for lunch at a Dairy Queen, although Lamont ate little.

"Aren't you hungry?" Matilda asked him.

"Oh yeah, but I don't like to eat much when I'm competing. I'll eat tonight after the rodeo."

As two-laned Highway 412 snaked westward, the scenery became wide open, with the sky overhead like a huge blue bowl. Utility poles traveled concurrently with the highway as the land stretched out into what seemed like infinity. It wasn't all that different from where Lamont's place lay, but there were more trees around Claremore. Matilda, however, gawked, and he remembered she'd been raised in East Texas, on the edge of Louisiana.

"I almost feel like I'm part of a wagon train, heading off into the unknown," she said, seated beside him. "I like this open country."

He grinned. "Kinda grows on a person."

"Are you excited for tonight?"

Lamont lifted one hand off the steering wheel and waggled it. "A little nervous, a little scared. Mostly, I'm looking forward to it, and I'm glad you're with me."

Although he'd spent years traveling from one rodeo to another through the season, sometimes as many as a hundred, most of the time, Lamont had done it alone. In the early years, especially when Logan competed too, his parents had often come along for the show. By the time they died in the plane crash heading for Prescott, he'd made his own way to each rodeo. Remy would sometimes decide to come watch him ride, but only the bigger shows in the large towns. She hadn't been one to travel by truck, either, and when she did show up, she flew into town using her daddy's private jet. Over the years, Lamont had had a few rodeo romances and a handful of girlfriends but never one who rode with him. Tilly's presence meant the world to him.

"I'm happy to be here. It's been years since I've been to a rodeo," she told him. "I think I was still in high school."

After they checked into the hotel, they headed to the rodeo grounds, and Lamont tried to see it through Tilly's eyes. As far as he knew, Paisley hadn't been to a rodeo either and if Shayne had, it probably hadn't been a great experience since he would have been with Teddy Anderson. He told them as much as he could, noted it was the richest rodeo in Oklahoma, and that most of the riders were, like him, top riders and champions. Then, with Logan at his side, he hauled his favorite saddle and gear down to the chutes.

For the first time in years, the prayer moved Lamont, and so did the National Anthem. Since it was his first appearance this season, everywhere he went, cowboys and cowgirls greeted him. While he shook hands, slapped backs, and gathered many welcomes, Lamont paid more attention to the stands where Tilly sat with his family. Shayne stood up on the bleachers and waved his cowboy hat over his head so Lamont lifted his hat high in return.

Once he prepared for his first ride, everything else faded into the background. Lamont tuned out the music, the announcer's voice, and the crowd noise to focus on his ride. He'd drawn a crossbred gelding, the product of a quarter horse dam, and a Percheron named Clown Prince. As soon as Lamont settled into the saddle, he lifted one arm, and Clown Prince bucked into the arena. The feisty gelding seemed bred to buck, tossing Lamont every which way, but he held his seat for the full eight seconds and earned a score of 77, a good start to the evening.

Lamont ended the first night in first place, a little saddle sore but in a good mood. At the truck, he stowed his saddle and gear in the back. Tilly met them with both kids in town, grinning.

"That was fantastic," she said with enthusiasm. "You were awesome!"

"I managed to stay on most of the time," he told her. "And I didn't get hurt, so it was a good night."

"You finished in first place, Dad," Shayne cried.

"There's still tomorrow," Lamont replied. He slung an arm around Matilda, and when she leaned against him, he maneuvered her into a kiss. Until now, he'd kept his romantic interest on the lowdown, especially around Shayne but if they had a shot at a future, the kid had to know sooner or later.

Tilly put her arms around his neck and kissed him back. Shayne whooped.

"Way to go, Dad!"

Logan laughed. "Want to go eat, Buddy?"

"I could use a steak," Lamont told him. "Let's go."

The small town of Guymon brimmed full even at the late hour. Traffic clogged the major streets as they headed for a steakhouse open to catch the rodeo business. They lucked into a big corner booth that could fit all of them. Lamont savored a large T-Bone. Logan chose a sirloin strip with a baked potato. Both the kids had cheeseburger baskets, and Matilda ordered chicken fried steak. It filled the plate, and she could eat no more than half of it.

"Help me out," she said, nudging Lamont. "Eat some of it."

He shouldn't, and he knew it. Already full of the big steak, a huge salad, a hefty portion of fries, and Texas toast, he didn't have room, but he didn't want to disappoint her, so he downed the remaining half plus a good chunk of mashed potatoes with cream gravy. Stuffed, he predicted that a stomachache was in his future, and he was correct.

Morning came too early, and the alarm he'd set on his phone roused him. Lamont sat up stiff and more than a little sore. His back ached, and the knee he'd injured in the past protested. A long, hot shower and some ibuprofen eased most of his discomfort. Logan had been up for hours, long enough to go downstairs for the complimentary breakfast.

"Tilly and the kids are down there," he told him when he returned carrying a paper cup of coffee.

"What do they have?"

"Make your own waffles, doughnuts and granola bars, cereal and milk, fruit, plus bagels and toast," Logan said. "Not bad."

It would do, Lamont thought. He didn't have time for more.

They managed to catch the last of the rodeo parade. A quick sandwich at a fast-food place equaled lunch, and then Lamont headed to the arena. Shayne begged to go to the carnival, so Logan volunteered to take the kids. Tilly found a seat in the arena bleachers, and Lamont rode in the afternoon competition. This time, he got bucked almost before the horse's hooves hit the arena but shook off the dirt, uninjured. That earned a lower score, but in the evening, he stayed on for the full eight seconds, this time with a score of 85.

He finished up in first place with one more round scheduled for Sunday afternoon.

Matilda frowned over that night's late supper. "I guess I didn't realize we wouldn't be back for church."

"I'm sorry, honey," Lamont said. This time, he ordered a smaller steak with a baked potato and he resolved not to eat anyone else's leftovers. "I guess I should have told you."

"Shayne's got school on Monday, too."

"We'll get back by bedtime on Sunday," he told her, hoping that they would. "The next rodeo is in Claremore, and school will be out by then, so it won't be a problem."

She took a bite of her hamburger steak and then frowned. "What about the rest of the season?"

Logan chuckled. "You haven't told her yet?"

"Told me what?"

Lamont cut and ate a bite of steak, then washed it down with tea. "I ain't had a chance, brother. Tilly, I won't be riding much longer. Logan came up with an idea for us to raise rough stock on the place. It's going to take some effort to get up and going, but I like it. There may be times when we deliver stock to rodeos or stay as pickup men, but I hope to hire some guys for that. It'll be a business I can do and stay home most of the time."

Although she smiled, it seemed weak. "That sounds wonderful, Lamont."

"I like it, Dad. Can I get a horse?"

"We'll have horses, kid," Lamont promised. "And you can have your own."

Paisley grinned. "Me too?"

"If your daddy says so, yeah."

Since the restaurant was adjacent to the hotel, Logan gathered up the two youngsters with the promise of an ice cream cone on the way back, leaving Matilda and Lamont alone.

"What's got your drawers in a knot?" Lamont asked her, cutting right to it.

She hadn't said three words since he told her about raising rough stock.

"I'm tired," she said, but he saw through the words.

"And what else? Is it raising rough stock or missing church?"

Matilda wiped her mouth and tossed down the discarded napkin. "Both. I was counting on church, and I wish you'd told me about raising stock."

"Honey, he only told me two days ago, but I like the idea."

"I guess that means he's going to keep living with you."

Lamont sighed. "No, it doesn't. He's planning to bring in a mobile home and live in it. I told you I want you to stay, Tilly, and I meant it."

Her expression lightened a fraction. "What about church?"

"We'll find one here and go in the morning."

That brought a smile. "I'd like that."

"Then we'll do it. How'd you like the rodeo tonight?"

"I'm impressed, but I was worried when you fell off."

Lamont laughed. "That mare bucked me off. I didn't fall."

They walked hand in hand back to the hotel. If it hadn't been for church, he would have suggested that they sleep late but instead, Lamont promised to be up. All he had to do now was track down a church.

CHAPTER SEVENTEEN

The church Lamont found was small and traditional, but he didn't enjoy the service as much as he'd hoped. He didn't think Tilly did either. Logan straight out said that he wished he had slept late instead, and the kids had no opinion either way. There wasn't anything wrong with the church, but they were visiting strangers, and although a few people welcomed them, most didn't.

More than a little bummed that the service hadn't been what he expected, Lamont bought dinner for everyone but ate little. He never did when he had to ride, and the rodeo would get back underway at 2 p.m. Dogged with fatigue and a steady headache, he wished he'd never got back into riding saddle broncs. Lamont had been content with his decision to quit, but here he was, six hours from home, facing another round he'd rather skip. If his ranking hadn't remained in the top ten for that event, he would have been tempted to bail and head back.

By the time he was in position to ride, it had begun to rain. Steady showers turned the dust of the arena to mud, and Shy Girl, the horse he drew, was anything but. The mare unseated Lamont within the first two seconds. He heard his bad knee pop when he went down and knew that he'd sprained it.

Logan had watched from the chute and met him. "Are you hurt? You're limping a little."

Lamont winced. "I sprained my bad knee. It'll be all right. Let's get out of here and go home."

"You'd better get it looked at."

Although he resisted, Logan insisted, so he let the rodeo medics check it. They agreed it appeared to be a sprain, so Lamont gathered up his saddle and gear. "Go get Tilly and the kids," he told his brother.

Matilda greeted him with a smile that faded when she noticed he favored his right leg.

"What did you do?" she asked.

"Sprained my knee, that's all," he told her. "It's nothing serious."

It wasn't, but it hurt like the dickens, and he thought it might be swelling a little. By tomorrow, there would probably be a bruise. Once home, he'd rest the knee. Right now, he could use some ibuprofen. Tilly provided some, watching him, her forehead creased with worry.

"Is Dad okay?" Shayne asked, when he ambled up.

"I'm fine, kid. Get loaded, and let's head for home."

"What about eating?"

He'd promised another meal after the rodeo. "We'll stop on the way back."

Once he got behind the wheel of his old truck, the knee twinged, but he didn't complain.

"Are you able to drive?" Tilly asked.

"Sure," he replied with a confidence he didn't feel. "If it gets hurting too much, I'll let you take the wheel."

Tilly nodded. "All right."

That surprised him. "You won't mind driving a truck?"

She shook her head. "No, should I?"

It still sometimes amazed him that she wasn't the city girl he'd taken her to be when she first arrived. She'd still had some New York City ways, and he'd never forget the way she freaked out when they headed home from the airport but most of the time, Matilda had a level head.

"No, I suppose not."

They stopped a little more than halfway back and grabbed a quick meal. Lamont could walk and tried not to limp, but Tilly insisted on helping him. She linked her arm through his and let him lean on her. That made him feel like an old man or an invalid, but at the same time, he appreciated the concern. After they'd all eaten burgers and fries, he handed her the keys.

"You can go ahead and drive," he told her. "When we get to Tulsa, if you want me to take over, I can."

"I'll be fine," she told him. "Remember, I've been living in New York for the past few years."

"Did you drive in the city?" he asked, knowing she hadn't.

"Well, no, but I drove the kids around while you were in Bartlesville with Logan."

She had, and he knew that.

"All right, but ask me to drive if you need me to," Lamont said. "I appreciate this, honey."

Her small hand stroked his cheek, and then she stood on tiptoe to kiss him.

"I'm just sorry you got hurt."

Rain dogged them until they reached Tulsa. Between the weather and the supper stop, they didn't reach Lamont's house until after ten. The kids had both fallen asleep. Logan carried his daughter inside and put her to bed. Matilda rallied Shayne enough to walk him to his room, put on night clothes, and crawl into bed. They both returned to help Lamont put his saddle and gear away.

"I'll take the couch tonight," Logan told him. "You need your own bed."

Too tired to protest, Lamont nodded. "Thanks, bro."

Although he meant to be up early, he slept later than usual. When he woke around eight-thirty, he noticed the newer truck wasn't in the driveway. He hoped Logan or Tilly had taken Shayne to school. When Lamont stood, his sprained knee protested, so he dressed in slow movements. As he walked into the living room, he heard Matilda's voice and realized she must be on the phone.

He wasn't trying to eavesdrop, but he sat down in the living room to give her some space, although he could hear her side of the conversation without any effort.

"All I have are clothing, some pictures, and a couple photo albums," Matilda said. "And some knickknacks with sentimental appeal. If you want to take over the apartment, you can have everything else. If you don't, I need to call so the landlords know I'm not coming back to stay."

During a pause, Matilda laughed. "I don't miss the city, Amber, not really. I haven't talked to Delphine since she fired me. What? No, I haven't seen any of the publicity about Bellissima's upcoming wedding or the cake that I failed to make for the engagement party. I don't really care. Hang on, I'm gonna put the phone on speaker because I can't hear you very well. What was that?"

"Have you found a job out there on the frontier?"

"Not yet, but I haven't been looking."

The other woman had a distinct NYC accent, sharp and nasal. "What else is there to do except watch the grass grow or something?"

Tilly laughed. "I'm getting to know my nephew again. He's a fantastic kid, really."

"Aren't you bored out of your mind?"

"Not hardly. I like it here. Remember, I'm from East Texas."

"Girlfriend, I'd hate it. You'll get burned out on cows and pickup trucks and horses."

"I don't think so. I just spent the weekend at a rodeo and loved it."

"*Rodeo?* I'm flying out there and rescue you. Don't you

hate living in some cornpone motel?"

"I haven't stayed one night in a hotel other than after the rodeo," Matilda said. "I'm staying with Lamont, the man who's adopting Shayne."

Lamont stood up. He'd listened too long already and, favoring his right leg, walked into the open kitchen area. Tilly sat on a high stool at the countertop, dividing the dining space from where she cooked.

"Sounds like a dorky name, La-mont. What is he, a redneck?"

Matilda giggled. "He's a total hunk, and he's a good man, Amber. I'm...," her voice trailed off when she noticed him.

"You're what?"

"Nothing. I need to go. I got tons of things to do but if you'll box that stuff up and ship it, I'll send you the money and owe you one."

"You'll owe me more than that," Amber replied. "I'll do it, but I'll miss you, Matilda. I bet you'll be back."

"You'll lose," Tilly said. "Bye, Amber, and thanks."

As soon as she tucked the phone into her pocket, she slid down from the stool and stood in front of Lamont. "How's the knee?"

"It's been better," he told her with a grin. It hurt like the dickens, but he hadn't been this happy in a long while. If he understood what he'd just heard, Tilly wouldn't go back, not even to get her stuff and she liked it here. *She thinks I'm a good man and a hunk,* Lamont thought and savored it.

"You shouldn't be on your leg with a hurt knee," she said. "Go sit down. There's coffee in the pot, and I made biscuits and gravy. I'll bring you some pain relievers, too."

"Thank you, sugar," he said. "There's something else I really need, though."

Her brown eyes focused on him. "Sure, anything. What is

it?"

Lamont took one step closer and put his arms around her. Then he kissed her, sweet and soft. Her lips melted beneath his, and she sighed. "I need some lovin',"

Maybe it didn't help his knee, but he didn't notice how much he hurt when he was smooching Matilda. After several kisses, she helped him to the den, and he settled into his recliner. He drank the coffee she brought and downed the ibuprofen tablets, washing then down with the brew. After she brought him a bowl of biscuits and gravy, she curled up on the couch across the room.

"How much did you hear?" she asked.

"I wasn't trying to listen," Lamont replied. "Enough to hear it sounds like you're not going back to New York."

A smile lit her face. "That's right. I'm not. My friend, Amber, is going to box up the things I want to keep and send them out here. I gave her your address."

"That's fine, honey. Where's Logan?"

"He took Shayne to school, then said he was going to Bartlesville so he could list the house with a realtor. Paisley went with him. They'll be back by supper time, if not before. He said he wanted to talk to Jacob, too."

Their cousin Jake Wills was the sheriff's younger brother. Like Lamont, he'd ridden in his share of rodeos for years until an injury sidelined him. He'd never gone back on the circuit but the last Lamont knew, he'd been delivering rough stock to rodeos through the region. "That's good. If he wants, maybe Jake can come to work with us."

"Your brother said something about that." Matilda put her hand on his knee, her touch light and gentle. "He also said if you need to go to the doctor, I can take you or he will tomorrow."

"I don't need a doctor. They'd just tell me to rest the knee, put ice on it a few times a day, and that it should heal in a few weeks."

"I hope so. Don't you have the first of those adoptive parent classes this week?"

Lamont had almost forgotten. "Yeah, I do. First one is tomorrow night. I can't miss that."

"You won't. Want another biscuit with gravy?"

He nodded. "Sure, it's delicious."

The ibuprofen dulled the pain, but Matilda hovered like he was seriously injured. Lamont had to admit he liked being cosseted a little, but he didn't want to play the invalid. She made an ice pack for his knee after breakfast and served him a turkey sandwich at lunch.

"What's for supper?" he asked.

"Meatloaf, scalloped potatoes, green beans with bacon and onion, and peach cobbler," Tilly said.

With delight, Lamont told her, "That's one of my favorite meals."

"Logan told me."

Because she insisted, he lounged in the recliner most of the day, channel surfing and reading. Matilda flipped through recipes on her e-reader. In mid-afternoon, Lamont stood up.

"I'd better go get the kid from school."

"I can do that," Matilda said.

He reached for her hand. "Honey, if I don't go, Shayne's likely to think I'm worse hurt than I am. Now that I'm his dad, he might worry and I don't want him doing that. I'm going but if you want to go with me, get your purse and let's go. We can't be late."

They arrived later than he usually did, so their place in the pickup line was farther back. From the truck, Lamont glimpsed Shayne, his face grim, as he held back from the other students, leaning against a bench as he waited. When they pulled into view, however, his expression changed, and he grinned.

"I was afraid you weren't coming," he said as he climbed into the seat. "I thought you might have ended up in the hospital or something."

"No way," Lamont said and exchanged a look with Matilda. "I messed my knee up a little, but it's not that bad."

Lying might be a sin but fudging wasn't, not to save the feelings of a boy. Driving to town and back didn't help the knee any. It still hurt when the over-the-counter meds wore off, and he knew he would favor it when they got home.

Even so, Lamont sat at the table and drilled Shayne on this week's spelling words instead of retreating to the recliner. Tilly brought him a fresh cup of coffee and some ibuprofen. He liked working with the kid and watching her put the finishing touches on supper.

Logan returned with Paisley as Tilly set the table, bringing Jake.

"Jake's in," Logan told Lamont as he sat down at the table. "He knows a couple of other guys who may want to hire on to bring the stock to the rodeos."

"Jacob," Lamont said as he shook hands with his cousin. "That's great. I'm hoping to be here on the place more than I'm out on the road."

"I hear you're becoming a family man," Jake said with a grin.

"Getting there," Lamont replied. "Meet my kid, Shayne, and his aunt, Matilda."

Supper was the best Lamont had eaten, ranking high even with Tilly's cooking skills. Her meatloaf was perfectly seasoned and topped with the red gravy he loved. The scalloped potatoes were tasty, and so were the green beans, but her peach cobbler, topped with real whipped cream, melted in his mouth.

After the meal, once the two kids were in bed and Jake had headed home to Nowata, Lamont stretched out in the den.

He had changed into a T-shirt and shorts for the night. When his knee twinged, he rubbed it and noticed the black bruise that covered most of it.

"That looks sore," Logan said as he joined him. "Got the house up for sale now. Realtor thinks it has a good shot at selling quickly."

"That's good. I'm glad you thought about Jacob. We're gonna need help with this thing."

"True," his brother said, then sighed. "I did something else today, too."

"What's that?"

"Paisley and I picked out the mobile home we're buying. I put a down payment on it, so they'll hold it until we're ready. It'll be a while, probably."

Logan showed him multiple photos on his phone of the three bedroom, two bath late model single wide mobile home. A far cry from the large two-story house in Bartlesville, it appeared homey enough, and Lamont vowed he'd do his best to make sure they settled in without any trouble.

"Looks fine," he commented. "Paisley like it?"

His brother nodded. "She does, as long as we can make her room a pink paradise."

"That's doable."

"Definitely."

Matilda joined them but stopped short when she caught sight of his knee.

"It bruised!" she cried.

"I figured it would."

"Does it hurt?"

Lamont chuckled. "Yeah, honey, it does."

She dug out some arnica cream from the medicine cabinet and rubbed it into his knee with careful hands, keeping her touch light. Then she wrapped an elastic bandage around it. "That should help. If you're ready to head to bed, I'll help you," she told him.

His brother stood. "I'll clear my stuff out of your room."

"I'd rather just stay right here," Lamont told them. "I'm comfortable, and it's less hassle."

Logan debated it, but Lamont convinced him it was fine. Lamont wished he'd grabbed a blanket but it'd be all right, he figured. It was May and shouldn't be cold.

Tilly returned, dressing in her granny gown, carrying blankets and pillows. She tossed a light cover over him and tucked a pillow behind his head. Another went beneath his knee. "How's that?"

"Better," he said. "Night, honey, and thanks."

"You're welcome," she said as she made up a place to sleep on the sofa beside the recliner. "I'm going to sleep in here tonight."

Although he liked that very much, he said, "Aw, you don't have to do that, Tilly."

"I want to be here if you need help getting up if you need to use the bathroom or need anything, Lamont. I wouldn't sleep in the other room, worrying and wondering."

"Thank you," he told her.

After she settled into place and turned off the lamp, Lamont reached out and took her hand. He held it as he fell asleep, and when he woke up, their hands remained linked. When he needed to go use the bathroom, Tilly woke before he asked. She helped him hobble through the quiet house and then assisted him back to the recliner. She got a fresh ice pack for his knee and more ibuprofen. Then she kissed him on the forehead. "Go back to sleep, Lamont, if you can."

With his knee hurting and her proximity, he didn't think he could, but the pain reliever worked, and he did.

In the morning, the knee still hurt, and the bruise had

turned more colorful, purple mingling with the black. It had also swollen, making it more uncomfortable. Despite that, Lamont was in good spirits. He'd completed his first rodeo, and after one more, he could quit. The new endeavor with his brother excited him, and he was eager to get it underway. His kid called him Dad, and the woman he cared about more than any he'd ever known was here to stay. He wouldn't have to make a trip to the Big Apple or fret while she did.

Despite his injury, Lamont made it to the first parenting class with Tilly behind the wheel. Even though she wasn't the one adopting Shayne, he insisted that she attend it too.

Afterward, he suggested they stop for ice cream.

"Sure," Matilda said. "I want a parfait."

"I'll buy you whatever your heart desires, honey," he told her and meant it.

His courtship had begun, whether she realized it or not.

CHAPTER EIGHTEEN

May burst into bloom with sunny skies, warm days, and cool nights. With three weeks until the local Will Rogers Stampede rodeo, Lamont slowed his pace. Although he'd never been one to enjoy downtime or be idle, he took a few days to let his knee heal. By the end of the week, he could hobble without much pain, although he still favored it. That didn't keep him from working every day, making sure every inch of fence was in place before they brought in any horses. He worked together with Logan, and after school, Shayne usually joined them for an hour or so before they quit for supper.

At the same time, Lamont had a load of gravel delivered, and in slack moments, they raked it flat for the mobile home site. Next week, the electric cooperative would bring in the lines and he'd hired someone who could tap into the already existing well. As soon as they finished securing the fence, Lamont and Logan put up a larger corral and then added three bucking chutes. For now, they cleaned out the largest barn and made it into a place for at least four horses. A new pole barn went up, and the brothers did most of the work. On his day off, Davy lent a hand, and Jake was there every day.

On a Wednesday evening in the second week of May, a delivery van brought Tilly's boxes from New York. The three large cartons contained everything she considered important.

Sweaty and weary, Lamont came in from working all day to find the living room in complete disarray. Matilda sat cross-legged on the floor, the contents of one of the boxes spread around her. She glanced up and made a face. "I'm sorry, Lamont. I thought I'd have at least some of it put away by the time you came home."

He stepped around some photo albums and trinket boxes. "It's okay," he told her, even though it wasn't. Lamont liked order, and even as a bachelor, he'd kept things fairly neat. This upheaval was temporary, so he could handle it. Besides, it meant she planned to stay, and he'd put up with a lot more to have Tilly here.

"I don't have supper started," she cried. "It's later than I thought."

"Honey, I've told you that I love your cookin', but you don't have to make every meal. Why don't we drive over to church? Didn't you tell me they have a meal on Wednesday nights?"

Tilly smiled. "Yes. We could go to it if you want. Where's the kids and Logan?"

"Coming right behind me. Let me clean up really quick, and we'll go."

The Wednesday Night Meals wouldn't have been his first or second choice. Lamont would have chosen to drive into Claremore to eat supper at a restaurant. If not, then he would've been happy to go pick up something to bring home. But he knew Tilly had been wanting to attend one of the church suppers, then stay for Bible study, so he offered to go, and she was pleased.

Each day, Lamont drew a little closer to the Lord, although he still had some reservations. His late-night talk with God at the hospital chapel had been a beginning, and he'd managed to pray a couple of times. Because Matilda liked it, he took her and the kid to church every Sunday without fail.

For a small donation, they ate tater tot casserole, corn pudding, and frosted banana bars. It didn't come close to Tilly's cooking, but it filled him after a long day working outside, so he didn't complain. Afterward, sitting beside Matilda for the prayer service and Bible study, Lamont struggled to stay awake. The topic, however, caught his attention – faith versus works.

It wasn't a brand-new theme for him – raised in church, he'd heard the debate often, but on this evening, it made sense. As the preacher shared a verse from the Bible that faith without works was dead, Lamont understood for the first time. As Brother Cartwright expounded on that theme, citing verses from James, he also asked the reverse – were works without faith any good? His answer was that they were empty, and guilt reared up in Lamont's heart.

He did good things, always had. After all, he was on his way to adopting Shayne. When Logan needed him at his side in Bartlesville, he was there. On the circuit and off, Lamont had always followed the Golden Rule – doing to others what he'd like done to him. He had a reputation for being fair and kind, usually good-tempered. Now, it seemed that might not be enough.

Once home and after the children were in bed, Logan retired for the night. Lamont had returned to sleeping in the den until his brother's mobile home arrived in a few weeks. Tired but not sleepy, Lamont sat out on the deck, staring upward at the stars, seeking answers or at least a clue on how to find his faith.

Lost in thought, he failed to notice Tilly until she rested her hands on his shoulders.

"Hey," she said. "You've been awfully quiet today."

Lamont liked her touch. "Just thinkin'."

"I'll get my mess cleaned up, I promise," she said as she came around to sit in the chair beside him.

He turned toward her. "I ain't worried about it, honey. I know we're stacked in here right now with Logan and Paisley but once they get moved into their own place, things will settle down."

Tilly sighed. "I thought maybe you were mad about my

stuff all over the living room."

"Not at all," he said. "Tonight's Bible study got to me, started me thinking, wondering if I'm a good person."

"You're a fine man, Lamont," she told him. "You're talking about the faith without works is dead message, right?"

With a nod, he reached for her hand and wrapped his around it. "Yeah. I'm kind of lacking in the faith part. I think I might be moving back in that direction, but sometimes I don't know."

"I think you are," she said, her voice as soft as the spring breeze that ruffled his hair. "So much has happened in such a short time."

"You ain't woofin'," Lamont replied with a laugh. "Sometimes I have to stop and just take it all in."

"Same," Matilda replied. "I'm glad to be here, though."

Remembering an old Johnny Horton tune his grandpa used to play, Lamont said, "It's a long rocky road that has no turning."

Then he wondered if it would make sense to her, but she smiled, so maybe it did.

"I'm going to read for a while before I go to sleep," she said, rising. "I'll see you in the morning, Lamont."

He stood, too. "Good night, Tilly. Tomorrow will be another long day getting the place in shape to raise stock."

"Don't forget, there's another pre-service adoption training class tomorrow evening," she told him as she leaned close to plant a light kiss on his cheek.

Lamont had forgotten. "I'll be there if you'll come with me again."

"I will, but where will Shayne be?"

"Logan can watch out for him," he said. Then he kissed her lips, tender and light. "Good night, honey."

He woke to rain on Thursday, which slowed the outdoor

work. Still sleeping in the den, Lamont groaned as he tossed off the blanket and sat up. He squinted at the clock, and when he realized it wasn't quite 5 a.m., he considered trying to go back to sleep. That wasn't his nature, though. Once awake, he was up for the day.

Moving with quiet steps, Lamont made coffee and poured a cup. Since they wouldn't be doing anything outside until the weather improved, he settled down at his desk, tucked between the kitchen and den, and pulled out his bills. After his first sip of black coffee, he donned his glasses and fired up his laptop. His routine never varied. First, Lamont checked his bank account, then took the accumulated bills and paid them. He'd paid everything with an imminent due date by the time he'd finished his coffee. As he rose to refill his cup, Tilly came into the kitchen, twisting her hair up with a plastic claw clip.

"Good morning, honey," he said.

"Good morning," she returned, then stared. "I've never seen you wear glasses."

He'd forgotten he had them on and removed them. "I don't, except for when I do close work," he said. "I didn't use to need them at all. I know they make me look like a nerd."

She giggled. "No, they don't. Don't be silly. You look like a handsome college professor or an author."

Lamont liked the compliment. "Do I?"

"Yes." As she spoke, she lifted the coffee pot and filled his cup. "I didn't think you'd be up this early."

"Once I'm awake, I'm up," he said with a shrug. "So, I paid some bills. I don't know what Logan and me will do today since it's raining."

"I figured we'd go look at a stock trailer I saw for sale in the free shopper paper," Logan said, strolling into the kitchen barefooted. "It's over near Grove. We're gonna need one, really, we'll need several."

Lamont topped up his cup again. "Yeah, we do, and that's not too far. I wanted to take Shayne over to see Har-Ber Village one of these days, but he's got school."

"Buddy, we'll have plenty of time for that later on," Logan said.

"I'm up for it as long as we're back early – I have my parenting pre-adoption class this evening."

His brother sat down on a stool at the bar that divided the kitchen from the dining area. "I plan on it. We should be back before lunchtime."

"All right," Lamont said. "Do you want to go, Tilly?"

She turned from the skillet with link sausages frying. "I'll stay – that way, if for some reason you're not back, I can pick up Shayne. Besides, I need to figure out something for supper."

Over sausage, eggs, and toast, Lamont had an inspiration. If his brother and the kids could manage, then he could take Tilly out for dinner before class. The more he considered it, the more it appealed. He craved couple time with her, needed it. So far, their relationship had been anything but ordinary. She'd arrived in Oklahoma thinking she'd pick up her long-lost nephew and take him back to the Big Apple. That first night, she'd been irritable and difficult and Lamont had been ready to take her back to the airport. He'd found her pretty, however, and by the next day, when she cooked breakfast, and her demeanor changed, he realized he liked her.

Now, he was far past that and knew it. Lamont wanted to date her and to use an old-fashioned term, court her. He dreamed about dinners for two, a night at the movies, a walk in the park, or even a baseball game. Taking her to a rodeo – one where he wasn't competing – would be fun. Lamont wanted to stroll with her in the rain, cuddle with her on the couch watching television, and visit a flea market just for fun.

Lamont wanted her to be happy, well, and safe. He liked

it when her face lit up in a smile, and the way she demonstrated concern for him gave him a warm, rich delight. *I love her,* he realized, *I love Tilly.* If he could spend the rest of his life at her side, wake up to her beside him, eat her fine cooking, and share his soul, he'd be content.

The revelation rocked him a little. He'd never felt this way, not even for his one-time fiancée Remy. Although he didn't know what he'd do about that in the short term, Lamont decided he should start thinking about the long haul.

He caught Logan before they left for Grove and asked, "Hey, do you mind watching Shayne this evening? I've got that adoption class, and I'd like to take Tilly out to eat first."

Logan grinned. "No, I'm happy to do it. She makes you happy, little bro, and that's worth a lot. I'll buy the kids some chicken nuggets or something."

"Thanks," Lamont said. "Let me go ask her, and then we'll head out."

Matilda sat at the kitchen bar, reading a cookbook with a fancy cake on the cover. She glanced up when he approached. "I thought you'd gone."

"Almost," he replied. "Would you like to go out for dinner before that class?"

"All of us?"

Lamont shook his head. "No, honey, just you and me."

Her smile lit her face. "Yes, I'd like that very much."

"Then it's a date," he said and leaned across the bar to kiss her. "Where'd you get the cookbook?"

"From my stuff," Tilly answered. "Sometimes I miss baking specialty cakes, but these are too elaborate for the family."

Family. Lamont liked to hear that about his family – hers now, too.

"I'll see you later," he told her.

The brothers took his old Chevy truck, already equipped

with a trailer hitch. Grove wasn't far, not much more than an hour away. The resort town sat on the shores of Grand Lake, but the guy selling a horse trailer lived just east. It was in good shape, and the price was right, so they bought it.

"I suppose I should get a truck," Logan said on the way back. "It would be more practical for raising stock."

"I've got two trucks," Lamont replied. "That old Ford Ranger of Dad's still runs. It looks a little beat, but you can use it if you want to keep your Lincoln. It wouldn't hurt to have a car around, too."

"I'd like that," his brother told him. "Maybe I can fix the old Ranger up a little."

The rain continued and when they were halfway back, a thunderstorm rolled in with heavy showers that slowed their progress. They stopped for an early lunch in Adair, at the junction of US 69 and Oklahoma 28. As they munched deli sandwiches, Lamont's phone rang. He didn't bother to read the caller ID, just answered, thinking it must be Tilly.

"Hey, honey," he said.

"Hey, yourself," his sister said, laughing. "What are you doing?"

"Me and Logan are grabbing lunch while we wait out a thunderstorm," Lamont told her. "We just bought a horse trailer."

"That's why I called," Lanelle said. "I talked to Suzi and she tells me you two are starting a rough stock company."

"We are," he replied, realizing they'd never told their sister. "It's Logan's idea, but I'm in. He's moving down here to the home place, and I won't have to ride broncs anymore."

"Hallelujah!" Lanelle sounded jubilant. "I'm glad about that. I shouldn't have to talk to my bestie and cousin's wife, though, to keep up with you two."

Lanelle could always make him feel like he was five years old, caught misbehaving. "I'm sorry, Sis, it's been crazy busy."

"That's what I hear. How's your knee?"

"It's good, now."

"I hope so. We figured on coming down Memorial Day weekend, decorate the family graves, and see you. Is that okay?"

"Sure. If you come Friday or Saturday, you can watch me ride, too."

After a pause, Lanelle said, "I thought you just told me you weren't riding anymore."

"That'll be the last one. I'm already signed up to compete in the Will Rogers Stampede," Lamont told her. "Then I'll be retired, co-owner of Fortune Brothers Rough Stock Company."

"Can't you back out?" Her voice sounded strained.

"I don't know, maybe. I'm kinda looking forward to it," Lamont said. "It'll be my swan song."

"Don't say that," Lanelle cried. "Swans are supposed to sing their best right before they die."

A little annoyed, he replied, "It's just a phrase, Sis. It doesn't mean anything. Besides, swans don't sing."

Across the table, Logan glanced up and sighed.

"I don't care," Lanelle said. "Cowboys do die, though."

"What in the world brought that up?" Lamont asked. "I'm not fixin' to die."

His sister drew an audible breath, then told him, "I have a feeling, Lamont. I've had it for a while now. Don't ride."

A shiver snaked down his back. Lanelle sometimes had what she called "feelings," intuitions that some might call a premonition. She'd tried to talk their folks out of flying to Prescott, urging them to drive instead. They didn't listen, and they died. Just before the tornado destroyed the original farmhouse, she'd called Lamont on the circuit and told him not to go home. Sometimes, like those examples, she'd been exactly right. At other times, she had vague forebodings, something she couldn't quite pinpoint. Then when some mishap occurred, she swore that's what she had been worried about. Lamont had never been sure if her feelings were actual precognition or just a worrywart's concern.

"I probably will, Lanelle," he said.

"I wish you wouldn't," she replied. "I don't know if it's the rodeo or what, but I'm afraid something's going to happen."

"Are you sure it's me?" Lamont asked.

"No," Lanelle told him. "But I keep worrying about you."

"You always do, Sis," Lamont told her. "Look, I'm gonna hang up. The rain's slacked off, and we need to get back on the road. I'll talk to you later. Love you."

"I love you, Lamont," she said. "Tell Logan the same."

As soon as he ended the call, Lamont shared her message and told him what their sister had said.

Logan shrugged. "We should have thought to tell her about raising rough stock. I'm glad they're coming down, but I wouldn't get your drawers in a knot over Lanelle's feelings. I know she's been right, but she's been wrong, too. Besides, she didn't have one about Tatum."

"True," Lamont replied with a nod. "Let's get down the road. I think the storm's over."

By the time they pulled in at the home place, the sun shone, and it had become humid. Tilly came out of the house to meet them and to see the horse trailer. Although Lamont told her that his sister had called, he didn't mention her dire concerns, afraid Tilly might side with Lanelle. If Matilda asked him not to ride, he might not but Lamont realized he wanted this last competition. He wanted to end his three-time championship on a high note, in an arena at his hometown and at a rodeo he'd attended all his life.

Lanelle had planted a seed, though, one that would gnaw at him for the next few weeks, never quite forgotten or out of his mind.

CHAPTER NINETEEN

The weather turned hot by the week leading up to the Memorial Day weekend. By then, Logan's mobile home had been delivered, set in place, and had all utilities in working order. They'd bought several horses, two Quarter horses, and two paints, one of which would be Shayne's horse. Everything was in place to raise stock after Lamont's final rodeo.

After a romantic dinner on Thursday night at an Italian eatery and Lamont's revelation, he became closer to her. Although Logan and his daughter often joined them for a meal, Lamont's house reverted to home for three, and he got his bedroom back. Matilda managed to assimilate her possessions into the house, her clothing in the closet and dresser. Some of her other things were tucked into the spare bedroom, recently vacated by Paisley. Most of the pink had gone with the little girl to her new bedroom.

Matilda wanted a job. Lamont wasn't opposed although he wasn't sure she would find a position that satisfied her in Claremore. Since she admitted that she'd waited tables, both in Texas and again in New York City, her experience wasn't broad. She could serve as a chef, even a cook, but her forte was baking beautiful, delicious confections. If she broadened her horizons to include Tulsa, she'd have a stronger chance at finding a job but Lamont didn't like the idea of her traveling through heavy traffic each day. Maybe it was old-fashioned, but he'd like it if she chose not to work. He liked having her there when he needed her, and he enjoyed the tasty meals she prepared. Lamont did understand she needed her own identity, too, and before he would ask her to become Mrs. Lamont Fortune, it would be a good idea for Tilly to have her own niche in Oklahoma.

After writing a new resume, she searched for suitable jobs.

The closest to what she'd done as a career was a sous chef job at an event center in Tulsa, but although she got an interview, she wasn't hired because the manager told Tilly she had too much experience. Several regional casinos had openings for a line cook, and there was a position in the high school cafeteria. Other than that, her choices narrowed to a discount store employee, working part-time at a daycare center, or outbound telephone sales at a call center. Miss Ava from church, who owned a florist shop, said she might consider Tilly.

"I could arrange flowers," Matilda told Lamont one evening after supper as they lingered in the dining area. "And I could wait on customers, even deliver arrangements. I'd rather cook or bake, though."

"Maybe something will turn up," he said. "School's out this Friday and Shayne can work with me. Logan's got a high school girl from church to babysit Paisley."

She sighed. "If the flower shop doesn't work out, I guess I can work phones like anyone else," Tilly stated. "Maybe if I got a job at a casino restaurant, I could move up to chef after some time."

Lamont glanced up from the table where he'd spread out the local newspaper and several area free shopper papers. Logan brought them home as a potential search for livestock or equipment.

"Honey, I think you'd be great at whatever you're hired to do," he told her. He stretched and winced because his muscles were stiff.

Tilly hung up her dish towel and stood behind him, kneading his tight shoulders with her hands. "You're working so hard, and I feel like I'm goofing off."

"That's silly," he returned. "You keep the house cleaner than it's ever been and cook three meals a day unless we go out or pick up something."

"I like it, but I feel like I'm playing house," she told him. "You and your brother are working so hard. I know it's costing a lot to get started, too. I want to help, not be a financial drain."

Playing house. The phrase caught his attention. Lamont remembered when his sister liked to play house, enlisting Logan to serve as her pretend husband and giving him the role of the baby. It hadn't been long before he rebelled, and she'd had to use her dolls instead. Now, two things struck him – he wondered if Tilly had played house as a little girl and the realization that his heart desired making a home with this woman, no games, no pretending.

For now, they were roommates, although he wondered how people, especially at church, saw them. Did they consider the three of them to be a family, or did they think of Lamont with Tilly as a couple? The social worker had questioned if this was her residence, and at the time she'd asked, it hadn't been. Now it was. Although for years he would have said he didn't care what anyone at church thought, Lamont realized he did. And he didn't want anyone to think he and Tilly were living together as man and wife without God's blessing.

"After I get a job, maybe I could look at an apartment or something," Tilly said, interrupting his thoughts although it was along the same line. She sounded hesitant as if it was something she didn't really want to do.

If there had ever been a time for honesty, to be open, Lamont though, this was it. "I don't want you to move out," he said.

Her dark eyes met his. "I really don't want to go, Lamont. It's just that I'm afraid people are talking about us. I worry they think we're living in sin, to use an old-fashioned phrase, and we're not."

"Then stay. Don't worry about what people say."

"I try not to, Lamont. I don't want their gossip to affect the adoption, though."

"The lawyer said it doesn't matter, not legally."

"Still…"

Lamont rose and pulled Tilly to her feet. He would ask her to get married, he decided, but not now. He wanted to get a ring and to make popping the question a romantic experience. He did, however, want her to know how he felt. "I love you, Tilly," he said, his eyes locked with hers.

When her eyes filled with tears, he worried that maybe she didn't feel the same, that he'd misjudged her emotions. His heart almost stopped beating until she offered him a smile. "I love you, too, Lamont, so very much."

"You make me very happy, honey," he replied. Then he kissed her, slow and sweet, so she would feel cherished. "Let's just ride it out for now – we'll figure it all out."

Tilly nodded. "We'll give it to God."

Although he smiled, he was afraid. "Sure, baby," he answered, although he knew he held back.

As she finished putting the kitchen to rights, Lamont returned to the ads. One stood out, and he didn't know how he could have missed it until now.

Ready to go, turn-key bakery for sale by owner. Downtown Claremore location includes all equipment and inventory. Selling due to retirement and planned relocation. Price negotiable, discount for cash. For more information, call. Lamont remembered the place, a small bake shop a block or so off the main thoroughfare. As a child, his mom ordered their birthday cakes there and sometimes bought them a cupcake or cookie as a treat. It would be perfect for Tilly, he thought. She could bake cakes, cupcakes, maybe cookies, and build up a good business. Lamont figured it would solve the job dilemma and make her happy. He tore out the ad with careful fingers and folded it. Tomorrow, he'd call to inquire. Buying a business for her now would be one thing and might be seen as questionable. The last thing he wanted to do was to look like a sugar daddy.

Is that you, God? Is this an answer to prayer? Lamont wondered but didn't say anything aloud. A plan formed – he'd buy the bakery for her, he would pick out a ring, something maybe Logan or even Lanelle could help with, and after his last rodeo, he would ask Tilly to marry him. He could wait two busy weeks, Lamont thought. It would go quickly with getting their rough stock company launched. School would be out by then, and life would settle down. Now that he'd decided, Lamont's heart brimmed with anticipation.

The days flew past, each one full. When he wasn't working with Logan on the place, Lamont went out to Bud's to ride a borrowed bronc. He got dusted more than once, and his knee twinged a bit, but he ignored it. He could tape it up and ride that last time, he figured. On Thursday nights, he took Tilly out for a meal, then they attended the class together.

On the Monday before the rodeo, he and Logan headed down to Tulsa. They planned to check out some tack but the real purpose was to buy a ring for Matilda. After visiting several jewelers, Lamont realized he wanted something unique. At a small shop that created their own designs, he found the perfect engagement and wedding ring set. The engagement ring boasted a full-carat diamond flanked by smaller ones, but the wedding band had both diamonds and turquoise stones.

"This is perfect," he told Logan.

"I think she'll like it," his brother said.

Lamont chose a matching turquoise wedding band for himself. He ached to propose the second they returned home, but he didn't. He tucked the ring into one of his dresser drawers.

Lamont also bought the little bakery and decided it would be the perfect place to ask Tilly to be his bride.

Shayne's last day of school was Friday. Since Lanelle and her family promised to arrive in time for the rodeo that evening, Lamont offered to grill steaks at home afterward. He bought thick strip steaks, hamburgers and hot dogs, huge baking potatoes, and Tilly made salads as well as a delicious lemon cake. She also baked chocolate cupcakes with peanut butter icing.

Since the rodeo ran from Friday through Sunday, Lamont planned to take Tilly to see the bakery on Monday. Since his time would be taken, on Thursday, he headed into town and got everything ready. Although the place had been cleaned to show when it was for sale, Lamont did a little more. In the front, there were four tables in front of the glass-fronted display case so he removed all but one, leaving the round table with two of the wire-backed chairs. The back of each chair formed a heart, and he thought they were often called "ice cream parlor chairs."

Lamont bought a lace tablecloth for it and a pretty crystal vase. Before he brought Tilly, he would put a single pink rose in it. He ordered other flowers, the white peonies and pink snapdragons he'd bought her before, to place around the room. He also picked up rose and vanilla-scented votive candles that he would light before their arrival. Once there, he would ask her to sit at the table and then ask her if she would marry him. Once the ring was on her finger, then he'd tell her he'd bought the bakery for her.

Lanelle called him on Wednesday morning. "We'll be there early on Friday," she told him. "Bradley wants to get an early start."

He laughed. "It's only a two-hour trip," he told her. "Shayne's school gets out at noon and once I pick him up, come out to the house for lunch. After the rodeo, I've got steaks to grill too."

"That sounds like a plan," she said, then after a pause. "I suppose you still plan to ride, Lamont."

Although he'd thought about it often since their last conversation, he hadn't found any reason not to compete. "I am unless I get a sign that I shouldn't," he told her. Lamont wasn't sure if it was considered a prayer but he'd asked God for that. So far, nothing had happened to convince him otherwise.

Lanelle sighed. "Oh, Buddy, I wish you wouldn't. I'm going to pray that you get your sign."

He really didn't want to talk about getting hurt or worse, so he changed the subject.

"I bought Tilly a ring," he told his sister. "I'm going to pop the question probably Monday."

"That's wonderful," she cried. "Oh, I'm so happy for you. Are you taking her someplace special to propose?"

He chuckled. "You might say so. I bought her a bakery."

"A what?"

"Remember that little old bakery downtown where Mama used to buy our birthday cakes?" he asked. "Okie Cakes And Things? It's small but pretty sweet. The owners sold it so they can retire and move to Arizona. In New York, Tilly was a specialty cake chef. She's been wanting a job, but she hasn't found anything, and I found out it was for sale, so I bought it."

"Oh, my goodness! Does she know?"

"Not yet, and I hope she likes it."

"I can't imagine why she wouldn't. When's the wedding?"

"All that's up to Tilly," he replied. "I'm up for whatever she wants. I'd marry her the next day if she'd let me, but I figure she'll want a wedding."

Lanelle asked how the rough stock business was going, then inquired about Logan and Paisley.

"They're hanging in there," Lamont said. "They both have good days and then not so great ones. I think getting settled into their own place has helped them both."

"Good. I'll see you Friday, then."

The closer it got to Friday, and his last bronc ride, the antsier Lamont became. He couldn't shake a heavy dread and wondered if he should pay attention to the feeling or ignore it. *Something's gonna happen,* he thought. *I just don't know if it's me or what."*

He didn't mention it to Tilly, although on Thursday evening, she joined him in the den.

"Are you nervous about the rodeo?" she asked, settling down beside him on the couch.

"A little, maybe," he told her. "I'll be glad when it's behind me. The suspense is about to kill me."

"Will you miss it?"

Lamont shrugged. "Maybe a little, but it's not like I won't be around rodeo. We'll be raising rough stock, and for the first year or so, we'll be delivering it until we hire more hands to do it for us. That means Logan and I will be pick up men at plenty of rodeos, although there's not much danger to that."

Matilda smiled. "That means we can still come to some rodeos," she said. "I like the idea, and so does Shayne."

"The kid's horse crazy right now," Lamont told her. "We've been teaching him to ride that paint pony I bought him. Named him 'Mickey Mouse'."

"Like Soda's horse in 'The Outsiders'?" she replied. "That's cool. I saw him reading it."

"It's a good book," Lamont said. He'd read it when he was a teenager, and it made an impact on him. It also made him glad he didn't live in Tulsa.

After everyone else was in bed, Lamont lingered. He walked out on the deck and gazed upward at the stars that spangled the sky. Beneath them, he felt somehow small and very human. He had a conversation with God. Some might call in praying, but he liked to think of it as a casual man to man talk about things.

"Lord, if I'm not meant to ride in the rodeo this last time, let me know. You're gonna have to make it obvious because I can be a little thick-headed at times. Doesn't have to be a burning bush or a whirlwind but unless it's big, I may not realize until it's too late. I want to thank You for everything in my life, this place, my family, this kid that's become my son, and this woman who I hope will become my wife. I've taken some wrong turns, and I know it, but I think I'm on the right path now."

He savored those moments of peace, then went to bed.

Lamont woke edgy on Friday, restless and uneasy. He tried to shake it over breakfast. Shayne was excited because it was the last day of school, and classes ended at noon.

"It's my last day as a seventh grader," he stated as they ate scrambled eggs with toast. "After today, I'll be in eighth grade."

"Making progress," Lamont said. "Next, it'll be high school, buddy."

"I can hardly wait!" Shayne said, then switched subjects. "Dad, can I have Jeff over for a sleepover next weekend?"

Jeff had become Shayne's best friend. "I don't see why not," Lamont told him. "I'll have to talk to his mom or dad first, though."

Shayne fist-bumped him. "All right!! Can we go? I want to get there early."

"I'll get the keys," he said. "Get your backpack."

"Don't need it today," the kid cried as he dashed out the front door.

Lamont lingered to kiss Tilly. "I'll be back as soon as I drop him off. I love you, honey."

She turned toward him and put her arms on his shoulders. "Same, Lamont."

Before he returned, he stopped by the supermarket to buy

snacks and a few other things. His sense of dread weighed heavy on him. *Maybe Lanelle's right, and I shouldn't ride,* he mused. He remained so distracted that Logan offered to pick up both kids when school was dismissed. Lamont stayed home to wait for Lanelle's family. Tilly had taken two loaves of French bread, split them, and built sandwiches. One was ham with several different cheeses. The second had ham, turkey, salami, and bologna with tomatoes, lettuce, onions, sliced green peppers, and more cheeses. Just in case any of the kids turned up their noses, she also had a jar of peanut butter ready with a loaf of store-bought bread. She'd made potato salad, and Lamont brought three kinds of chips. Tilly baked snickerdoodle and classic chocolate chip cookies.

Lanelle, Bradley, and the kids came to the house before Logan returned. Their safe arrival relieved a little of his anxiety – they were all right, he thought. Now, he just had Tilly, Shayne, Logan, Paisley, and himself to worry about. At lunch, although the food was tasty, Lamont ate very little, and Tilly noticed.

"What's bugging you today?" she asked, a frown creasing her forehead. "You're so uptight."

He covered his face with one hand and rubbed it. A headache pounded inside his skull. "Honey, it's just a mood. It'll pass."

"That's not what Lanelle told me."

Lamont groaned. "I didn't want her to say anything."

He leaned against the sliding glass door that led out onto the deck. Tilly placed her hand on his back. "I'm glad she did. Lamont, she says she's got a promotion that someone's going to get hurt, and she thinks it's you, at the rodeo."

"She doesn't know for sure what it is," he told her. "Sometimes she's specific with her feelings, but most of the time she's not."

"Is that what has you all worked up?"

"Yeah, sugar, it is."

"Don't ride, then," she said. "I don't want you to get hurt, Lamont."

A sigh escaped his lips. "I'd rather not get hurt myself, but it ain't simple, Tilly. If I don't ride, I still might get hurt doing something, and it might not be me."

Matilda leaned against him. "You're worried about the rest of us. That's why you're fidgety and pacing the floor."

Lamont turned and pulled her into his arms. "Yeah, sugar, that's it."

"What are you going to do?"

"I don't know yet," he replied. All he could do, he figured, was wait for the shoe to drop where it did. That might be in the arena or it could be someplace else. Maybe it was him, but it could be anybody he loved. That was what bothered him most of all.

CHAPTER TWENTY

Shayne begged to show Lanelle's kids, eight-year-old Samuel and ten-year-old Grace, his horse. "Can I, please?"

"Either me or Logan needs to be out there," Lamont said. "I don't want you messing with the stock alone."

"Uncle Logan is in the barn, I think," the kid replied. "Paisley, too. Come out and watch me ride."

Any other time, Lamont would, but he shook his head. "I gotta start getting ready for tonight," he told Shayne, although he hadn't decided if he would ride or not. If so, he needed to clean up, shave, and get dressed. His head ached from lack of sleep. Since his knee still grumbled a little, Lamont needed to tape it to avoid any further damage. The arena gates wouldn't open until six, but it was already after two.

Shayne's face fell, but he accepted it. "Okay, Dad. We won't be gone too long."

"Be careful," he said. "And don't ride Mickey Mouse. Maybe you can show off tomorrow to the kids."

Thirty minutes later, Lamont rooted through the kitchen cabinets, looking for some aspirin or acetaminophen. Matilda came through with a basket of clean laundry.

"What are you looking for?"

"Something for a headache," he replied.

"Look in the smaller cabinet to the left of the sink," Tilly told him.

Lamont had just popped three tablets and washed them down with sweet tea when he heard Grace scream and Logan shout. He dropped the glass in the sink, where it shattered, then ran outside toward the noise. Until he halted when he saw Shayne on the ground, he didn't realize Tilly had been behind him. "Oh, dear Lord," she said, gasping after her wild dash. "He's injured."

Logan knelt beside the boy in the corral, so Lamont joined him.

"I'm here, kid," he said, his voice breaking with emotion.

So was everyone else, all wide-eyed with concern.

Shayne managed to roll over and sit up, clutching his right arm. "Dad, it hurts."

"It's broken," Lamont said. He'd had enough fractures to tell from the way the arm hung crooked that it was a break. "Try not to move it."

"It hurts more when I do," Shayne moaned.

"I know it does, buddy," Lamont replied. "We gotta get you to the hospital, but we'd better splint it first."

"What do you need?" Logan asked.

"I'll get the stuff," Tilly cried. "I'll be right back."

She returned with a pair of wooden spoons, a balled-up dish towel, and some adhesive medical tape. "Do you want me to do it?"

"You probably have a lighter touch," Lamont said. "Though I can."

"Let Dad do it," Shayne moaned. He had tears in his eyes from the pain.

Lamont built a splint quickly, then taped it in place. "Can you walk, kid?"

Shayne nodded and stood. Lamont put one arm across the boy's shoulders as they walked toward the driveway.

"I'll drive," Logan announced. "Paisley, stay with Lanelle, okay?"

"I'm coming too," Tilly told them. She'd grabbed her purse at some point, and she carried Lamont's wallet in the other hand. Lamont helped Shayne climb into the front of the club cab, then he crawled into the backseat beside her.

"Are you sure it's broken?" she asked en route. "Maybe it's just sprained."

"I heard it crack when he hit the ground," Logan answered. "I'm pretty sure it's broke."

Lamont nodded. "It's busted. I've had too many broken bones not to recognize one. Is it your first, Shayne?"

"Yeah. I'm kind of scared."

So was Lamont, but he wasn't going to admit it. "Don't be, buddy. I'll be right beside you all the way, I promise."

"Okay."

At the local hospital, Lamont got Shayne checked in, and then they waited. The kid sat between him and Matilda. With her head down, he thought she must be praying, and he did a little too. When asked, Lamont provided basic information, including Shayne's name and address.

"Thank you, Mr. Sawyer," the employee on duty said. "What about an insurance card?"

"It's Lamont Fortune," he replied. "Not Mr. Sawyer. Right now, he's my foster child, but I'm adopting him. I'll just pay for whatever treatment he needs."

"If he's a foster, then Sooner Care should take care of the costs," the woman told him. "Do you have his Medicaid card or number?"

"I probably do at home, with all the paperwork," Lamont told her. "I can call the social worker and get it, or I can just give you my debit card number."

"All right, Mr. Fortune. Now I have some questions about Shayne's medical history."

Frustrated, Lamont said, "Could he be treated first? The kid's in pain."

Besides, he didn't know anything about the kid's past

medical history, and he doubted Tilly did either. Lamont took a seat, shoulders taut with tension.

"Anything I can do to help?" Logan asked.

After scrubbing his face with both hands, Lamont nodded. "Yeah, can you call David and tell him to get ahold of that social worker? I think I'm supposed to report if the kid gets hurt or sick. I don't need anything that might slow the adoption process. And someone better call the rodeo organizers and tell them I've got a family emergency."

"Will do," Logan said. "I'm gonna step outside to call, but I'll be here. Soon as you know anything, Lanelle wants to know too."

"Tell her I ain't bronc busting and that it wasn't me, but Shayne."

A nurse stepped out and called Shayne's name, so Lamont and Tilly took him back to an exam room. As they entered, the nurse held up one hand. "I'm sorry, but just one of you can be back here with him. Who's it going to be? Mom or Dad?"

Lamont didn't correct her, but Shayne spoke up, "Dad, stay, you promised."

"I did, buddy, and I'm here," he said. "Tilly, honey, we'll be out as soon as they get him fixed up. I'll text you if I find out anything."

She planted a kiss on Shayne's cheek and kissed Lamont's lips. "I love you both," she said. "I won't be far."

"I love you, sugar."

As they waited for the doctor, Shayne's temperature was taken, and he was weighed. Lamont sat in a very uncomfortable chair against the wall. The tiny cubicle made him feel claustrophobic, but he steeled himself to be patient. Shayne sat on the exam table, wearing a miserable expression.

"Am I in trouble?" Shayne asked after they'd both been silent for a few minutes.

"Naw, of course not," Lamont told him. "You're hurt, kid, and that makes me worried. What happened?"

"I wanted to show Sam and Grace how I could ride, but I didn't ask Uncle Logan like you said," the boy stated. "I saddled Mickey Mouse and rode him around the corral twice before he got spooked, and I fell off."

"What startled him?"

"I think it was a bee flying around," Shayne said. "I don't think it stung him, though. Right before the bee, Uncle Logan came running over. I think he was gonna chew me out for being on Mickey Mouse, but then I lost my seat and fell."

That must have been when Grace screamed, and Logan hollered, Lamont thought. "All cowboys fall sometimes," he told the kid. "You saw me hit the dirt at Guymon."

"I still want to be a cowboy."

"You'll have plenty of time for that. We're raising rough stock, and you can help once you get over this. I'm proud of you, Shayne. You're tough as any cowboy."

The compliment brought the first faint grin he'd seen on Shayne's face.

"I hear we've got a cowboy in here," the doctor said as he entered. "I'm Dr. Beshara, and you must be Shayne."

"That's me."

"Tell me what brought you to the ED today."

Shayne held up his arm, then winced as he told the story.

Dr. Beshara examined the arm which Lamont noticed had swollen within the makeshift splint. "I believe you do have a fracture, but we'll go get an X-ray and find out."

An hour later, the diagnosis was confirmed, and Shayne could leave. He had a broken ulna bone in his lower right arm. The doctor put a splint in place along with a sling. "As soon as the swelling's down, he'll need to return for a cast. That should be Tuesday."

"Do I bring him here?"

"Yes. He'll be in the cast for 6-8 weeks. For now, through the weekend until Tuesday, keep the arm propped on pillows when he's sitting or lying down. It will be painful, but you can put an ice pack on it for no more than twenty minutes up to three times a day, but keep it dry. Wiggle your fingers once in a while and eat healthy."

"What about pain pills?"

Dr. Beshara shook his head. "I don't like to give them to children. He's twelve? I can give him a pain shot now to minimize the discomfort, but once he's home, over the counter pain relievers will do the trick."

He handed Lamont a printed instruction sheet. "You don't need to make an appointment to come back for the cast. I'll see you Tuesday. If the pain becomes severe, or he gets sick to his stomach a great deal, or the swelling doesn't go down, bring him back immediately."

"Will do," Lamont replied. "Thank you."

They walked out into the early evening sunlight once Shayne had received the shot. Tilly hovered close to her nephew as Lamont explained everything the doctor said. Since the pain medicine might make Shayne sleepy or groggy, he rode in the back with Tilly.

"Do you want to drive?" Logan asked, offering Lamont the keys.

"No, I'll call Lanelle on the way," he said. His headache had returned, worse than ever, and now that the initial crisis was over, Lamont's hands shook. This, he realized, was the event he'd been worried about.

"How is he?" Lanelle said when she answered her phone.

"Shayne's all right, just hurting," Lamont told her. "He's got a fracture, the ulna bone in his lower right arm. No other injuries, thank God. I have to bring him back Tuesday for the cast because right now, his arm's a little swollen."

"So, you're not riding in the rodeo?"

"No, sis, I'm not. I would have to have been there an hour ago," Lamont said. "Logan called to tell them I wouldn't be there. Shayne's more important than one last ride anyhow."

"I knew something was going to happen," she stated.

"Yeah, but you thought it would be me," he replied. "I'd rather it had been instead of the kid. We'll be home soon, and we'll get the grill going."

"Bradley already has," Lanelle told him. "Burgers and dogs are done, keeping warm in the oven. I baked the potatoes. Tilly already did the salads and desserts."

"I'll do the steaks, then," Lamont said. He might not be picky about everything, but he wanted his steak cooked just right.

"I'll holler at him to wait."

Shayne fell asleep on the way home, aided by the pain shot. Lamont had Logan pull close to the side entrance and toted the kid into the den. He placed him in the recliner and arranged pillows beneath the injured arm.

"Whatcha doing?" the boy asked, sounding sleepy.

"Getting you settled," Lamont told him. "Thought you might want to bunk in the den for a few nights because it's easier with your busted arm. I'll sleep on the couch in case you need anything."

"Or I can," Tilly said. "Are you hungry, Shayne?"

"Maybe a little."

"I can fix you a burger," she told him. "Do you want a baked potato or chips?"

"Chips, I guess. And soda pop."

Lamont followed Tilly to the kitchen. She pulled a grilled hamburger from the warm oven, added some ketchup, mustard, pickles, and cheese, and then tossed some chips onto the plate.

"Want me to take that to him?" Lamont asked.

Matilda paused, pouring pop into a tumbler with ice. "I can do it. Are you cooking the steaks?"

He nodded. "Yeah, I'd better go do it."

First, though, he needed a new round of over-the-counter meds for his head. Tilly noticed as he counted out the tablets.

"Is your head still hurting?"

"Pounding like a drum," he told her.

"Let me grill the steaks, then."

"I don't know…"

Tilly folded the fingers of one hand against his cheek. "I'm a chef. I'll do them however you prefer, I promise."

"Medium rare," Lamont said. Lanelle must have cleaned the broken glass out of the sink, he noticed. "Just don't cremate it."

"I won't, Lamont." She made a cross on her chest.

"All right," he said.

"Go sit with Shayne while he eats," she told him. "See if he wants to sit outside. I'll bring you some sweet tea."

Since Shayne, now more alert, did want to eat on the deck, Lamont trailed him with his plate. He got him settled at one end of the table and sat down beside him. Tilly winked as she came through with the platter of steaks.

"If the other kids want to eat, let them," she said. "Everything's in the house."

Lanelle rose. "Come on, Samuel and Grace. Paisley, too. Let's go fix your suppers."

They returned with loaded plates and settled around the table, so Lamont moved to give them more space. He sprawled on the bench so Tilly could join him, sipping tea as his head eased down a few notches. Shayne ate his burger and chips, then downed the Pepsi, a good sign.

He cut into his steak and cut a bite. The seared meat melted in his mouth, tender, with the inside as rare as he preferred.

"That's perfect," he told Tilly. "Absolutely perfect, better than I would have done."

"I told you," she replied, grinning.

The other adults joined the kids at the table. They had almost finished the meal when Sheriff David Wills strolled around from the front and mounted the steps to the deck. Behind him, Donna Wellington followed, wearing a sour look on her face.

"Davy, there's a couple extra steaks," Lamont told his cousin. "Or burgers and hot dogs if you'd rather. You, too, Ms. Wellington."

"I'll take a steak, with thanks," the sheriff said. "I'm off duty but I came out with Donna because she insisted she had to see Shayne tonight."

"I have to make certain there's been no abuse," she said, prissy as her pursed lips.

"There's not," Lamont told her. "Where were you when this kid lived with his stepdad, who treated him like an afterthought or an outright nuisance?"

Although he kept his tone mild, he meant every word.

Tilly bristled, but before she could speak, Lamont put his hand over hers and shook his head.

"Let it go," he whispered. "Or we'll just make her madder."

"You've read the hospital notes," Davy told the social worker. "You can see with your eyes that Shayne's fine and that it was a legitimate injury. The boy took a tumble from his horse."

"I'll make my own report," Ms. Wellington snapped. "How did this happen?"

Logan stood. "He was riding his horse this afternoon, wanted to show off his new skills for his cousins…

"*Cousins?*" the social worker cried. "What cousins?"

Lamont grinned as his brother crossed his arms and didn't back down. "In the Fortune family, when we get a new member, we're all family. My daughter is Shayne's cousin now and so are

Lanelle's kids."

Shayne smiled and pushed back his chair to stand. "This is my family, ma'am," he said. "All of them. Uncle Logan is telling you what happened. I fell off my paint horse when a bee buzzed past. Dad stayed with me at the hospital, even in X-ray."

Donna Wellington stared, mouth open. "Well, I never," she stated. "I don't believe I've ever seen a family close ranks like this with a foster child before. It's admirable but unusual."

"That's a shame," Lamont said. "Would you like a steak or a hamburger, Ms. Wellington?"

"I really can't accept," she said. "It could be considered an effort to sway my opinion. I'll leave you to your meal. Thank you, Sheriff, for coming out. I appreciate it."

Although David had already removed his trooper-style hat, he mimed tipping it. "Just part of my job, Donna. And for the record, in case you've forgotten, they *are* my family."

Although Lamont had planned to cook out after the rodeo, it would have been late, and this was much better. He'd almost forgotten the rodeo. The weekend now loomed ahead, open and free.

I can take her to the bakery tomorrow instead of waiting until Monday, he thought. *I can propose sooner.*

A delightful anticipation filled him. Since he now had more time, maybe he would add dinner along with candles, flowers, and rings. Shayne would heal, and the terrible foreboding had vanished. Full of a good meal, content with Tilly beside him and family around him, Lamont relaxed. Maybe that was why a verse from Romans popped into his head, unbidden, "And we know that all things work together for good to them that love God, to them who are called according to his purpose."

Lamont didn't realize he'd spoken aloud until Tilly smiled. "Romans 8:28," she said. "And yes, they do."

"Seems like it," he commented. All his fears were gone,

and everyone was alive, mostly well. Tomorrow, he would ask this beautiful, awesome woman to become his wife, and he was launching a new business. Soon, he would have his first son in His family had gathered, and the future lay ahead, filled with possibilities for the first time in a very long time.

Family, built on a foundation of faith. His mother used to say that, but after she was gone, Lamont tried not to think about her or his dad. Their loss left such a huge hole in his life and heart that he couldn't, but now, remembering, he liked it.

"Family, built on a foundation of faith," he told Tilly. It was worth repeating.

By then, dusk had fallen, and it was almost dark on the deck. Her brilliant smile in response lit the night like a candle in the darkness. She nodded and laid her head on his shoulder, cozy and seemingly content. So was he.

CHAPTER TWENTY-ONE

On Saturday, Lamont awakened early and, for a moment, was disoriented until he remembered he had slept in the den. He glanced at the recliner where Shayne still slept. The kid had awakened twice during the night, once thirsty and the second time asking for a pain reliever. Following the doc's advice, he had dosed him with ibuprofen. Thankful that his injuries hadn't been any worse than a broken arm, Lamont rose and stepped out onto the deck. He turned to admire the eastern sky, beautiful as the sun rose. The blue sky was highlighted with golden light that bathed the few clouds with glory.

He spent a few minutes in conversation with God, still not quite ready to admit he had returned to prayer. Just talking to God was casual and simple. Lamont asked God to bless his marriage that Tilly would say 'yes' to the question, that Shayne would heal without any difficulty, and that the new rough stock enterprise would prosper.

The morning breeze was cool, although it would warm up later. Lamont shivered in the white T-shirt he wore with sweatpants and headed inside. He inhaled the aroma of coffee and headed to the kitchen.

"Good morning, Lamont," Tilly said and handed him a cup. "How's Shayne?"

"Still asleep," he replied and kissed her. "Good morning, honey."

"Since you aren't riding broncs, what's your plan for today?" she asked.

Lamont grinned. "I need to go to town this morning to take care of a few things," he replied. "Later, I thought maybe Shayne and the other kids might like to go see a movie or something."

He had shared his plan with his sister in a late-night phone call, and she had suggested the outing. She also came up with the idea that Tilly would ride with her and the children into town, and then she would drop Tilly at the bakery because she would be meeting Lamont.

Her fingers curled around the handle of her mug as she nodded. "That sounds awesome. Are you coming back to go with us?"

"Probably not," he told her. "I thought, too, maybe we could go out for dinner, just you and me."

"I'd love that," she said. "It's a date."

Logan brought Paisley over for breakfast, and although Saturday morning cartoons no longer aired anywhere Lamont could name, he put in a DVD with classic cartoons for the kids to watch. He ate two of Matilda's biscuits, using them to make egg and bacon sandwiches, then paused the 'toons to show Shayne the rings.

"I'm going to ask your aunt if she'll marry me," he confided.

Shayne grinned. "That'll make her my mom more than my aunt."

Lamont hadn't thought about it, but he nodded. "I suppose it will."

"I'm glad, Dad. We'll be a real family."

His mom's words popped into his head again, family with a foundation of faith.

He tousled the boy's hair with one hand. "We already are, kid, but it'll seal the deal."

Lamont packed his best Western-cut suit, a favorite shirt, and a string tie into a garment bag. Tonight, he wanted to look his best for the occasion, but he wasn't about to leave wearing his finery. He toted the clothes out to his old truck and then came back inside.

"Hey, sugar, I'm heading out," he told Matilda. "What do you want to eat tonight?"

"As long as I'm with you, I'm not picky about the food," she replied.

He snugged her close. "C'mon, don't be difficult. Tell me what you want, and we'll have it."

Matilda tipped her head back to gaze up at him. "All right, then. I've been craving Tex-Mex food – street tacos made with steak and some tamales."

Comfort food, he thought, and it sounded delicious. "That's what we'll have then, honey. I'll see you later. Dress pretty, would you?"

Her eyes narrowed, and she scrutinized his face. "What are you not telling me?"

Lamont feigned innocence. "Nothing. Give me a kiss, then I need to git."

Tilly offered her lips, then linked her hands behind his neck for a slow, sweet kiss. "I love you, Lamont," she told him.

"Love you too, honey," he said and walked out humming Jake Owen's song *Up There, Down Here*. He was just a seasoned cowboy, but Tilly was his angel.

At ten, Lanelle and her family met him at the bakery. Lamont took them on a short tour and then showed his sister the rings.

"Oh, those are exquisite," she cried. "I've never seen diamonds with turquoise before, but it's beautiful."

"I hope Tilly thinks so," he replied. "What about the rest of this?"

He had the candles in place to light later, vases ready to receive the flowers he would pick up, and plates laid out for the dinner he'd order in. Lamont planned to use one of the ovens to keep the food warm until they were engaged and ready to eat. His fancy clothes in the garment bag hung on a hook behind the kitchen.

"It's perfect and very romantic," Lanelle told him. "I didn't know you had it in you, Buddy."

Lamont laughed. "I didn't until I met Tilly."

"What do you want us to drop her off?"

"After the movie, I guess, four or five o'clock. Make sure the kids don't give it away. Shayne knows – I told him this morning."

Lanelle hugged him. "I'm very glad for you, Lamont. Are you nervous?"

Although he hadn't expected to be, he was now that he would pop the question in a few short hours. "A little."

He would have skipped lunch if Logan hadn't come by to lend a hand. When his brother learned he wasn't going to eat, he insisted on buying them a small cheeseburger each. "You don't need to faint, all weak with hunger," Logan teased. "What do you need me to do?"

"I don't know. I've got most of it ready except for the flowers and the food."

"I can pick up the flowers if you want, bro. I don't have anything else to do."

"You could have gone to see the movie."

Logan chortled. "I'd rather be here. I'll leave before they drop Tilly off and I'll pick up something for supper, then follow them back. Are y'all coming to church in the morning?"

Lamont nodded. "Tilly wouldn't have it any other way and we can announce our engagement."

He donned his Western-cut suit jacket, black jeans, and a soft blue shirt with pearl snaps instead of buttons with his favorite bolo tie. Lamont combed his hair multiple times, wanting it to lay down just right.

By three, he had the flowers arranged the way he wanted, peonies and snapdragons in vases on the glass case and by the cash register. One arrangement sat in front of the window overlooking the sidewalk. Lamont placed a single red rose in the vase on the table, covered with the lace tablecloth. The sweet aroma of the posies filled the space, and all he had left to do was fire the candles.

Logan had picked up the food – street tacos, tamales, rice, beans, chips, salsa and queso dip from their favorite local Mexican restaurant. He also brought a jug of sweet, iced tea. Lamont shifted the food from the foam containers and put them in a warm oven in foil pans.

"Bradley just texted they're leaving the theater," Logan said. "So, I'm leaving. I'll see you back at the house."

Lamont nodded. He lit the candles with trembling fingers, then waited. He thought he had it all planned out in his head, but now, he wasn't sure. Mouth dry, palms perspiring, he fingered the ring box in his pocket and waited. He knew she had arrived when he heard Lanelle's van, a babble of excited voices, and the van door slide shut as Tilly exited it.

The silence echoed around him, and he wished, too late, he'd thought about music. He didn't have time to think about it much because the bell over the front door jingled, and Matilda walked into the bakery.

She took his breath away, beautiful in a navy dress with a lace overlay and a soft chiffon jacket. Her hair was swept up and secured in place with a clip. Lamont caught a whiff of her perfume, rose tonight not lavender. Matilda stopped and gazed around the bakery.

"Hey, honey," he said, finding his voice. "You look beautiful."

"You look very nice, too, Lamont," she said. What

happened to dinner?"

"We'll get to that," he told her. Despite the flowers and the candles, he could smell a hint of the Mexican food and wondered if she could. He stretched out his hand to her. "Come here, sugar."

Tilly walked across the tile floor with slow steps, her eyes large as she took in the scene he'd set. "I don't understand."

The last thing he wanted was to cause confusion. Lamont had prepared the words he wanted to say, but he would probably bumble them. He didn't want to lose the moment. When she reached the table, he dropped down on one knee. He did his best not to wince since it was the one he'd injured at Guymon.

"Matilda," he said, using her full name. "I never realized how lonely I was or how empty my life had become until I met you. I didn't know helping a boy in trouble would change everything, but it did in the best way. I love you, honey, and I don't want to ever wake up without you. I want to go to sleep beside you and hold your hand for the rest of my life. It's you I want to kiss when I'm feeling down or tired, to help me when I'm sick, and to smile when I'm happy. Tilly, honey, will you marry me?"

She met his gaze, but when her expression didn't change, his heart wrenched. Maybe she would refuse, he thought, and if she did, he didn't think he would ever get past the heartbreak.

"Lamont Fortune," she said. "I started to fall in love with you the first time I heard your voice on the phone, and when I saw you that night at the airport, I was overwhelmed. I didn't expect you to be so good-looking and so I fought the attraction. I thought I'd be here and gone back to New York with Shayne but God had something better in mind. I expected to feel like an intruder in your life, but instead, I felt like I was coming home. I figured out you're a good man, too. I love you more than I ever dreamed I'd love anyone, so yes, Lamont, I'll marry you."

Relief rushed through him, so powerful he almost toppled

over, so he rose. Lamont managed to fumble the ring box from his pocket and opened it. "Sit down, sugar," he said. "Give me your left hand."

He slid the engagement ring onto her finger, as she gasped. "It's beautiful."

"Wait till you see the wedding ring," he told her. "It's got diamonds and turquoise."

"Kiss me," she whispered and stood.

Lamont wrapped his arms around her and fused his lips to hers. He let his mouth cherish hers, cradling her close because she was the most precious thing in his life. A pure, sweet love filled him and he did his best to share that through his kiss.

Afterward, she shifted her hand to admire the ring in the candlelight. The diamond sparkled. "It's so pretty, Lamont."

"I'm glad you like it, honey. You make me so happy I want to holler out loud."

"Holler all you want," she replied with a laugh. "Looks like we're alone."

"We are, and dinner will be served as soon as you're ready."

Matilda took a few steps around the room. "This looks like a bakery. What did you do, rent it for the evening?"

He drew a deep breath. "No, honey, I bought it for you."

She stumbled. "For me?"

Lamont shrugged. "You've been looking for a job. I didn't want you to end up decorating cakes or frosting donuts at a supermarket or doing phone sales, or even arranging flowers for Miss Ava. I know what a fine cook you are and that your cakes are something special. I want you to be happy, so when I found out this bakery was for sale, I bought it. The price was low for a business. What do you think?"

More than once, he'd seen birds smack into a window by mistake, then recover but hop around dazed. Tilly appeared just as befuddled. She walked over to the display case and touched it, then turned to him. "Is this for real? This is my place? I can bake cakes and other things here?"

"To your heart's desire, honey. My mom used to buy our birthday cakes here when we were kids. Sometimes, if we were good, she'd bring us here for a cookie or cupcake."

"What's the name of it?"

"Okie Cakes And Things," Lamont told her. "But you can rename it whatever you want, Tilly's Sweet Recipes or something."

"I'll keep that name," she replied. She came back to where he stood. "I like it, but I love you. Lamont, if I didn't already, I'd love you for this. Thank you."

Embarrassed but pleased, he responded. "*De nada,* honey. Sit back down, and I'll serve dinner."

They enjoyed the food but Lamont basked in her company. This lovely, wonderful woman would be his wife. Neither got in a hurry, and they lingered over their supper. Afterward, Tilly explored every inch of her new establishment, exclaiming over the large kitchen, pleased with the variety of pans and utensils. When it was time to head home, she gathered up the flowers to take with her while Lamont blew out the candles.

At the house, all the kids were still up, and he realized it wasn't that late. His brother and sister were both on hand, offering congratulations.

On Sunday morning, Lamont rose early and surprised Tilly by making waffles. His dad had done that most Sundays, something he'd almost forgotten. It seemed funny, but in gaining a family, it was almost like he had his parents back. He could enjoy the memories and although he would miss them forever, he would no longer try to forget they ever existed.

Having the woman he loved and would marry, the kid that was his son in his heart, his brother, sister, brother-in-law, nieces, and nephew fill two pews made Lamont's heart full. He had avoided church for too long, he realized, but he belonged here, with these people.

After church, Tilly asked to visit his parents' graves. Lanelle brought silk flowers but Tilly placed a bouquet fashioned from the flowers Lamont bought her on the grave. Lamont showed her where his grandparents and other family members lay, then Lamont bought them a late dinner at a local buffet restaurant.

"When will the wedding be?" Lanelle asked once they were back at Lamont's.

"We have to talk about it," Tilly said, sitting within the circle of Lamont's arm.

"I'd marry you tomorrow," Lamont stated. "But we have to get a license and all that."

"I'd like a church wedding," his fiancée told him. "I want a dress and everything."

They had gathered in the living room and from where he sprawled on the floor, Shayne spoke up. "You could get married on my birthday."

"That's awful soon, Yankee Doodle," Lamont replied. He knew from the adoption paperwork that Shayne had been born on the Fourth of July. "I'd rather you have your birthday for your celebration. We'll think about it, though."

The kid hadn't stopped grinning since they shared their news. "Then how about your birthday or Aunt Tilly's?"

"Mine isn't until January 6," Matilda told her nephew. "And Lamont's is in November."

"November 21," Lamont said. "We have plenty of time to decide on a wedding date. Let's decide what we're all doing the rest of today and tomorrow."

"I thought I might go wet a line," Logan said. "Good weather for fishin'."

Full of dinner and lazy, Lamont said, "Are you gonna take

the boat out?"

"Naw, just go to Claremore Lake for a little bit. Does anybody want to come?"

Lanelle exchanged a glance with her husband. "We're planning to head home before long. Since we've visited the cemetery, Bradley figured we'd miss a lot of the Memorial Day traffic if we go today."

"Aw, Mom," Samuel groaned. "I'd like to go."

"You can come back anytime," Logan told the child. "Remember, I live here now too. You could even come and stay a few days if your parents approve."

"I think that's possible," Lanelle said. "Maybe you could come for Shayne's birthday and the Fourth."

Lamont hated to see his sister's family leave. "Sure, he could. Any of you can. We'd be glad to have you."

Although Lamont invited her to come along, Matilda declined.

"I want to get some ideas for the bakery and the wedding," she told him.

Lanelle's family departed, and Tilly stayed with Paisley. Lamont, his brother, and Shayne gathered up their gear and spent a few hours fishing at Claremore Lake. He kept an eye on the kid since the broken arm wouldn't be in a cast until Tuesday, but Shayne was careful. He wore the sling that the hospital provided without complaint.

They returned, windblown, sunburned, and sweaty but content. Between them, Logan and Lamont had caught a dozen bass, big enough to eat. Shayne, due to his injury, hadn't caught anything, but he wore a smile.

On Tuesday, Lamont took Shayne back to the hospital, where the kid got a blue fiberglass cast. Although Shayne complained his arm still hurt, the doctor pronounced he was doing well. Afterward, Lamont offered ice cream, but Shayne had another idea.

"Can we go see Aunt Tilly's bakery?" he asked.

"Sure." Lamont had dropped her off on their way, delighted to see her grin.

They found her taking inventory and exploring every nook.

"This is really sick," Shayne exclaimed after he'd seen the place. "When will you open?"

Tilly sat down at one of the tables in front. Lamont had returned the others after his proposal, so there were six. "I'm not sure," she replied. "I need some time to get organized. I'll need a business license, baking supplies, and to figure out a menu. I think I need to hire a couple of people to help. I'm going to make wedding cakes and those must be delivered, then set up at the venue. It wouldn't hurt to have someone to work the counter, too."

"I'll help out when I can, honey," Lamont told her.

"Except if you're at a rodeo with some of the stock," she said.

"That won't be as much this season as next year," Lamont replied. "Logan will do some of it, and we hired our cousin Will. We plan to hire more hands, too."

Shayne chimed in. "I can work for you."

Lamont smiled. "Sure, you can, this summer and even after school. How long until you can open the doors, Tilly?"

"A month, at least," she said. "I really want to set the wedding date first, though."

"Then we will," Lamont told her as he put an arm around her. "Let's go home and figure it out."

Summer arrived with heavy heat and high humidity, but for Lamont, life was good. Ronnie Upton, his attorney in the adoption process, clapped her hands with glee when he announced he not only had started a rough stock company with his brother but had also purchased a bakery.

"That's perfect," she cried. "That strengthens your adoption case – you own two businesses now."

"That's not all," Lamont told her. Now that he wasn't on the circuit, he sometimes wore his beat-up oldest cowboy hat around town. He spun the Stetson between his hands. "Tilly and I are engaged."

Matilda offered the lawyer a smile and displayed the ring.

"Even better," Ronnie said. "I'll see if we can't get the adoption hearing moved up."

"I'd like that," Lamont replied. "The kid would too."

On the way home from another pre-adoption class, Matilda sat beside him in the truck.

"Let's not mention the chance the adoption might be granted sooner to Shayne yet," she suggested. "He'll just get disappointed if it doesn't."

"Agreed," Lamont replied. "We've got a lot coming up, like his birthday. I thought I'd throw a big party for the family and any friends he wanted to invite. We can have it at home or anywhere. I could rent someplace in town or even in Tulsa."

"Where?"

He shrugged. "A party venue, maybe skating or rollerblades, or rent a movie theater or take a gang to the zoo."

Snuggled up to him, Tilly laughed. "I think he'd like having it at home more, Lamont. I'll make a special cake, and we can have pizza, or we can grill burgers, whatever he wants."

When consulted, Shayne made his choice. "I'd like to be here, Dad," he told Lamont. "And I want Aunt Tilly's homemade pizza and one of her cakes. Plus, I want tons of fireworks."

"Then you'll have all of it," Lamont promised the kid, planning to provide that and more.

Shayne's thirteenth birthday would be one he could always remember. He would see to that.

CHAPTER TWENTY-TWO

The last Saturday in October dawned with clear skies and the loveliest dawn Lamont thought he'd ever seen. Skies as blue as the turquoise in the wedding rings provided a background for the rising sun, framed with clouds touched with brilliant gold and soft rose. He stood on the deck, gazing at the sky, missing Tilly. After last night's wedding rehearsal, she had gone back to the hotel with Lanelle's family to honor the old tradition that the groom shouldn't see the bride before the wedding. Matilda's friend Amber had flown in from New York City, every bit as edgy and sophisticated as he'd expected. Amber possessed a wicked wit and sarcasm. Both flavored her conversations, but Lamont realized he liked her anyway.

Lamont cradled a coffee mug between his hands and sipped. Although Tilly had left cinnamon rolls he could heat for breakfast, he hadn't eaten and didn't know if he would. His habit had been not to eat before he rode and he wanted to follow the same rule on his wedding day. Behind him, the house remained silent. Shayne had slept at Logan's last night so that the groom and his two best men could get dressed together.

He thought he'd enjoy the quiet but didn't. It reminded him of all the years spent lonely and how empty his life had been. Until first Shayne, then Matilda became part of his everyday existence, Lamont hadn't known what he lacked. Although he'd always been in communication with his brother and sister, they had been distant. Having Logan, brother and best friend, as a partner, living at the home place restored the sense of kinfolk he'd lost. Although losing Tatum had been tragic, they'd bonded during that difficult time.

Last night at the rehearsal, he'd left his old truck and rode home with Logan. Lamont fully expected some of his rodeo buddies and old friends would tie tin cans to the back and tack on a 'just married' sign or two.

Since the wedding was scheduled for 11 a.m., they left for the church at nine, already sporting the Western cut tuxedos Lamont rented for the occasion.

"I look more like an old West gambler than a groom," he commented after seeing his reflection in the mirror.

Logan laughed. "You clean up nice, little brother. Shayne here, he looks like a movie star."

The kid hooted, and so did Lamont. "It's the shades," he said since Shayne wore a pair of mirrored sunglasses. "That's what gives him the Hollywood look."

It would be a day of surprises. He hadn't seen his bride's gown and anticipated it with delight. Tilly would be lovely no matter what style she'd chosen. Lamont had a huge surprise for her – a week-long honeymoon. As far as Tilly knew, they would spend two nights in an upscale Tulsa hotel, then return home but Lamont had made other arrangements.

The ladies had decorated the church the day before. Pink and mauve bows decked each pew as well as a rented tall candelabra. White peonies and roses, pink roses, and miniature purple roses that matched the bridal bouquet were arranged around the sanctuary.

Just before eleven, when most of the pews were full, Lamont took his place at the front of the church, flanked by Logan and Shayne. Brother Alec Cartwright took his position as his wife played Mendelssohn's wedding march on the piano. As the guests rose, Lamont faced the back of the church. His nieces, dressed in pink lace, led the way, scattering flower petals as they walked. Amber came next with a measured walk, pausing after each step, and then Lanelle followed with a bright smile.

Matilda appeared, and Lamont forgot anything else. She wore a lovely white gown with puff sleeves to her elbows above a full skirt. A veil cascaded from her head, and although he found her beautiful every single day, as a bride, she was magnificent. Something about the dress seemed familiar, and it hit him when she was halfway down the aisle. He'd seen it in photographs because his Granny Fortune had worn it in the 1960s, and then his mom had been married wearing it. Touched by the gesture, he teared up as he watched Tilly make her graceful way to him on his cousin David's arm.

Since Tilly had no family, Davy had offered to walk her down the aisle. Lamont stepped into place beside her and reached for her hand. Her small fingers slid within his, and she offered him a smile. He gazed into her face as they repeated their vows. For Lamont, he meant each word with all his heart. He slid the ring onto her finger, then she put the band on his.

"I now pronounce you man and wife, Mr. and Mrs. Lamont Fortune," Brother Cartwright exclaimed. "Lamont wants to say a few words before he kisses his bride."

Only Logan knew what he intended. Tilly frowned at him but Lamont turned with her to face their guests. "Shayne, come join us," he said.

The teenager came down and stood on Lamont's left with Tilly on his right.

"All of you here are special to us," he began. "You came here to see us married, and now we are, but there's more than that. I think you all know Shayne here, but what you don't know is that yesterday, the adoption was final. I don't just have a wife, I have a family now and a son. I'd like to introduce you to Shayne Michael Fortune."

Applause echoed through the old church as Shayne turned

to him. Tilly shifted position, and the trio hugged. All three wept with joy.

"I love you, Lamont," Tilly whispered to him. "I didn't know you were planning this, but I'm glad you did."

Shayne detached, grinning, and stepped back with Logan.

Lamont took Matilda into his arms and kissed her. "Now it's all official," he announced. "Come on back to the hall. We've got lunch for everyone, fried chicken and all the fixings, plus the most beautiful wedding cake I've ever seen, one my wife baked herself."

They hurried to change out of their finery in two of the larger Sunday School classrooms. Lamont met Tilly in the hallway. "Do we really have to stay?" he whispered with a wink.

"Of course we do," she told him with a smile. "At least till we cut the cake."

"What about all those gifts?" he asked. "Do we have to stay for that?"

"Logan can take them home for us," Tilly replied. "As long as we send thank you notes, it'll be fine."

Seated at the head table, they dined on crisp fried chicken, mashed potatoes, milk gravy, corn, and biscuits, but Lamont hardly noticed the taste. His focus was on his bride first, followed by his family. After the meal, came the wedding cake.

The cake that she'd baked stood four tiers high, each one a delicious white cake with a chocolate filling decorated with white frosting topped with icing roses that matched the colors of Tilly's bouquet. She'd fashioned each one by hand. Lamont had watched her craft the roses, impressed with her talent. Following tradition, they saved the top layer for their first anniversary, and after sharing a taste with each other, Tilly and Lamont cut the cake. Lanelle took over serving, assisted by Amber.

Although she wore too much makeup for Lamont's taste with crimson lipstick and eyes enhanced with smoky kohl, he had to admit she was beautiful. Her bright blonde hair was lighter than his and much shorter, worn in a tousled do that could have come straight from the pages of a fashion magazine. He watched as she served Logan a large piece of cake and noted that her hand caressed his brother's as she handed him the plate.

"Enjoy, Logan," Amber said.

Faint pink flushed his brother's cheeks, and Lamont stared, surprised. If he wasn't mistaken, Logan found the city woman attractive. He wouldn't act on it, not so soon after Tatum's death, but the fact Logan demonstrated interest provided hope for the future.

"Interesting," Tilly whispered beside him.

Lamont grinned. "Oh, yeah, very."

After a few toasts made with fruit punch, they prepared to leave.

"I'm gonna miss you, Dad," Shayne told him as he hugged the kid. "Aunt Tilly, too."

After hugging the kid, Lamont nodded. "We'll be back in a few days, kid. Don't give Logan or Paisley any trouble, you hear?"

"I won't," the boy promised.

Tilly tossed her bouquet before they exited, and Amber caught it, mouth open wide with shock.

Hand in hand, Lamont and Tilly dashed outside to his truck and climbed inside while the guests pelted them with birdseed. Once seated beside him, Tilly turned to him.

"Will we really be gone a few days?" she asked. "I thought we were spending the night in Tulsa, then coming home."

"Change of plan," Lamont replied although it wasn't, not for him. He'd made reservations near one of his favorite places, Natural Falls State Park. The 77-foot-high natural waterfall cascaded down over rocks in a beautiful setting. Although visitors had to hike down a sometimes steep trail to reach it, Lamont ranked it as the most peaceful place he'd ever been, as well as a spot where he felt close to God. They would stay the first night in adjacent Siloam Springs, Arkansas then visit the waterfall early on Sunday morning. From there, he'd booked two nights in a vintage hotel in the Victorian village of Eureka Springs, an hour and a half north in the Ozark Mountains.

"Where are we going?" Tilly questioned. She sounded eager, not upset.

"Ask me no questions, and I'll tell you no lies," Lamont responded, using an old saying his dad had been fond of using.

Matilda cuddled close to him and smiled. "I'm happy to go wherever you take me, husband."

Lamont savored the word and all it meant.

Although the hotel was nothing out of the ordinary, the room was spacious and pleasant. After an early dinner at a local steakhouse, Lamont made love to his bride for the first time, all the sweeter because they hadn't until now. With tender kisses and gentle hands, he made Tilly his wife in every way. Afterward, he held her close as they slept.

In the morning, he woke up hungry, and they breakfasted downstairs before heading out to Natural Falls State Park. Early on Sunday morning, they were the first to visit and had the spectacular waterfall to enjoy alone.

"It's called Dripping Springs," Lamont told her, sheltering her in the circle of his arms. In late October, it was chilly. "I've heard that it was considered a sacred place to the Cherokees."

"I'm almost afraid to say a word," she replied. "It's so peaceful and beautiful here. I feel like praying."

His heart overflowed with love for this discerning woman. "I'm fixing to pray, honey," he told her. It was the main reason he'd come here. It wasn't just to share the natural splendor with his bride but to offer a prayer to the Lord.

Matilda nodded and sat down on a bench near the

waterfall. Lamont stepped forward, then sank to his knees, then removed his hat. He spoke from his heart, although he'd given a great deal of thought to what he wanted to say.

"Dear Lord, I come to you with hat in hand, humble in my heart, ashamed for how I've been but determined to be a better man, one who loves and serves You. I turned away from You when times turned hard, when I lost my folks and a tornado destroyed the family homeplace, when I got hurt riding rodeo, and when I was all alone. I thought I'd lost everything but now I see, I didn't. You were never distant from me—I was far from You. Right before things got better, everything got worse. I thought I'd found a woman to marry, and she bailed on me when I was busted up and in the hospital. I came down with the worst flu I ever had, and I never felt so alone in my life. Then, a kid came into my life, my son Shayne, out of a situation worse than mine. Through him, I met my helpmate, my love, my wife, Tilly. Through her, I came home to church, and I found life again, life everlasting through Your mercy and grace. I've been too proud, and I failed to trust, and I was lost. Now I'm found. In the book of Joshua, it's written, "Choose ye this day whom ye will serve – as for me and my house, we will serve the Lord. Thank you, God, for all You have done for me and all that You will do. Bless my marriage, my family, and our business endeavors, and let us always work for your glory, not our own. Amen."

A few tears trickled down his cheeks as he spoke, his emotions raw.

"Amen," Tilly said. She came to stand beside him and offered her hand so he could rise.

Lamont stood and kissed her. In this holy place, it was a benediction, one as powerful as the vows they'd spoken in church. No other words were necessary as they climbed the steep path, but at the overlook, an elderly couple stood gazing down at the waterfall.

"Good morning," Lamont told them with the tip of his hat. "It's a fine morning."

The old man, simply clad in faded overalls, nodded. "It is, and that was a good prayer, cowboy."

Lamont hadn't imagined his voice would carry, but in the hush of morning, apparently, it had. "It's what's on my heart," he replied.

"Praise Jesus," the man's wife said, a pretty matron in a flowered dress. "You're that saddle bronc champ, aren't you? Lamont Fortune out of Oklahoma."

Startled to be recognized, he nodded. "Yes, ma'am, that's me. This is my wife, Tilly Fortune."

"We're Ralph and Dorothy Thayer," the older man said. "We watched you ride many a time, young man."

Uncertain what to say, Lamont told the man, "Thank you. All that's behind me now. My brother and I are gonna raise rough stock, and my wife has a bakery in Claremore. If you're ever out that way, come by and see her at Okie Cakes And Things."

"We will," Dorothy Thayer replied. "We live up near Ramona, not so very far."

The quiet blessing and joy of the morning remained with Lamont for the rest of the day. They spent two pleasant days in Eureka Springs, then returned home to begin their life together.

Two years later.....

Sweaty, filthy, and weary from working with bulls for rodeo rough stock, Lamont called it quits after lunch at the corrals.

"Done already?" Logan asked, removing his battered straw cowboy hat to run one hand through his hair. "It's still early."

"I thought I'd go pick up Tilly at the bakery," he told his brother. "She ought not even be there, but she wanted to finish decorating a wedding cake. I told her she ought to let Madison do it, but Matilda is stubborn."

"How many weeks is she now?"

Lamont sighed. "Thirty-seven, so she swears she won't have the kid for another two weeks, but I'm not so sure. Are you picking up Paisley?"

"Planning on it. Do you want me to get Shayne at the high school?"

"Yeah, if you don't mind. Otherwise, he'll walk over to the bakery, and Tilly will be home long before then."

He drove the newer truck because it had a smoother ride for his wife's sake. He strolled into Okie Cakes And Things to find Madison providing a single-layer chocolate cake from the case to a customer.

"Where's Tilly?" he asked.

"In the back," Madison said. He'd hired the young woman as help for Tilly after she became pregnant. "I'm glad you're here – she said she was thinking about going home early."

Concerned, Lamont ducked into the kitchen. His petite wife stood beside one of the prep tables, a piping bag in one hand and the other pressed against her belly.

"What's the matter, honey?" he asked.

She grimaced. "The breakfast burritos we ordered in didn't agree with me. My stomach's hurting."

"Are you sure it's just a stomachache?" he asked. "Or is the baby coming?"

Tilly rubbed her abdomen. "I don't think so. I should have known better than to eat two spicy burritos."

Lamont put his hand on her belly and felt it tighten. "Is your belly cramping?" he asked, worried.

She nodded. "Yeah, that was a bad one. Let me do these last few roses, and you can take me home. I'll feel better there."

"Sugar, I think you might be in labor."

"Oh, no, I doubt it," she said and then turned to him with a strange look on her face. "Lamont?"

"What is it?"

Tilly stared down at her feet as fluid gushed from beneath her dress to puddle on the floor.

"Unless I wet myself, I think my water broke."

His calm vanished. "I need to get you to the hospital, honey."

She insisted on completing the last three flowers before Lamont convinced her to leave. Her suitcase, packed for the event, was at home, so he called Logan.

"What's up?"

"Tilly's in labor, but her bag's at the house. Could you bring it to the hospital for me?"

"Sure, no problem. Do you need me to get the kids early?"

Lamont tried to collect his scattered thoughts and focus. "I don't know. Maybe."

Logan laughed. "Calm down, Daddy. It's gonna be fine."

At 9:47 p.m. on the 27th of October, their daughter came into the world, six and a half pounds of beautiful. Lamont sat beside his wife and once cleaned, a nurse handed him the baby wrapped in a blanket.

"Hello, Annamae," Tilly told the child and kissed the tiny forehead. The baby opened bright eyes and then bawled.

"Annie, you're a pistol," Lamont said, laughing, giving the baby her nickname.

He became serious when he held his daughter for the first time, such a small, precious bundle. "I've never held a baby this small," he told Tilly. "Scares me a little."

"You're not going to break her," his wife replied.

By the age of three months, it was apparent that Miss Annie Fortune would be as fair as her daddy, with Lamont's blond hair and blue eyes. Although only her mama could soothe her to sleep with a song, Annie rested content in her father's arms. Her first word at the age of nine months was not Mama or Da-Da but Shayne, which pleased her big brother very much.

For her first birthday, Tilly baked a three-tiered pink frosted cake covered with fondant butterflies in pastel blues, yellows, and greens. All the Fortunes gathered for the party, and Tilly's friend Amber flew in from New York.

As his daughter giggled and smeared frosting through her curls, they sang 'Happy Birthday,' and then, with Tilly's help, Annie blew out the single candle.

Lamont grinned. He knew what no one else did – another child was on the way. His family continued to grow. Both the bakery and the rough stock endeavor prospered. Life had a sweetness and a joy unspeakable, one that went beyond words. He knew contentment and love for his wife, his children, his family, and his Lord. The words of his prayer at the waterfall were never far from his heart or lips.

His happiness brought a brightness to his days and a lightness to his step.

This was his treasure, he thought, and where his heart would always live.

Lee Ann Sontheimer Murphy is a former newspaper editor and reporter who makes her home in the Ozarks. As a widow with three grown children, her focus is on writing romance novels that range from sweet to heat, from contemporary to historical. She has written more than twenty-five novels and novellas, along with a variety of non-fiction and freelance works. A native of St. Joseph, Missouri, where the Pony Express began and outlaw Jesse James met his end, she is a graduate of Crowder College and Missouri Southern State University. She lives in what passes for the suburbs in far southwestern Missouri, a little north of Arkansas and just east of Oklahoma.

www.ingramcontent.com/pod-product-compliance
Lightning Source LLC
Chambersburg PA
CBHW032035240626
47154CB00003B/925